FOREVER

He embraced her hungrily, kissing her soft lips and neck. Her head was swimming as she clung to him, never wanting to let him go. Oh, how wonderful his strong arms felt, safe and good.

He stripped her of her clothing, both of them oblivious to the chill of the night. His fingertips traced her face, her neck, then on down . . . "I love you," he declared huskily, "and, for the first time, I'm going to make love to you with no ghosts between us. We've a right to it Julie, because we've committed our souls. You're mine now . . . for always."

THIS SAVAGE HEART

PATRICIA HAGAN

AVON
PUBLISHERS OF BARD, CAMELOT, DISCUS AND FLARE BOOKS

THIS SAVAGE HEART is an original publication of Avon
Books. This work has never before appeared in book form.
This work is a novel. Any similarity to actual persons or
events is purely coincidental.

AVON BOOKS
A division of
The Hearst Corporation
1790 Broadway
New York, New York 10019

First Avon Printing, November, 1984

AVON TRADEMARK REG. U. S. PAT. OFF. AND IN
OTHER COUNTRIES, MARCA REGISTRADA, HECHO EN
U. S. A.

Printed in the U. S. A.

WFH 10 9 8 7 6 5 4 3 2 1

For my nephews, David Hagan and Dwain Hagan, with love.

❧ Chapter One ❧

1864

THE soft gray mist rose eerily from the churning river, creating the illusion of ghostly creatures writhing in the throes of a mystical dance, whipped into frenzy by the chilling January winds. Darkness was fast engulfing the Texas plains like a giant black hand.

Myles Marshall stood on the riverbank, a worried frown furrowed deep in his forehead as he watched the horses straining to pull the wagon through the ripping current.

They had begun the crossing at first light, twenty-seven wagons lined up, and it was already late afternoon. As feared, the winds had picked up furiously, whipping the water into a churning frenzy, making the crossing even more precarious. An hour earlier, a

1

wagon had tipped over and been swept down-river, its occupants—Sajem Holland, his wife, Eritha, and their children—barely saved from drowning. The wagon had disappeared into the seething foam, along with the four horses pulling it. There had not been time to cut the horses free.

Threatening clouds taunted them, portending a dangerous storm, probably by dawn. They had to have all the wagons across by sunset, and three still remained. There were two Conestogas, Myles's and Elisa Thatcher's, and a smaller wagon belonging to Myles's sister, Julie.

Myles turned and looked at his wife, who was sitting on the wagon's wooden seat, holding the reins and trying to stop her hands from trembling with cold and fear. Their eyes met over the team of six horses, and she smiled confidently. As always, Myles's whole being was filled with love for the tiny, courageous woman he had married in late August, just after the wagon train left Savannah.

Myles knew himself blessed. No matter the miseries and discomforts they had encountered along the way, he had yet to hear one word of grievance from Teresa. He marveled at her endurance, especially so because she was carrying a child. She calculated it would be born after they reached their destination in Arizona. Her roughest time was still ahead, for they could not possibly arrive before April, and then only if the going was much easier than it had been.

He had seen the miserable expressions etched into the weary faces of other married men on their harrowing trek west, heartaches inflicted by their nagging, complaining wives. Yes, he was blessed.

"Myles, perhaps we should wait till morning to cross," Teresa called, her voice hopeful. "At dawn, the waters will probably be calm."

Myles shook his head and pointed to the storm clouds. "We've been lucky they haven't broken by now, honey. There's snow in those clouds. Heavy snow. We could get marooned here. No, I'm afraid we're going to have to cross over now, all three wagons."

He shifted his gaze to Elisa Thatcher's wagon. The Conestoga, with its broad wheels, wouldn't sink easily into mud, its floor curving upward at each end to prevent the contents from moving about. But unlike the other travelers, Elisa had her wagon packed to capacity with what she often referred to as "priceless family heirlooms." Myles snorted. The only thing priceless out there on the trail were food and water. He'd be damned if he'd endanger himself by hauling around all that fancy furniture and crystal. Teresa and Julie had been inside the wagon and told him what they'd seen.

He saw Elisa's driver, the old Negro called Micah, shuffling around in little circles, kicking up sand with his scuffed wooden shoes, hands jammed into the pockets of worn, frayed trousers, his white head shaking. Everyone knew Elisa gave him a hard time, always yelling that he couldn't do anything right, how she should have left him behind in Georgia to starve along with the other freed slaves, how he should be grateful she was letting him go to Arizona with her.

Elisa saw Myles looking, and waved, smiling broadly. He lifted an arm wanly in response. Despite her foul disposition she was a pretty woman. Long golden curls delicately framed sculptured features. Her eyes were smoky blue, with long lashes she knew just how to lower teasingly whenever a man was around. Still, Myles did not like her, and he couldn't put his finger on the exact reason why. The other women criticized her often, calling her a conceited, spoiled brat, too used to getting her own way. Elisa let everyone know that her husband was a lieutenant in the U.S. Cavalry at the post they were headed for in Arizona. She was always hinting that invitations to balls and parties she planned to give would be hers to hand out—or not—as she chose. He was glad Teresa didn't care about things like that, because he had had enough of fancy balls and teas at Rose Hill when it had been in its glory.

Thinking of Rose Hill made him look at Julie, standing beside her smaller wagon behind Elisa's. He felt a rush of pride. Lord, what that little one had been through in the past four years! It made him sick every time he thought about it. He hadn't been there when their mother talked her into agreeing to marry that impostor, Virgil Oates, who swore he had the necessary connections to get Rose Hill cotton through the Federal blockade and save their plantation from ruin. Before then, Myles had been forced to flee the hangman's noose. Everyone knew of his lack of sympathy for the South's cause, and no jury would have given him a fair trial after he killed the men who had assaulted Julie, an attack precipitated by revenge on Myles's political views. So he had not been there to stop Julie from sailing to Bermuda on a blockade runner, en route to England and marriage to Virgil. Thank God a bizarre set of circumstances had intervened and she'd never made it, and the wedding had never taken place.

Myles could see the hopeful expression on Julie's face as she watched the Field wagon near the opposite bank. Even in that drab dress of simple gray muslin, her rare and delicate beauty shone. Her sleek black hair was braided, but he knew that when she brushed it that night it would fall wistfully around her lovely face, and her emerald eyes would sparkle despite her weariness.

Or would they? Myles chewed on his lower lip. Lately he had seen a strange despondency in his sister. It had begun, he recalled, shortly after they left Brunswick, Georgia, in the fall. Myles was completely perplexed. He had seen her face suffused with joy when they discovered that their wagon master was to be none other than Derek Arnhardt, the man Julie was in love with. Of course, she had never said as much, but Myles just had a gut feeling about it.

He recalled how Derek had come riding in on that big golden palomino, heading straight for their wagon. The cry went up, "It's him, the wagon master! We're on our way!" They had been waiting for the person who would lead them west, away from the misery of the Civil War, and when Myles recognized Derek as their savior, he couldn't believe it. Julie looked as though she had seen a ghost.

Myles jumped up to shake Derek's hand and found himself in for another shock. Their cousin, Thomas Carrigan, came charging up on horseback to laugh at Myles's expression and tell him he was the assistant wagon master. The two of them watched as Derek reached over, took Julie in his arms, lifted her into his saddle, and rode away with her. It was some time before they came back.

Myles had told Teresa the story of Julie and Derek Arnhardt. Derek had been captain of the blockade-runner *Ariane,* the ship Julie had sailed on her way to marry Virgil Oates.

Derek kept her from completing her voyage, holding her for a ransom Virgil never paid. The Yankees blew up the *Ariane* and made Derek walk the plank, but Julie slipped him a knife so he could cut his ropes and swim to safety. Later, she found her way back to him. By then, Myles had returned to Rose Hill to learn that Virgil had married their dying mother. Myles was still a wanted man, and Virgil set the law on him, and he had been sent to the infamous Libby Prison, in Richmond.

Thank God Thomas had been one of the soldiers at Libby, and he had managed to help Myles escape. He nursed Myles until he could get around, and they went in search of Derek, trying to find Julie.

Myles shook his head in bitter reflection. Things had not turned out well. When Derek finally found Julie, it was obvious that something bad had happened between them. Julie had never told her brother exactly what it was, but he knew she was hurt, deeply hurt. She had been forced, somehow, to betray her own people. He did not prod her for specifics.

Anyway, Myles sighed as he continued to stare at Julie; she had been sinking deeper and deeper within herself since they'd left Brunswick, four months earlier. Almost every night he and Teresa talked about it. Teresa couldn't get Julie to tell her anything. "But it must have something to do with

Derek," she kept saying. "I can tell by the way they look at each other—or rather, *don't* look at each other. They're like total strangers, but they were in love once."

"I *think* they were in love," Myles said, bewildered. "I can't be sure. All I'm sure of is that they went through a lot together. But Julie has always kept her troubles to herself. We were always very close, but there was a part of her she never shared with me or anybody else. I guess . . . if she and Derek are meant to be together, they will work out their problems."

Julie looked up to see Myles staring at her and started walking toward him. He hated that she had insisted on keeping the little wagon they had started out on and driving it herself. Both he and Teresa had assured her she would be more than welcome to share the Conestoga he had bought as soon as they got married, but Julie said newlyweds should be alone. Besides, she was capable of handling the wagon by herself. Derek had not liked it, and they'd had some words over her insistence, but Myles stayed out of arguments between Derek and his sister.

Julie worriedly greeted him, "I don't like the idea of our being stuck over here, away from the others, if that storm decides to break. Do you think we'll get across today?"

Just as he was about to answer, there was a distant cheer, and they turned to see that the

Field wagon had made it across the churning river. Immediately a rider on an exhausted horse started back through the water toward them, and Myles said worriedly, "I have a feeling we're about to find out."

"It's Thomas." Julie nodded toward the rider. He was shivering with cold, his pant legs soaked with the icy waters of the Colorado River.

"Get going and be careful," he said to Myles. "Let Teresa take the reins and you hold onto the guide rope. If you stay in a straight line and hold steady, the horses' hooves and the wagon wheels can stay on the bottom. Veer off the least little bit and you'll get caught in the current."

Myles hurried to his wagon to tell Teresa, and Julie turned toward her own wagon. But Thomas called to her, "Get in your brother's wagon, Julie, or Mrs. Thatcher's. We're leaving yours behind. Arnhardt says if the storm doesn't break tonight, we can come back for it in the morning."

"But what if we can't come back?" she protested. "That storm looks bad. And we might wake up to find snow on the ground. I'm not losing my wagon and my team!"

Thomas shook his head. "I'm sorry, Julie. There's no time to argue. Those are his orders. Now please, just get in another wagon. If there's anything important in yours, tell me and I'll get it for you now."

"This isn't fair," she said tightly, green eyes flashing. "I was way up in line ready to cross. I should have crossed at midday, but Derek kept sending word for me to fall back so the larger, heavier wagons could go. They took my place. Now my wagon is the one to be left behind. That's not right."

"You can argue with him later." Thomas sighed. "I've got my orders, and now you've got yours. We're wasting time and there *is* no time. Now, do you want anything out of your wagon or not?"

She shook her head, eyeing him steadily. After a moment he moved away. She watched as he rode back to the river, guiding Myles's wagon by the guide rope stretched between the banks and tied to trees.

Hearing running footsteps, she turned to see old Micah. "Miz Marshall," he called. "Miz Thatcher say for you to come on now. We's fixin' to cross."

Julie walked straight to her own wagon, hoisted herself up, and took the reins in her hands. "So am I." She smiled down at him. "You and Mrs. Thatcher go right ahead. I'm not leaving my team and my wagon."

Having heard Julie's declaration, Elisa Thatcher leaned out of her wagon and called, "Leave her be, Micah. Let her make a fool of herself, if that's what she wants."

Julie pretended not to hear. Her grip on the reins was firm, her gaze straight ahead.

When Myles was midway through the river, Micah moved his wagon into the water. It had become quite dark, and Julie had to strain to see the Thatcher wagon. All she had to do, she told herself, was stay close behind Micah.

It seemed hours before Micah's wagon reached mid-river. When it did, her nerves taut, Julie popped the reins and moved the eager horses forward. They were right behind Micah, and it was so dark that Derek couldn't see her there. By the time he realized she'd disobeyed his order, she and her wagon would be safely across.

Julie could barely see the gray canvas of the wagon ahead of her as she urged her horses down the gentle slope of the riverbank and into the black, churning river. The horses balked as they felt the icy water, and she snapped the reins again, hard. Wind whipped about her face, making her eyes burn and tear. Blinking furiously, ducking her head against the wind, she gripped the reins tightly and forced her team onward into the water.

Suddenly the wagon gave a sharp lurch to the left, and she realized, terrified, that the mist was descending so quickly that she couldn't see anything at all. Elisa's wagon was no longer visible, and she had planned to follow that, because there was no one beside her to grasp the guide rope. But the rope *had* to be there, she knew that. Wrapping the reins around her left hand, continuing to pop them up and down to force the horses forward, she moved along the rough wooden bench to the right, groping for the rope in the mist. It wasn't there.

The horses stumbled, this time more sharply, and Julie realized they were floundering. The wagon and the horses were all afloat. She had gotten off the track, into a place where the water was too deep for the wagon wheels to touch bottom. Freezing water flowed across her feet, rising to her calves. Then suddenly she was thrown sideways, the reins torn from her as she groped for the seat, trying frantically to stay in the wagon.

Ahead and, oh, too far to her right, cheers of triumph rose above the crash of the river. Myles had made it. But she saw how far from his wake she was. She had been caught in the current and was being swept downriver. She groped for the reins, then gave that up and held tightly to the sides of the bench, struggling to keep from being thrown into the water.

Another cheer. Micah had made it across. They all sounded so far away. Too far. She screamed, screamed long and loudly, but the sound wasn't enough, and the waters rushed over it. Just then, the wagon lurched over into the thrashing waters.

At the destination point on the riverbank, Derek was helping haul up Elisa Thatcher's wagon. He froze. Had he heard a scream? He ran along the bank. Thirty yards or so downriver, he saw a wagon, bobbing and rolling in the mist, the black figures of horses struggling. Was he seeing right? Without thinking, he threw himself into the churning foam, calling on every shred of strength to take him through the churning current. He called Julie's name—who else could it be?—and felt a stab as he heard her feeble cry.

Behind him, in the distance, Myles shouted, "Hang on, Derek, I'm coming!"

"Stay back!" Derek yelled, hoping he could be heard.

He stretched out his right arm, and his fingertips touched a flailing hand. He jerked her to him. Holding her neck in the crook of his left arm, hearing her desperate gulps for air, he shouted, "The river bends just below here. We'll let the current take us in. We should touch ground soon. Stretch your legs. Feel for it."

Gasping, she struggled, choking now and then, for she had gone under once and swallowed a great deal of water.

They were swept along, the river apparently playing with them. They were tossed and rolled like twigs. "The bottom!" Derek suddenly cried. He pushed forward with all his power. Then, when the water had subsided to chest level, he pulled Julie into his arms and carried her through the water and up the bank. Gently, he laid her down on the ground.

Julie coughed and gasped, her body convulsed by a deep chill. Derek knelt beside her, running his hands over her to feel for broken bones. "Are you all right? Do you hurt anywhere?"

She shook her head and gasped, "I'm just out of breath. I must have swallowed a lot of water when I went under. The wagon turned over."

Faintly, from far away, Myles's voice reached them. Cupping his hands around his mouth, Derek hollered that they were both safe but would have to wait until daylight to return to the others. He turned back to Julie. "Stay here. I'll try to find some kind of shelter for the night."

Trembling with fear and cold, Julie lay there as he moved away, deep into the darkness. A little later he returned and carried her to the shelter of an overhanging ledge. She watched his huge shadow as he moved about, gathering wood, building a fire, the ledge sheltering them from the howling wind. She waited for him to unleash his anger at her, but instead, once he had the fire going, he said casually, "Take off your clothes, Julie."

She drew her knees up to her chest. "I'll do no such thing!"

As though addressing a child in the throes of a tantrum, he said patiently, "You can't sit there all night in wet clothes. I'll put your things by the fire, and they should be dry before long."

He stepped into the shadows and soon reappeared. In the firelight, he was naked.

"Why are you embarrassed?" he grinned. "We were marooned on an island once, and we frolicked naked for quite some time. You didn't mind then."

"That was then," she snapped, not really knowing what to say. "Things have changed. Or maybe they never were the way we thought they were. Maybe everything just seemed the way we wanted it to be."

He shook his head wearily. "Don't you think you've caused enough problems for one night? Thanks to you, we're stuck here, wet and cold, and a big storm is about to break. We've got to try to get back across in the morning, come snow or rain or hell frozen over. Now take off your clothes so we can get them dry."

"There wouldn't be this trouble if you hadn't tried to keep me from taking my wagon across," she said bitterly. "You hated my having my own wagon, and you didn't think I could handle it."

"You couldn't," he pointed out brusquely,

"so now it's gone. I just hope the horses made it across all right. We can't look for them in the dark. I tried to tell you all along that a woman isn't capable of handling a wagon and a team on such a rough journey. You've destroyed a good wagon, held everyone up, and damned near gotten yourself drowned. Now take off your clothes!"

He was right. Julie began to work the buttons on her dress, but the cloth was soaking wet and her fingers were numb and stiff. Finally she had peeled everything off. She handed him her clothes, covering her breasts with her arms. Then she shrank farther into the shelter of the overhang.

Derek stretched the wet things out near the fire. She hated herself for the rush she felt at the sight of his naked magnificence. She had always thought his body a sculpture of proud, masculine flesh, and the sight of it again flooded her with memories of glory she'd known in those strong arms.

His back to her, he murmured, "You're going to have to come close to the fire, Julie, and get warm."

She was already quite warm from looking at him, but she was determined he would never know that.

He sighed. "Julie, you know me well enough to do better than that. When I tell you to do something, I expect you to do it. Now get over here, or I'll drag you."

She stepped toward the warmth of the fire. "What do we do now?" she said icily, giving her braids an angry toss. The nerve of the man!

He held out his arms to her, his handsome face mirroring amusement. "You are going to lie next to me, so we can keep each other warm."

He laughed softly at her astonishment. "Don't worry, I'm not going to seduce you. We're going to sleep, Julie."

Blast him, his arms did look so inviting. There was nothing to do but walk over and lie down beside him. Arms still folded across her chest, she turned her back against him, lying spoon-fashion. He wrapped himself around her, his thighs beneath her buttocks, and held her close. When his lips touched her ear and she felt the warm tickle of his breath, she began trembling.

He pulled her closer still and whispered, "Julie." When she went rigid, he said, "It doesn't have to be this way, misty eyes."

She struggled in his grasp. "Please. Just leave me alone, Derek. I just want morning to be here quickly. Please."

His voice was strangely sad as he said, "When I was a kid I'd go to bed real early on Christmas Eve, wanting to fall asleep quickly so the night would hurry and be over. I wanted to wake up and find Christmas. But you know, that was the one night of the year

17

sleep wouldn't come, because I was so excited." He pressed his lips gently against her ear and whispered, "You always were stubborn, Julie."

She felt the heat of his desire, and it was agony. She prayed for sleep and was furious when it did not come. When she heard Derek's even breathing, knowing that he was able to sleep, she was even angrier.

The night wore on, and Julie lay awake. Several times she tried to move from Derek's arms, but at her slightest movement, he gripped her harder, holding her tightly against him as he slept. And all the while she was tormented by wanting him, yearning beyond endurance for the very man who held her close against him. She wanted to feel him inside her, to know once again the joy he had given her before.

She blinked back her tears. She could not give in to her yearnings no matter how painfully they seared her. Not now, and perhaps never again. For she acknowledged that Derek Arnhardt could never love her—not in the way she needed to be loved. She needed to be loved completely. He was not capable of giving all of himself to her. Maybe he was incapable of giving everything to any woman.

She passed what remained of the night watching the fire die out, and holding tightly to her sadness.

sleep *sudden* I *dozed* because I *was* *so*
tired. *He* *pressed* *his* *hot* *mouth* *against* *mine*
his *hand* *moved* *up* *my* *thigh* *and* — (illegible)

❧ Chapter Two ❧

THEY were standing up, both naked, bare flesh touching, the thick, dark down of his broad chest tickling her taut nipples. She stood on tiptoe, and he stooped to allow his erect shaft to slide teasingly between her thighs. A moan of delight bubbled from her arched throat as he touched that fire source between her legs. Hot flames ignited her loins.

Ever so gently, he lowered her to the ground, moving his body over hers. His mouth crushed her lips, then withdrew a little to tantalize her mouth gently with his tongue. She spread her thighs, bent her knees, and yielded herself. At his first, probing thrusts, her hands groped for his firm, rounded buttocks. How she loved to feel his hips moving while he pounded into her, as waves pound against a shore.

She received him, all of him, marveling at the giant roar building within. How beautifully her small body received his magnificence.

Again and again he pummeled into her, and her buttocks rose to meet him. Her fingers dug into his flesh urging him on. Never let it end, she cried silently. Never let this moment end. . . .

"Julie, wake up. Thomas is starting to cross with the horses."

She looked around wildly, sitting bolt upright. The world was gray and cold. Everything came back in a rush. She shivered.

Derek was standing several yards away, beyond the sheltering overhang and the embers of the fire. He was dressed, his back to her, straining in the dim light of a stormy dawn to see Thomas making his way across the river, leading two horses.

Snowflakes shimmered above the water before falling to dissolve and die. The storm was just starting. There was time to get across the river and join the others. And, she realized, there would have been time to get her wagon: Derek had been right.

She scrambled to her feet, pushing at the wild strands of hair, and hurried into her stiff, dried clothes. Derek turned around and gave her a lopsided grin. "That must have been some dream you were having, Julie. The sounds you were making were . . . Anybody I know?"

"I don't know what you're talking about," she said flatly, turning away quickly so he wouldn't see her face. She could feel her cheeks flaming. Had she cried out his name? Oh, Lord! If he ever knew of the dreams that came too often, the dreams that tortured her!

He walked over. Cupping her chin, forcing her to meet his fiery gaze, he said, "Damn it, woman, why do you have to be so stubborn? What we had was good—and you know it. I can feel the longing in you. I see it in your eyes. You were dreaming about me just now." He paused to take a ragged breath before continuing, "I dream, too, Julie, and I'm not ashamed of it. I admit that I want you more than I've ever wanted any woman. Why do you deny us?" He gave her a gentle shake, then released her. She said nothing, and a long silence enveloped them.

"Julie, damn it, answer me!" Derek commanded angrily. "We haven't talked since we had that fight—"

"There's nothing to talk about." She cut him off in a weary voice. "We argued because you thought we were going to pick up where we left off—in bed. It can't be that way. It *won't* be. I won't let it. It's not enough."

"I've never lied to you, Julie," he said quietly. "I told you I never intend to marry, no matter how beautiful or pleasurable I find

21

a woman, and I find you both. I have told you that I desire you more than I've ever desired any woman, that I want to keep you with me always. More than that I can't give. That has to be enough."

"Well, damn you, Derek Arnhardt, it isn't enough!" she exploded, jerking away from him. "I won't be any man's mistress. Who do you think you are, expecting it? I'm not some . . . some trollop."

"I happen to care for you a great deal," he told her simply. "And I believe I can make you happier than any man you could marry. Marriage doesn't make for happiness forever. Look at the couples on our wagon train. Some are completely miserable. They don't love each other. Maybe they never did, but *if* they ever did, the love is dead now. Yet they're stuck with each other for the rest of their lives. They have children. Their lives are interwoven now whether they want it that way or not.

"That wouldn't happen to us, not my way. I'd work at making you love me, because I'd know you could leave me anytime. We wouldn't take each other for granted. Our love would never die away to ashes like that dead fire over there."

"Some married people *are* happy," she countered. "Myles and Teresa are happy."

"They just got married a few months ago! But maybe they're going to be different. For their sake, I hope so." He took a deep breath. "You love me, Julie. I know you do. And I know you're not a trollop. You're a lady. If I've ever made you feel like less, I'm so sorry. Lord knows I taught you what it means to be a woman." He grinned.

"Yes, you did," she agreed. "I won't deny it, I love for you to make love to me. But, Derek, that's not all there is to life. And understand one thing right now. . . ." She glared at him. "I'm not husband-hunting. I don't believe a woman can't make it without a man. I'm going out west to start a new life—for myself. If somewhere along the way I fall in love with a man and he falls in love with me and we want to marry, fine. But that is not my great need in life. Can you understand that? Or are you too conceited not to think every woman wants to marry *you?*"

He smiled, slowly and infuriatingly. "Now that we understand each other so well, why don't you move into the supply wagon and be my mistress, at least until we get to Arizona? We've got a lot of long, cold nights ahead of us, Julie."

When she remained silent, he decided to smooth over that last ill-considered remark. "At least let's be friends," he offered with a faint smile.

She drew away. "Derek, I don't think you know me at all," she said through a veil of tears. "I'm not the same woman I was during the war years. I'm stronger now."

He shook his head. "No, Julie, you're wrong. You're weaker now. When the war started you were strong, but it left you weak. You're afraid, afraid to be a woman . . . and goddamn it, I pity you more than I can say."

He walked away, then suddenly turned and murmured, "Your eyes really are misty now. You can't lie about it, can you, Julie?"

She blinked back the tears as best she could.

A few minutes later, Thomas came ashore, waving and calling. After dismounting and turning the horses over to Derek, he rushed over to Julie. "Are you all right? Damn! You had us scared to death! A fool stunt that was! Your horses made it ashore, thank goodness, but your wagon's gone. Myles is fit to be tied. You can bet he'll have plenty to say to you. And poor Teresa, we thought she'd never stop crying."

She was sorry Teresa was upset, especially in her condition. "I didn't want to lose my wagon," she told Thomas feebly. "But I did. I'm sorry I caused everyone trouble."

"Let's go," Derek called. "The snow's getting thicker. We've been lucky so far."

Julie started toward Derek, but Thomas caught her arm and drew her back, to speak to her alone. He whispered hoarsely, "Julie, you know how I feel about you, how I've always felt. Last night, did you and Derek . . . ?" He swallowed hard, forcing himself to ask, "Did you make up?"

"Nothing has changed, Thomas," she said firmly, meaning both that she and Derek had not been lovers and that there was also no chance for a love affair between her and Thomas. Thomas was a dear, and she loved her wonderful cousin and friend, but there could not be more between them.

He nodded sadly, understanding, and said tightly, "Let's get going. The snow is really getting bad."

They reached the other side easily enough, and Myles lifted Julie down from the horse. Shivering with cold she gratefully accepted the warm blanket Teresa held out to her, giving her sister-in-law a guilty look. They hurried to the camp fire, which hissed irritably against the assault of the snow. Julie nodded in silent agreement as Myles admonished her for her foolishness, interjecting apologies whenever he paused for breath. She was grateful for Teresa's smiling presence. Julie had done what she felt she had to do. Teresa understood that.

Others gathered around, some condemning by their stares. A wagon train, understandably, didn't welcome unnecessary trouble. Julie appreciated that. But what was done was done. She was sorry and hoped they knew it, but it was she who had lost her wagon and supplies. Surely that was punishment enough?

The train was much smaller than when they'd left Brunswick in the fall. There'd been fifty wagons then. God, what a sad lot they'd been, gaunt, bedraggled soldiers, spared the further agonies of war only because of their wounds. The women grieved for the past and feared the danger ahead. Many had fallen by the wayside, unable to continue the treacherous journey. Some, like Teresa's grandparents, had succumbed to illness. Julie had wept at the graves of all of them, and the people who remained were dear to her. She counted twenty-six wagons in the snowy mist. She did not want her friends angry with her.

"Julie needs dry clothes," Teresa interjected as Myles continued his censure.

"All right," he said sighing, giving his sister a hug to let her know she was forgiven. "Just please, in the future, obey the rules— whether you like them or not. Okay?"

Julie nodded and went with Teresa to their wagon. Inside, she gratefully accepted a dress of thick wool, then reached eagerly for the tin of hot coffee Teresa offered.

After a few quiet moments, her sister-in-law shyly began, "I am so very sorry for what you had to endure, Julie, and I'm thankful you're safe. Don't be hurt by what Myles said. He's just upset because he was so worried.

But he'll get over it, and so will everyone else."

"Everything he said was true. It was stupid of me."

"What about Derek?" Teresa asked hesitantly. Julie glanced up sharply, and Teresa said hastily, "I mean, was he very angry?"

Julie nodded.

"He didn't hesitate to jump right in that icy water," Teresa rushed to explain. "He pushed everyone else out of the way."

"He's wagon master. That's his job."

Teresa, gathering her nerve, stated flatly, "It was more than that, and you know it. Forgive me if I'm interfering, but Myles has told me about you and Derek. It makes me sad to see you so unhappy. Is there no way the two of you can . . . can . . . ?"

Blinking furiously, Julie gulped the coffee, then set the empty tin aside. "No. Derek is a strange man, Teresa, and I doubt he'll ever love any woman enough to marry her. I can't accept less."

"But he loves you!" Teresa cried. "The way he looks at you! And he didn't hesitate to risk his life to save you."

Julie gazed at Teresa. She loved her, loved that gentle, sensitive, trusting person. Suddenly, she felt the need to confide, and she told her, "Derek wants me to be his mistress. I refuse, Teresa. As much as I love him, I won't accept that.

"Besides," she added tartly, "I can survive without a man."

"Even in the wilderness?"

"I won't marry a man just to take care of me, either. I will marry only for love, and . . ." She fell silent, staring at Teresa in wonder. "You aren't shocked that he asked me to be his mistress?"

Teresa laughed and shook her head. "Not at all. From what I've seen of Derek Arnhardt, I believe he would want a mistress instead of a wife. Now, Myles might be shocked and angry that he would ask such a thing. But I'm a woman, Julie, and even though I love your brother with all my heart, I can appreciate the fact that Derek is quite a man. Frankly, I don't see how you can refuse him. I imagine he'd really know how to make a woman feel like a woman."

There was a long pause before Julie said, "Now I'm the one who's shocked. I've always taken you to be so prim and proper."

"You're teasing me," Teresa grinned. "You aren't surprised at all."

"I suppose not," Julie admitted, "but just try to understand how I feel. I won't accept Derek's offer, and the best thing both of us can do is forget that we ever loved."

"And do you think you can do that?" Teresa asked. Julie didn't answer.

A moment later, Esther Webber came in, carrying a fresh pot of coffee. "I'm so thankful you're safe," she told Julie. "We turned over yesterday, you know. We lost everything. I'm just glad to be alive."

Julie accepted the coffee gratefully. She liked Esther well enough, but the woman did love to gossip—and Julie felt that was a waste of anyone's time. Sure enough, Esther began to report what people had said in criticism of Julie.

"I know some people are mad at me," Julie said softly. "In time, they'll get over it."

Teresa chimed in. "Just as soon as something else happens to give them something else to talk about."

Esther, a plump woman whose eyes glittered with excitement when she had special gossip to impart, feigned disgust as she lowered her voice conspiratorially. "I think it's terrible what some of the women are saying."

Julie and Teresa exchanged looks.

Esther shook with eagerness as she rushed on. "It's absolutely sinful to suggest that, just because you and Captain Arnhardt were alone all night on the other side of the river, something immoral went on. They even say you planned the whole thing so the captain would save you and you'd have to spend the night on the other side, that you've been throwing yourself at him since we left Brunswick. Isn't that terrible?

"After all," she continued, eyes blinking, "we all know you are a lady, and the captain

29

a gentleman. He would certainly not take advantage of a situation, and you wouldn't stand for it if he did. It's just nasty gossip is all it is. I'm sure there's a special place in hell for people who talk that way." She smiled at them.

Julie was stunned, speechless, staring at her incredulously. Teresa was instantly furious. "Who would dare say such things? Esther, you tell us right now who is responsible. Myles will want to speak with them. And I'm sure the captain will set them straight. We will not stand for slander."

Esther's smile faded. "I'd rather not say." She picked nervously at her cloak. "I don't want to cause trouble."

"Well, you already have," Teresa snapped. "How many other people have you told about this? Really, Esther, you're just as bad as a person who starts gossip when you spread it around."

"Well, pardon me!" Esther cried. She rose to leave. "I thought I was doing you a favor, coming to let you know. Now you blame me for it! I had nothing to do with it."

Teresa said calmly, "If you refuse to tell us who started this ugly talk, then at least do Julie a favor and not spread it any further."

Forcing her anger below the surface, Julie said, "Esther, would you be so kind as to tell me who would even think such a thing? I would like to go to them and tell them how wrong they are."

Suddenly the curtain covering the back of the wagon opened, and they looked down to find Elisa Thatcher glaring up at them. "I'll be glad to tell you, Julie," she exploded, eyes flashing, lips curled back in a snarl. "I said those things, and I said them because they're true. You have been throwing yourself at Captain Arnhardt since the day he rode into Brunswick. It's obvious to anyone who has eyes. You've been so brazen. Flirting with a man is one thing, but causing him to risk his life, holding up the entire wagon train because you want a chance to be alone with him all night, well, that's another matter entirely. My goodness, can't you just meet him after dark?"

Julie and Teresa were too stunned to speak, and even Esther Webber was shocked by the young woman's outburst.

Teresa was the first to recover. "You are very cruel, Elisa Thatcher. And very wrong. I demand that you apologize to my sister-in-law at once and stop spreading lies, or I will have to tell my husband and Captain Arnhardt about this."

"Tell your husband," Elisa taunted, hands on her hips as she swished her long skirt sassily. "Tell him what his sister is. I don't care. And Derek already knows the kind of woman she is. Shameless!" She pointed her finger at Julie and cried, "Wanton! You would be doing everyone a favor if you left the train at San Angelo. We don't want your kind!"

Julie was trying to contain herself. Oh, how easy it would be to give in to the fury and attack the haughty witch, rake her nails down Elisa's lying face. But she would not be goaded. "I have no intention of leaving this wagon train, Elisa, and if you don't get away from me right this minute, I am going to do something you will regret!"

Elisa's eyes widened, but she stood her ground. "I'm not afraid of you, Julie Marshall!" she told her, a slight tremor in her voice. "But I imagine you are adept at unladylike brawling, so I'll leave now."

Julie stood staring at her, and Elisa taunted, moving away slowly, "Maybe I can't make you leave the wagon train, but I can make you wish you had. I'll make sure that every wife knows you're a hungry man-chaser."

"What have I ever done to you to make you want to hurt me this way, Elisa?" Julie asked quietly.

"I don't want to associate with trash like you!" Elisa replied hotly, then turned and scurried toward her wagon.

Teresa put her arm around Julie's trembling body. "I am so sorry. Just try to understand that she's going through a very hard time right now, expecting a baby, her husband not here to be with her. I'm sure she'll apologize when she realizes what she's done."

Julie shook her head. "No," she murmured thoughtfully. "It's more than that."

"What do you mean?" Teresa asked. Esther was listening, and Teresa wished she would leave. She had witnessed the ugly scene and would waste no time making sure the entire wagon train heard about it.

Julie shared her apprehension over Esther, so she murmured, "I'll have to think about it."

What *had* provoked Elisa to hysteria? To say such vicious things about her and Derek?

Derek!

Elisa had referred to Derek by his first name. No one called Derek by his first name, not even Thomas, who was assistant wagon master. There was an air about Derek Arnhardt that commanded respect.

She nodded to herself. Yes, there was something there, something to evoke such rage from Elisa. Something.

❧ Chapter Three ❧

JULIE sat huddled next to Myles, a blanket wrapped tightly about them both. It was difficult to make out the lines of the wagons ahead, for the storm had unleashed its fury. Angry winds whipped white torrents, shrouding the world in whispered oblivion.

Myles had pulled the brim of his hat down as far as it would go, and still the icy snowflakes slapped his face. He leaned close to say, "If the wagons weren't tied together we'd veer off and get lost in this mess."

Julie shivered. "I wish Derek would let us stop for the day. Why must we continue in this storm?"

"It's best to keep moving. Keeps the horses warmer than if they were standing still in the snow and wind. It'd be hard to keep a fire going, too. He figures we're two weeks out of San Angelo, and we're running low on supplies. We need to get there as quick as we can."

"But what about tonight, when we have to camp?"

"Arnhardt told the men that we're heading into the base region of a mountain range, and he knows a place where there's high rocks to protect us from the winds. If the storm is still bad tomorrow, we'll have to sit and wait it out. I hope you ladies aren't very hungry." He gave her a quick, anxious glance. "We'll probably have to ration out food if we get snowed in."

"I'm not worried about me," she responded quickly. "I just want to make sure Teresa doesn't go hungry. She needs strength."

"I know she does," he said, and his voice was almost bitter. "I wish she weren't pregnant. Not now. This trip is rough enough on a woman without her expecting a baby."

Julie shared his worries. Teresa was so tiny and delicate. But she made her voice cheery. "She will do just fine." It was a confidence she did not really feel. "She figures the baby won't be born until June, and we should be in Arizona in April."

"I know, I know," he said, sighing impatiently, "but she's growing larger every day. She's so damn small, Julie. What if the baby is going to be a big one? And what if she delivers early? Hell, the roughest part is still ahead. We're heading straight into part of the Rocky Mountains.

"And Indian country," he added grimly, glancing at her to gauge her reaction.

Julie stared straight ahead and made no comment.

"I'm sorry. I'm not trying to frighten you." He turned his gaze back to the ghostly world before him. "It's just that I'm kind of scared myself, and I can't talk about it to Teresa. I have to pretend I'm brave and not worried about anything. Damn it all, I am scared—and I can't admit it to anybody but you. Maybe I'm just a coward."

Julie was furious. "Myles Marshall, you are anything but a coward! Have you so easily forgotten the reason you had to leave home? You faced up to Jabe Brogden and Wiley Lucas for what they tried to do to me! And your leg." She touched his right leg. "You limp because you took the charge of a wild hog to save my life when we were only ten years old. Don't you *ever* let me hear you call yourself a coward again!"

Her anger had warmed her blood, and Myles glanced at her flushed cheeks and laughed affectionately. "Dear, dear Julie," he murmured. "With your spirit, I don't know how I could be afraid of anything, not as long as I've got you beside me."

She smiled at him. "There's nothing ahead on this trail that you can't face."

"I've never had to face an Indian," he countered, "and we'll have to go through Chiricahua country."

She admonished herself for the effect his words had.

"The Chiricahua," he went on when she remained silent, "are part of the Apache nation. There are three bands of them, ranging from the Rio Grande to southwestern Arizona and from northern Mexico on down to Zuni and Acoma. They're savages, Julie. They like war, and they hate the white man."

"I'm sure Derek will keep a close watch on us," she said as stoutly as she could.

Myles moved a gloved hand to her knee. "Forgive me, honey. I'm not trying to scare you. Like I said, I can't talk about my fears to other people."

"We're going to be just fine." Julie forced a smile. "It's too cold for Indians to be roaming around anyhow."

He laughed. "I wish that were true."

Suddenly Julie said, "You know, even if it is dangerous, the snow is beautiful. I'd never even seen real, heavy snow before the war."

At the mention of the war both went silent. Then Myles said, "Why don't you crawl in the back and take a nap with Teresa?"

"I'm not sleepy. I'd rather stay out here with you. In this storm, four eyes are better than two. Besides, we'll surely get to that shelter before long, and I can sleep then."

"What about Arnhardt?" her brother asked suddenly. "Did you solve your differences?"

She sighed. Was everyone going to ask her about Derek? "No," she finally told him. "It will never work for us, Myles, and I really don't want to discuss it."

He ignored her protest and said earnestly, "You love him. He loves you." He said it matter-of-factly. "You're both stubborn, but you'll come to your senses one day."

"We all have a new life waiting for us in the Arizona territory, Myles. Perhaps it's best if we put the past out of mind. I intend to do just that."

"You love him," he said firmly. "You can never forget those you love."

She was silent for a moment, then said quietly, "I think I'll go back and see how Teresa is doing."

"Fine," he said, amused. "But remember, Julie, you can run from the past, but you can't hide from yourself."

Pushing aside the canvas, she stepped down into the wagon. Above her, the wagon coverings of strong white homespun hemp, arched over thirteen wooden bows, whipped and strained against the gale.

In the scant, gray light, she could just make out Teresa bundled beneath blankets. Moving quietly, she picked her way to her own mattress and prepared to lie down.

Patricia Hagan

"I'm not asleep," Teresa said, her voice muffled. She uncovered her face and sat up. "I guess I'm too worried about Myles being out there. Is he all right?"

Julie nodded. "I don't think we'll be going much farther today. It'll be dark soon. Myles says Derek knows of shelter ahead. We'll camp there.

"But how are you feeling?" she asked anxiously. "Can I do anything for you?"

"Yes," Teresa said, laughing. "You can wake me up in June, when the baby gets here. I think I'd like to sleep till then.

"No," she said quickly, sensing Julie's concern. "I'm fine, really. Don't worry about me."

"We can't help but worry, Teresa," Julie told her as she wrapped herself in a thick wool blanket. "The baby seems to be growing awfully fast. I hope he isn't going to be too big. You're such a tiny thing."

"I'm going to be just fine." Teresa grinned confidently, propping her elbows on her knees before her as she leaned back against one of the wooden support hoops. "It's going to be wonderful having Myles's baby, beginning a new life in the Arizona territory, leaving all the terrible war memories behind. I only wish Grandma and Grandpa had lived to have that new life. But we're supposed to think they have a much better life where they are."

40

Julie felt a wave of pity as she looked at Teresa's big, shining brown eyes. Teresa was a child in her exuberance but mature beyond her age in compassion and understanding. "I'm sorry your grandparents didn't make it, Teresa," she told her sincerely. "They sound like wonderful people."

"They were." Teresa nodded eagerly. "After my parents were killed, they took me in and treated me like their own child. They were so happy when Myles and I fell in love. But I think I knew from the beginning they wouldn't make it all the way. I think they knew it, too, but they tried—for my sake, really, to give me a new start."

Suddenly the wagon lurched to a stop, and the two young women turned anxious eyes toward the front. Myles appeared in a minute. "We're moving onto the plateau, one wagon at a time." He grinned. "Soon we'll have a fire going and food cooking."

As Myles stood there, the canvas pulled open, wind whipping snow inside the wagon. In a rare show of irritation, Teresa cried, "Myles, you're letting in the snow, and my seeds are going to get wet."

Julie watched, amazed, as Teresa moved her bulk over to a small packet lying on top of a carton. Retrieving the packet, she held it to her bosom as she snuggled back beneath the blankets. Myles looked at Julie and shrugged, then stepped back outside.

"What was all that about?" Julie asked curiously.

"My flower seeds." Teresa smiled proudly, holding up the packet. "My grandmother gave them to me to start a flower garden when we reach our new home. I guess they're just about the most important thing I'm carrying with me. I don't want anything to happen to them."

"Flower seeds?" Julie laughed incredulously, then saw the hurt look on Teresa's face and said, "I'm sorry, Teresa. It's just that I'm surprised they mean so much to you."

"Well, they do," she said. "They came from Grandma's garden back home, and she said that even though we might not be sure of anything else out here, we could be sure of having flowers in the spring. That means a lot to me, especially now that she's gone. . . ." Her voice trailed off, and she blinked furiously.

"I read once," she went on in a hopeful whisper, "that Napoleon said, 'Where flowers degenerate, man cannot live.' My flowers will grow, Julie," she whispered. "I have this picture in my heart of my flowers growing, and my child standing near the blossoms, laughing. The picture sees me through the sad times, the worried times. I feel that where my flowers can't grow, we can't survive, either. Can you understand that?"

"Of course," Julie responded awkwardly, taken aback.

* * *

As Derek had promised, the spot between the rocky bluffs gave shelter. There were even bare spots where the snow had not been able to reach, and a high, sweeping overhang afforded a nice, dry area for a roaring camp fire.

They pulled the wagons into a circle, making a corral where the horses could move about freely.

"Ration your food," Derek ordered. "We may be here a few days if this storm doesn't break soon, and we're still two weeks out of San Angelo. We have to make what we've got last."

Julie watched him speaking to the men, giving orders which were always quickly obeyed and never questioned. He had that affect, she reflected, exuding authority and commanding respect with only a gesture.

"I think we'll make a stew out of the dried venison we have left," Teresa was saying. "That will last awhile, and it will be good and filling. I'll ask Myles to get potatoes from the bin in back."

"He's got to feed the horses. I'll do it. You rest, Teresa."

Teresa sighed with exasperation. "I wish you would both stop treating *me* like a baby. The baby is inside me. I'm a grown woman, and I can do my share of the work."

Julie ignored her and set about making the stew. By the time it was ready, night had fallen, and the large camp fire blazed, dancing eerily in the snow-blanketed night. After they had eaten, the men brought out their whiskey and sat to one side of the fire while the women who did not have small children to see to gathered on the opposite side away from the men and their conversation.

Julie and Teresa sat off to the side, by themselves. Julie felt uncomfortable around the other women because of Elisa's tirade. It was warm by the fire, but the wind was harsh and they would soon be going to bed to burrow beneath blankets.

Esther Webber walked over and settled her heavy bulk next to Julie. Gently, she said, "I can tell you're feeling bad about what happened this morning, dear. Please don't. That little snob isn't worth your concern."

Julie merely looked at her, keeping quiet. Teresa did the same.

Esther, undaunted, rushed on eagerly. "I knew that girl in Brunswick, and she's just a troublemaker. Came from a wealthy family, she did, the Beckworths, and she and her mama were always lording it over everybody. Always giving balls and teas and acting like the Lord High Almighty when it came to picking out who was good enough to be invited."

She paused to take a breath, then continued. "Anyway, Elisa and Genevieve, her mother, made up their minds that they wanted Elisa to marry Adam Thatcher. Now he's a fine young man from a real nice Christian family. The Thatchers had money, too, but they didn't throw it around like Elisa's family. So Elisa got her hooks into Adam, and they got married. Then the trouble started."

Esther paused to gauge their reactions. Julie and Teresa were both listening raptly despite their intentions. Teresa urged her, "What kind of trouble? Go on, Mrs. Webber, please. I'd like to know what happened to that poor girl to make her so spiteful. Maybe it would help us to understand her."

"Understand, my foot!" Esther snorted. "There's nothing to understand. She's just a spoiled brat, just plain ornery.

"Adam said he couldn't hold to slavery, and he went off and joined up with the Yankees. I can tell you that didn't set well with Elisa's daddy. Jordan Beckworth had a big plantation, he did, owned a lot of slaves, and he didn't much like his son-in-law taking sides against him and his people. Well, Elisa told Adam to go on off to war and, when it was over, if he hadn't gotten himself killed, he could just keep right on going."

Teresa gasped. "But she's expecting his baby."

"I'm getting to that," Esther said excitedly. "See, the gossip was that Adam Thatcher was just tickled to death to get away from that hateful, willful girl, so when he rode off, he didn't look back. But then Jordan suddenly died of a heart attack. All the strain of the war, you know. Well, it came out that he was heavily in debt, and Genevieve didn't have sense enough to look after anything, so what little they did have after Jordan died ran out fast. Well, she and Elisa went to Adam's daddy and got him to call his boy home, thinking, probably, they could get some of the Thatcher money. Only it didn't work out that way. Adam and Elisa were together for a while, but then they had a big fight, and he left. It wasn't long after that Elisa found herself in the family way. So Genevieve took her to the Thatchers and told them she was their responsibility. Then she took off to live with her sister up in North Carolina.

"So," Esther gasped, out of breath from excitement, "Adam's daddy wrote him he had to do the right thing, and Adam wrote back and said he wouldn't come back to Georgia, that he liked it just fine with the cavalry out in the Arizona territory, and though he wanted to do right by the baby, Elisa would have to get herself out there. He wasn't about to go back to Georgia where folks hated him for taking sides with the Yankees."

Teresa sighed. "The poor thing. She's going to have a baby, but she can't be sure her husband wants her anymore. That's heartbreaking."

Esther lifted her chin. "If you ask me, she's getting what she deserves. You can be sure Adam Thatcher would never have anything more to do with her if she wasn't having his baby."

Julie's gaze was drawn to Elisa, walking over to Derek. Whatever was said Derek got up and walked with Elisa to her wagon.

Esther, also watching, cried, "That's what kind she is, a man-chaser. Everybody knows she's been running after the wagon master— and her a married woman expecting a baby. Disgraceful."

"You shouldn't jump to conclusions," Teresa admonished. "That's how gossip gets started. She probably wants Captain Arnhardt to check something on her wagon."

"Ha!" Esther clapped her hands together and rocked back on her ample bottom. "What's he checking in a wagon in the middle of the night? I've seen him slipping in there when he thought no one was looking, and Ramona Towles saw him sneaking out one morning just before daybreak. Now, tell me who's jumping to conclusions?"

"There could have been reasons," Teresa said as easily as she could. "He *is* the wagon master, after all. Besides, none of it is anyone's business."

Before Esther could start up again, Teresa nodded to her, smiled at Julie, and suggested it was time to sleep.

When they were inside their wagon and bedded down for the night, Julie whispered, "It doesn't matter, you know. Any of it."

"Of course it matters," Teresa said firmly. "But you can't let it bother you. I'm sure the captain has a good reason for visiting that wagon, and—"

"It does *not* matter," Julie repeated stiffly, miserable. "He can do whatever he wants. I just wish this trip were over and we were there. Oh, please, let's not talk about any of it again. Please."

She turned her back toward Teresa, whose mattress was on the other side of the wagon, and whispered a muted good night.

Yes, she told herself mournfully, it mattered. Something she had once read in the Bible raced through her mind then: "To the hungry soul every bitter thing is sweet."

She had been hungry. Derek's love had been sweet. Now only bitterness remained.

🦋 Chapter Four 🦋

WHEN the stygian night had faded to the gray shroud of dawn, the storm had abated. The snow had ended, leaving the hills and plains in alabaster glory. Julie peered from the wagon, thinking how beautiful the sight would be were it not a hindrance to them. She could hear the squeals of delighted children, begging for a few hours in that playground.

Myles brought hot porridge from the camp fire and told Julie and Teresa that Derek and Thomas had ridden out earlier to see whether the road ahead was passable. "If the sun manages to break through," he remarked hopefully, "the snow will start to melt. But we've still got to contend with mud."

"It could take days for the mud to dry up, even if the sun is strong," Teresa pointed out.

"Our supplies are running low. We can't just sit here, Myles."

"We won't," he told her, kissing her lovingly. "The going might be very slow, however. We'll have to stop and cut pine boughs to fill up mud holes as we come to them. We'll see what Arnhardt says when he and Thomas get back. No telling how long they'll be gone, but we plan on staying put till tomorrow."

They finished eating, and Teresa remarked that she would love to go for a walk. "I'm feeling awfully cramped and stiff from spending so much time in the wagon."

"Then walk we shall," Myles responded cheerily, and after she was bundled up, they left.

Restless, Julie decided to go for a walk on her own, and after dressing warmly, she climbed down from the wagon and smiled as she felt the soft crunch of snow under her boots. She delighted in every step, marveling at the wonderland. The air was crisp, and above the distant mountain peaks was a hint of golden light. The sun was coming out, after all.

The sound of crunching snow behind her made her turn. Arlo Vance was following her. Arlo, an enigma, had appeared out of nowhere as they left Louisiana and crossed into Texas. Alone with his wagon and six mules, he was happy and relieved to join their wagon train, citing the dangers of traveling alone.

He was heading for the Arizona territory, where they were going, so that was fine. But since his arrival, he had stayed to himself, seldom joining the men around the fire at night, never mentioning anything personal or explaining why he had started such a long journey by himself. One of the young boys had peeked into Arlo's wagon and reported there was little inside, just food and a few necessary provisions. This added to everyone's curiosity, for Arlo's wagon was large, with ample room for cargo. Why was he burdening himself with a heavy wagon he didn't need?

"Miss Marshall, wait up," Arlo called, his voice ringing clearly in the quiet snowy morning.

Julie told herself to be friendly. Why not? He was not a bad-looking man, of medium height, a bit heavy, in his mid-thirties. His hair was dark and hung loosely around his neck. He drew closer and she could see his eyes. Myles didn't like Arlo's eyes, she knew that. They were narrow and lacked warmth. His entire face looked threatening because of the strange scars all over his cheeks. He looked like a man who had known violence. But what man—or woman—hadn't known violence in recent years? She reminded herself to ask Myles about Arlo.

"Miss Marshall," he said again, standing before her, a wide grin twisting the scars into a macabre crisscross pattern. "I hope you don't mind me joining you. I was starting to feel closed in back there, listening to all those kids whining and their mothers screaming at them. Horses don't smell too good, either." He made a face and Julie laughed.

"Besides," he continued, "it's not safe for you to be out walking alone."

She raised an eyebrow. "What makes you say that, Mr. Vance? There's not a soul around for miles." She began walking again, carefully lifting her skirt to the tops of her boots as the snow got deeper and deeper.

"It's not always people you have to be afraid of. There are coyotes and wolves, and with all this snow, they can't be too choosy about what they eat."

"Really, Mr. Vance. You have a way of making a lady feel safe!"

He shrugged. "Please call me Arlo."

She stepped into a hidden drop-off, lost her footing, and pitched forward. He didn't move fast enough, and she landed on her face in the deep snow.

"That's another thing to watch out for." He pulled her to her feet and laughed at the sight of her snow-covered form. "I'm sorry. It's just that you look so funny."

Julie dusted at the snow, unperturbed. "I guess that ends my walk. I'll have to go change clothes now."

"Oh, it'll brush off easy enough." He dusted her shoulders, then moved to brush the snow from her chest. But he jerked back quickly as he realized he had touched her breasts. "I'm sorry," he offered, staring down at the ground. "Please don't think I was trying to be . . . uh . . ."

"I know," she said, embarrassed. "Tell me." She looked for another direction. "If you don't think I'm being nosy, what takes you west? You speak with a northern accent, so I don't suppose you're running from the Yankees."

His reply was surprisingly brusque. "No, I'm not."

"Forgive me. It's none of my business." She turned to walk back to camp, but he blocked her path, his gaze intense.

"I didn't mean to be short with you, Miss Marshall. I'm aware of the speculation about me, but I don't want you wondering. I mean, I'd like for us to be friends. I'm not trying to be forward, it's just that I don't know of any other way to let you know how I feel without coming right out and saying I'd like to get to know you better. I haven't got any courting skills, you see?"

Julie was surprised. She couldn't criticize him for being blunt, because she was often pretty blunt herself. "I'm flattered, Mr. Vance, but frankly, I don't foresee any opportunities for socializing on a wagon train."

"Will you at least stop calling me Mr. Vance?" he asked. "It makes me feel like an old man. And as for being social, what are we doing right now?"

She smiled up at him. "Walking in the snow."

"Well, we're getting to know each other, aren't we?"

"I suppose."

"That's a start. And when we get to San Angelo, there'll be a big dance. I heard the town always does that when a wagon train comes through. It's their way of saying welcome. Would you do me the honor of allowing me to escort you?"

A dance! Heavens, she couldn't even remember the last time she had whirled about a dance floor! The thought was so appealing. But what did she know about Arlo Vance? Myles wouldn't approve, for all the menfolk were leery of Arlo. Derek wouldn't like it, either. *That* thought gave her pleasure.

"You're hesitant." Arlo continued to smile hopefully. "It's because no one knows anything about me, is that it? Well, I'll be glad to go to your brother and tell him I have only the most honorable of intentions."

"That won't be necessary, Arlo. I am capable of making my own judgments about people." She wondered if Arlo sensed her doubts about him. Something she could not quite define warned her to be careful with his feelings.

His eyes widened just enough that she

could see the hope there. "You will allow me to escort you?"

"We'll see," she hedged, beginning to walk again. He fell into step beside her.

"Maybe it'd help you make up your mind if you knew something about me, knew why I'm traveling alone."

His voice suddenly became tinged with sadness.

"I was married once," he began softly, head bowed. "We had a little farm in Pennsylvania. It wasn't much, but we survived, me and my wife and little girl. We were happy. Then the war broke out, and I felt it was my duty to join up with the Union army. I thought Louise and Betsy would be safe, but there was fighting around Gettysburg, not far from our farm. I got there as soon as I could. It was too late." He swallowed hard.

"Please, Arlo," Julie said quickly. "Don't talk about something that hurts you. It's none of my business."

"But I want you to know," he cried. "It burns me, and the only way I can get any peace at all is to tell it to somebody who might give a damn, like you." He rushed on. "I went back to find my farm burned to the ground. Louise and Betsy had been shot like dogs. The damn Rebs didn't even stop with two bullets. They kept on shooting and filled them full of holes. They weren't part of the goddamn war, and Betsy was four years old. Now they're both dead."

"Oh, Arlo, I'm so sorry," Julie whispered, cut clear through. "What a terrible grief you must carry. Dear Lord, I am sorry."

He took a deep breath and looked up at the sky, gazing into the distance as though attempting to avoid the memories by looking far away into space. "That's why I'm traveling alone, Miss Marshall. I'm searching for some peace, and I'll keep on moving till I've found it."

After a silence she spoke. "Please call me Julie," she offered in a gesture of friendship. "I've known grief from the war, too, and I do understand."

"Then you'll do me the honor of allowing me to escort you to the dance?" he asked.

"Of course," she told him. "I'll look forward to it." The poor man wanted a friend, that was all.

Later, when she told Myles, he was instantly furious. "He's not taking you to any dance. I won't allow it. I'm the head of this family, and—"

"You're the head of *your* family, yours and Teresa's," Julie cried, her own anger rising. "I am in charge of my own life. You *don't* tell me what to do, Myles."

They glared at each other, and Teresa said, "Both of you, stop it right now! This is ridiculous!" To Myles she said, "Julie is capable of making her own decisions about her friends, and she should be allowed to do so without interference from either of us. If Mr. Vance proves to be undesirable company, I am sure she will end their relationship at once."

Myles scratched at the stubble of his beard. Teresa was right. And Julie wouldn't bend to his will, anyway. He just hoped Vance wouldn't bother his sister further. Damn it, he wished he knew what it was that bothered him about Vance. There was just something. . . .

Sudden shouts around them turned their attention to Derek and Thomas riding up the slope. They rushed outside to join the others.

"It's warming up," Derek told them, sitting atop his palomino, "and it doesn't look as though the snow will be a problem. If we move out right away, we can still make a few miles today, before the snow turns into slush and mud. Get ready to leave at once."

The men moved to harness their horses, and the women scurried to prepare for the journey. Julie hung back. She didn't know why, but for some unexplained reason she could not tear her gaze from Derek, who was staring at her intently.

Finally he dismounted and took a few steps toward her, but a woman's voice stopped him.

"Derek! I must talk to you."

Elisa Thatcher approached, and Derek was

forced to turn away from Julie and see what Elisa needed.

With a deep sigh, Julie left to help Teresa and Myles prepare for the day's trek.

❧ Chapter Five ❧

AT long, long last, they arrived in San Angelo. The townspeople were happy to see the wagon train, and after introductions to more people than Julie could possibly remember, Myles whisked her and Teresa to one of the town's few hotels, dismissing their protests that they would save money by staying in the wagon.

The next day, while Myles went off with the men to barter some of their horses for mules or oxen, Julie and Teresa shopped. Everywhere they went people were friendly, glad for the excitement of new faces, glad for an excuse to be festive despite the bleak winter.

There had not been much to choose from in the few shops, and Julie made up her mind not to buy a dress for the dance, to forego the ball altogether. She returned to the hotel and was surprised, a few hours later, by the delivery of a dress she had admired. Teresa had told Myles how pretty the dress looked on Julie, and that Julie refused to spend the money for it. Myles, bless his generous heart, had gone and bought it for her, explaining that after trading two of his horses and one of hers for oxen, there had been money left over.

It was a beautiful dress. Slip-on, puffed sleeves were fashioned to taper from her elbows to her wrists, and the points were meticulously embroidered in gold cord. The skirt was full and hung in thick drapes, a new style from Paris, which did not demand hoops—for which Julie was grateful. Hoops, as well as other fashion items, were unimportant and had no place on wagon trains.

The next day, an hour before the dance, Julie stood before the oval mirror and beheld the vision she was. The gown was of midnight-blue velvet, and the delicate gold thread embroidery around the bodice accented her black hair. She had labored for hours with a borrowed curling iron, twisting her long tresses into delicate spirals that graced the tops of her bare shoulders. Tiny ribbons that matched the dress were entwined in the curls.

A soft knock on the door brought Julie out of her reverie, and she heard Teresa's voice.

"Oh, you're beautiful!" Teresa exclaimed, clasping her hands in admiration as she

stepped inside. "Julie, I always did think you
were the prettiest woman I ever saw, and now
I know I was right!"

"Teresa, you're prejudiced," Julie said,
laughing. "You look lovely, too, Teresa. You
did a marvelous job on that dress."

Teresa looked down at her loose-fitting
gown of soft pink wool. "Are you sure you
can't tell where I let out the seams? I don't
mind looking pregnant, but I don't want to
look awkward, either."

Julie reached out to adjust the white ribbon
and bow Teresa had fashioned under her bodice to conceal the seam marks. "You do have
talent with a needle, Teresa."

"Uh-oh!" Teresa's eyes grew wide, and her
hands flew to her swollen stomach. "The
baby just kicked me. What am I going to do if
my bow starts jumping up and down?"

They looked at each other and giggled, delighted, but the moment was spoiled by the
appearance of Arlo Vance in the open doorway.

"I hope I'm not early," he said.

Julie's elation faded. She had told him she
would meet him downstairs, in the lobby.
Dear heavens, he was ornery, bent on doing
things his way without regard for what anyone else wanted. "It's all right, Arlo," she
told him in a tight voice as Teresa looked on,
puzzled. "But I did tell you I would meet you
downstairs."

He stepped inside and flashed a wide grin, his eyes raking over her possessively. "I knew you were going to look real pretty, honey. I wanted to escort you downstairs, to let everyone know you're with me."

Julie bristled. But, not wanting to make a scene, she told Teresa she would see her downstairs and then she allowed Arlo to lead her through the door and down the narrow, dimly lit hallway.

"This hotel is a dump," Arlo remarked with a condescending air. "Why didn't your brother put you in another one?"

She looked at him sharply. "Myles got rooms we could afford, and I see nothing wrong here, anyway. It's clean."

"Why didn't you tell me money was a problem?" he asked her pointedly. "I would be glad to put you up at my hotel. It's a nice place. No ballroom, but the rooms are bigger and furnished with newer things."

"I wouldn't dream of such a thing," she gasped, astonished. "Really, Arlo—"

"Shhh," he hissed. "We're about to make our grand entrance."

Standing at the top of the stairway, she could see that the lobby was already crowded. From the adjacent ballroom came the sounds of instruments being tuned. As she listened, she heard something that made her gasp with horror. Arlo leaned over the railing and yelled, "Hey, all you ladies and gentlemen down there! I want to introduce you to the prettiest girl in the state of Texas—Miss Julie Marshall."

Julie wanted the earth to open and swallow her. Never had she known such mortification. At least a hundred people turned to stare up at her curiously.

"Arlo, how could you?" she hissed, but he tightened his grip on her arm and started down the staircase.

If all those people hadn't been watching, Julie would have exploded. Arlo, she decided, was crazy, and she didn't known why she hadn't seen that before. He was also pompous. She wanted nothing more to do with him, but what could she do about that evening?

She saw the way some of the women were looking at her, and she wondered whether they were shocked by Arlo's behavior or had heard Elisa's gossip. She only wished she were someplace else.

Then she became aware of familiar eyes on her, of long, thick lashes fringing eyes as black as the Savannah River. Derek was standing to one side, strikingly handsome in a wine velvet coat, his coffee-colored hair curling slightly about the open-throated white satin shirt. He watched with a look of quiet amusement, his lips slanted, but she saw his nostrils flare ominously, his fingers gripping his brandy snifter.

Julie glanced away and tried to control the

nerves that threatened to make her explode. She had to get through the evening. Then, she would forget she had ever met Arlo Vance. But she *had* to get through the evening.

Arlo escorted her on into the oak-paneled ballroom, which was gaily decorated in streamers of red, white, and blue. In the center of the high ceiling, a large crystal chandelier cast mellow light onto the rose carpet below. To one side, the orchestra had set up their instruments on a platform. Along the other wall ran four white linen-covered tables, all laden with platters of sandwiches, fried chicken, fried sweet potatoes, and griddle cakes, as well as dozens of frosted cakes and succulent fruit pies, cookies, and several kinds of candy.

Arlo led Julie to the far corner of the room where a large crystal bowl was filled with bright crimson punch. The woman standing beside it smiled and gave them two cups filled to the brim, but her expression changed as Arlo took a big swallow from each cup, then set them down on the table. He pulled out a flask from his coat pocket and added whiskey to each cup. He held one out to Julie, but she shook her head and snapped, "No, I don't want any, Arlo. What is wrong with you, anyway? You are behaving terribly." To the hostess Julie murmured only, "I'm sorry."

"I'm going to have a good time tonight," he

said sharply, tossing his drink down in one gulp and helping himself to Julie's. "And so are you. Just relax. If other people don't like it"—he glowered at the woman who still stared at him—"they can go soak their heads."

"Oh, dear me!" The woman gasped, then turned and hurried away.

"Arlo!" Julie faced him, grateful that they were away from the others. "I thought we might be friends, but I find you are not the kind of person I want for a friend. You are unpardonably rude, and you embarrass me. I am sincerely sorry for the pain you suffered in the war, but carrying a grudge against the whole world is not the way to the peace you say you want. Now, if you will excuse me, I prefer not to be in your company. I wish you well, Arlo."

She turned to walk away, but he set his cup down and caught her roughly around the waist, slinging her toward him. "I won't excuse you," he growled, pulling her onto the dance floor. The musicians were playing a soft melody. "We're gonna dance."

Julie realized he was well on the way to being drunk, had probably been drinking all afternoon. If she made a scene, there was no telling what might happen. If Myles knew what was happening, there was no telling what he would do. It was best, she decided, to dance with Arlo for a while and then slip away from him later.

He held her much closer than decorum dictated, and she tried to pull back without being obvious about it.

"We're gonna have a good time," he muttered. "I'm gonna show those sons of bitches on that wagon train that Arlo Vance can have a pretty woman. They think 'cause I'm a Yankee I ain't good enough for them or for a Southern woman."

They danced in silence, and after a while he said, "I like to hold you. You feel good, Julie. Have you ever had a real man? I'll bet them Johnny Rebs don't know anything about satisfying a spitfire like you."

"Arlo, if you don't behave," she warned, "I'm going to scream."

"Good." He chuckled. "Maybe it'll bring that gimp-legged brother of yours over here so's I can smash his self-righteous face. Scream, Julie, but I'm not going to let you go."

How dare he call Myles "gimp-legged"? There was something terribly wrong with Arlo.

The dance ended, but instead of releasing her, Arlo continued to hold her, smiling down at her insolently as he waited for the music to begin again.

"Let me go, Arlo," she whispered between clenched teeth. "I don't want to dance with you. I find you offensive and anything but a gentleman."

"Well, I don't find you offensive," he said, laughing, blasting her with whiskey breath. "And I find you every bit a lady—and more. I'll just bet when you let your hair down and stop acting prissy, you can be real hot. We'll find out later."

She jerked against him in vain. There was nothing she dared say to him at that point. Should she scream?

"The lady promised this dance to me, Mr. Vance."

Julie looked up gratefully to see Derek towering above them, his brown-black eyes stormy. Taken by surprise, Arlo's hold upon her relaxed. With one quick jerk Julie freed herself and stepped quickly to Derek's side. His arm around her, so protective, had never been more welcome.

Arlo sized up the situation as quickly as he could. Arnhardt was too damn big. And as much as he'd had to drink, he wouldn't stand a chance anyhow. Soon he would see that Arnhardt paid for butting in. But for the moment he figured it was best to leave. With a last hungry gaze, he promised himself a chance someday to enjoy the delectable fruits of Miss Julie Marshall.

"Well, of course, Captain," Arlo said, giving Derek a polite bow. "The lady is all yours. Good evening to you."

"Thank you," Julie whispered gratefully. "You couldn't have come at a better time. He's had too much to drink."

"Vance has other problems besides drinking, Julie," Derek said somberly. "You would be wise to stay away from him." He took her in his arms and they began to dance.

"I know that now," she admitted. "I'm afraid what happened to his family has unbalanced his mind." She spoke absently. The nearness of Derek, having his strong arm wrapped tightly about her, was overwhelming. She was floating with a heady, dizzy feeling.

"Tell me," Derek urged. "No one knows anything about Vance. He just showed up one day and asked to join us. I saw no harm. But it helps to know a man in case he gives you trouble."

She told Derek the story as Arlo had told it. Then she said, "It's made him bitter toward all Southerners, I'm afraid." She repeated Arlo's caustic comments about the wagon train members.

"If he makes trouble, he'll get trouble," Derek said. Then his arms tightened, and he smiled. "You're ravishing tonight, Julie, ravishing."

Julie felt the familiar warm flush catapulting within her. It was so easy—oh, dear God, so easy— to remember those times in his arms, nights when they were alone. As she gazed up at his warm, sensuous lips, she could almost feel those lips. So many warm memories. . . .

He gazed down at her, suddenly amused. "What are you thinking about, Julie? Whatever it is makes you happy."

With her usual candor she replied, "I won't lie to you, Derek. I was thinking about how it was for us. It was good, right or wrong, and I will always cherish the memories."

"Would you care to make more memories?"

She stumbled, losing her step. "Why . . . no," she stammered, grasping for composure. "Derek, I was not insinuating . . . oh, I don't know what I mean!" Her cheeks were flaming.

Derek laughed, but it was a gentle laugh, not taunting.

Others drifted in, and the ballroom began to fill. They were receiving open stares. Arlo had positioned himself against a wall and was scowling at them. Abruptly, Derek stopped dancing, tucked her hand in the crook of his arm, and led her from the dance floor.

"It's a nice night, and we could both use some fresh air." He stopped by the punch bowl where another hostess ladled the crimson punch into two cups, handing them to Derek with a friendly smile.

Outside on the terrace, the night wind was cold. Stars, studding the sky like ice chips, seemed to chill the air even more. Julie shivered, hands trembling as she lifted the crystal cup to her lips to drink. "I guess it isn't so nice out here, after all, Julie. You're freezing."

"Anything is better than being back in there with Arlo Vance watching every move I make."

"Why did you agree to come to the ball with him, Julie?" he asked. "To make me jealous?"

She matched his smugness by asking demurely, "Did I succeed?"

He chuckled, moving closer. Lips brushed against her own as he murmured, "You little vixen." His mouth claimed hers. She resisted but only for a moment, then felt herself helplessly yielding.

Finally he released her, smiling in triumph. "You've been wanting me to do that, and don't lie to yourself about it." His eyes were challenging. "I feel you watching me, Julie, and I see the desire in your eyes. It matches my own. What we had was damn good."

He kissed her again, passionately, and when he released her, she was crying. Stepping back, she crossed her arms across her bosom and sobbed, "Yes, it was good, Derek. It was beautiful." Tears streamed down her cheeks. "Can't you leave me alone?" she whispered. "We both know we don't want the same things out of life, so why can't you get the hell out of mine?"

Suddenly he bent over and lifted her into his arms. "You don't want me to get out of your life, Julie, you want me in your life—on your terms. You're so goddamn stubborn, you deny us both pleasure because you want your way. But tonight, by God, it'll be *my* way."

He walked her swiftly across the terrace, down the stone steps, and into an alley behind the hotel.

"Where are you taking me?" she demanded. "Derek, put me down."

He ignored her.

They passed a drunk staggering in the alley, and then a tomcat searching for food.

He walked purposefully, and Julie lay in his arms, her head on his shoulder. "Derek, please let me go," she begged as they moved through the glow of a street lamp into the dark shadows of the main street. "Forcing me won't make me agree to be your mistress."

"Force you?" He laughed. "When did I ever force you, Julie? I won't force you tonight, either. But I'm going to make you realize you want me as much as I want you."

They reached the wagon train compound, and he walked directly to the large Conestoga used for a supply wagon, the wagon he lived in. With one quick movement he lifted her up and inside, pulling himself in right behind her.

Without preamble, he began kissing her, soothing her with caresses, and in a few minutes both were naked in the dark wagon.

His fingertips danced slowly down her belly, sliding easily downward between her thighs, sending spasms of pure pleasure into her. He knew just where to touch to cause her to moan with delight. Enraptured, she yielded, but mustered enough will to plead once. "No, Derek, don't do this, please."

His lips were devouring her breasts, moving between the swollen globes to tease. Raising his head, he taunted, "Take me, Julie. Put me where you want me," and he thrust his swollen organ against her thigh. "I'm yours . . . just as you're mine. Take me, misty eyes, all of me, if you can."

She could no longer deny the voracious need, and her fingers inched toward him as her heart urged her on. She wrapped her hand about him, and they sank to the floor as one. Spreading her thighs, lifting her legs, she guided him, gasping with delight as he thrust inside her. Bittersweet spasms of fire flamed within her belly. She hated him and hated herself, but, oh, he did have such power.

As he plunged inside her again and again, she clutched eagerly at his undulating buttocks, inciting him. Faster and faster he drove into her, carrying them to a realm of euphoric release.

Moments later he withdrew to lie beside her, cradling her head on his shoulder. Gently, lovingly, he caressed her face. She made no sound, and he did nothing to provoke her, for he wanted the moment of peace to last. He ought to have known better. Peace was never theirs for very long. She started to dress, and he said, getting up and putting on his clothes, "I'll walk you back to the hotel."

"I can walk myself," she said, then could not resist saying, "unless you want to go back to the ball in hopes of seeing Elisa. I suppose you love the way she fawns all over you."

"Elisa?" he said. "You think I would lust after a woman in her condition?"

"Her condition is temporary. Her marital status is not—but I doubt that her being married would stand in your way if you wanted to bed her."

"No, it wouldn't," he told her bluntly. "If a married woman I find desirable invites me to her bed, I don't have the scruples to turn her down . . . as long as her husband isn't *in* the bed with us."

He laughed at himself. She was about to say something cutting when Micah came running and peered into the wagon. At the sight of Captain Arnhardt standing with Miss Marshall, certainly imprudent at such an hour, Micah bowed his cotton-white head in embarrassment.

Derek was not one to explain his own conduct, so he simply said, "Yes, Micah. What is it?"

Micah slowly lifted his eyes. He looked afraid. "Cap'n, it's Miz Thatcher. She in a bad way. She hurtin'. She say fo' me to fetch you quick."

As Julie looked on in alarm, Derek touched his fingertips to his mustache thoughtfully. "It isn't time for the baby, so this means trouble. Run on into town and find a doctor. Is there anyone with her now, Micah?"

"She wouldn't let me get nobody but you. She say to get you and nobody else. She say she don't want none of them old busybody women around her. That was what she said, Cap'n Arnhardt."

"Right now she doesn't have any choice." He turned to Julie and told her calmly, "Go back into town with Micah and find Teresa and bring her here. Elisa can't have any objections to Teresa."

He hurried away, and Julie watched him disappear into the shadows. Why, she wondered, had Elisa sent Micah for Derek? Why hadn't she just sent for a doctor?

❧ Chapter Six ❧

JULIE rushed into the hotel lobby, ignoring the curious looks. She knew she was a sight—hair disheveled, gown mussed. Pushing through the throngs of people, she searched the ballroom until she saw Teresa and Myles standing beside the refreshment table. Both looked at her in alarm as she made her way over to them.

Myles quickly turned to grasp her elbow and lead her away from the curious before asking, "What on earth has happened?"

Julie explained, and in a minute she and Teresa were on their way to the wagon train compound, while Myles went in search of a doctor.

The two women were scurrying down the street when they heard Myles shouting, and turned to see him running from the hotel. He reached them, a look of deep worry on his face. "I'm sorry, but there's no doctor around. There's only one in this town, and somebody just told me he's been gone since early morning. A whole family is sick about ten miles out, and there's no telling when he'll get back."

Julie and Myles looked at Teresa, who was shaking her head. "I've never delivered a baby. I've never even seen one born."

"I'm sorry," Julie said. "I haven't, either. But maybe it isn't the baby. Maybe it's something else."

Myles went to find Esther Webber, and the two women continued on to Elisa's wagon, shivering against the cold. Micah was standing outside, shoulders hunched, eyes filled with fright. "I couldn't find no doctor, so I come back here. Is she gonna be all right, Miz Marshall? If it's the baby, will it be all right?"

"Micah, I certainly hope the answer is yes to both your questions." Julie patted his bony shoulder. "Pray for her. We'll do what we can."

She started by him, but he cried out, "If ever'thing thing ain't all right, will you see to it Captain Thatcher knows it won't my fault? His daddy told me to see to it Miz Thatcher got out to Arizona okay."

"No one is going to blame you for anything, Micah," Julie told him. "Now go somewhere and pray."

Before they could call out, Derek pushed aside the canvas at the rear of the wagon, a grim look on his face. "I hope the doctor's on the way. The baby's coming. I don't think it will be much longer. I wanted to move her to town, to a room somewhere, but hell, I don't think there's time. Did you find a doctor?"

"Dear God," Teresa gasped.

"The doctor's out of town," Julie said, "and no one knows when he will be back. Myles has gone to get Esther Webber."

A shrill scream from inside the wagon caused everyone to stiffen. Julie gave herself a shake and murmured, "We have to do what we can."

Swiftly, Derek lifted her and then Teresa up into the wagon. "I'll be outside if you need me," he offered, knowing, as they did, there was nothing he could do.

Elisa was lying on her mattress, her face drawn and pale, slick with sweat. Another pain slashed through her body, and she screamed, writhing and twisting, her nails clawing at the mattress. "I can't stand it. Get it out of me, please. Get it out!"

Julie knelt beside her. "Esther Webber is coming, Elisa," she told her. "She'll help. Please now, try to relax and stop fighting the pain. You might hurt the baby, and you're making it harder on yourself."

Elisa's lips curled back in a snarl. "You!" she hissed, drawing away, arching her back.

"Get away! I don't want you near me." Julie moved back, stunned by Elisa's violent reaction.

Teresa knelt down, reaching to give Julie a reassuring pat. "She doesn't know what she's saying, Julie. She's in so much pain, and she's frightened."

"I do know what I'm saying," Elisa panted, her swollen stomach heaving as she waited fearfully for a new contraction. "I don't . . . want . . . that bitch near me. Get . . . her away." Her shoulders rose from the mattress as she was caught in a fresh agony.

"Maybe I should wait outside," Julie whispered.

"No, you stay right here," Teresa told her firmly.

Elisa's body slumped. "Both of you can get out," she cried. "Where's Derek? I want Derek."

Teresa raised an eyebrow. "You've got a baby wanting to be born, and that's a woman's job, not a man's."

"Yes," Elisa cried. "The baby is going to be born, and then it's going to die. That's the way it should be, because I never wanted it."

"You don't know what you're saying," Teresa cried, wiping Elisa's brow with the hem of her skirt. "We'll do everything we can for the baby, and it's going to be just fine."

"I don't want you simpering over me, you fool!" Elisa lashed out at her, flinging her arm to knock Teresa away. "Leave me alone! I want this baby to hurry and be born and die so I can get my beauty back and find a man who truly loves me."

Fearful, Teresa moved back to kneel beside Julie. They watched as Elisa began to writhe and twist again. Her voice was strong as she cried out, "Never would have wanted me if it hadn't been for the damn baby . . . life is over . . . beauty gone . . . damn baby . . . no one to love me . . . no one. Damn you, Adam."

Teresa looked up, delighted as Esther Webber scrambled into the wagon. "Thank God you're here! We don't know what to do. The baby is coming."

Esther bent over Elisa and made a hasty examination, ignoring her protests. "Yes, it's coming," she said without alarm. "Tell the captain we'll need some hot water. Tell him to have a wagon ready, too. There's no time to move her into town, but as soon as the baby comes, we will."

Teresa moved to follow her orders, and Julie asked, "Is there anything I can do?" Then, "She doesn't want me here," she added hesitantly.

"Nonsense," Esther snapped. "I may need you. It won't be long now."

"I . . . I don't want her here," Elisa gasped. "Please, send her away."

"Oh, for heaven's sake!" Esther looked at Julie in exasperation. "Of all times for you two to be feuding! Go on and get out, then. Teresa can help me."

Gratefully, Julie went to the rear of the wagon. When Derek saw her, he helped her down. "I sent Micah for the hot water, and Thomas has gone to get the wagon ready."

Myles stepped from the shadows and asked, "Don't you think it'd be better if you stayed inside, instead of Teresa? I mean, in her condition . . ."

"I know, I know," Julie murmured. "Elisa doesn't want me in there. She hates me."

"I think I understand why." Derek's voice was so soft that only Julie heard.

She looked at him curiously, but just then Elisa screamed again, louder than before, a long scream, and then there was another noise—a weak, mewing sound.

"The baby," Myles breathed.

Micah had arrived with the water, and he stopped short, tears springing to his eyes. "Oh, Lawdy, I've heard many a newborn cry, and I know what this one sounds like—like it ain't gonna live. Lawdy, Lawdy, he's just too weak."

Teresa stuck her head out of the wagon and called, "It's here—a little boy," then disappeared inside.

Thomas brought a wagon up, ready to take Elisa and the baby into town, but Derek told him they would have to wait till Mrs. Webber thought it safe for them to be moved.

Myles could suddenly keep still no longer. Running angry fingers through his hair, he turned to Derek and said, "Look. You may think I'm sticking my nose in your business, but Julie is my sister and her welfare is my concern. I want to know why you left the dance with her and why she came back to the hotel looking like she did. I want to know"—he jabbed his finger at Derek's massive chest, undaunted by his size—"what you're doing to my sister!"

"Oh, Myles, please!" Julie blinked back tears of frustration and embarrassment as she stepped from Derek's side. "Stay out of my business, please. I'm a grown woman."

"And he's a grown man. And—"

"We have a right to our privacy, Myles," Derek cut him off gently. "I care for Julie a great deal, and I don't think I have to tell you that we were once very close. We've had some problems. I still care for her, and whether she'll admit it or not, she still cares for me. We're trying to work things out. Can you understand?"

Myles was treading in dangerous water and he knew it. He glanced at his sister, then nodded. "All right. But damn it all, these are tense times, and I don't need additional worries right now. You two worry me."

Derek nodded slowly. "I understand, Myles, and we'll try not to."

Julie turned away, miserable. But her self-

81

recrimination was pushed aside as Teresa appeared again, holding out her arms to Myles, tears streaming down her face. He helped her down, wrapping his arms around her as she sobbed, "The baby died. Oh, Myles, the baby died. He cried once, and then he just died. He was so tiny, hardly as big as my hand. Oh, God. . . ."

Myles held her, trying to soothe what couldn't be soothed.

Micah turned away, disappearing into the shadows, and the sounds of his harsh weeping echoed in the night.

They waited for long moments, and then Esther looked out and said to Derek, "She's ready to be moved, but she refuses to go anywhere until she has spoken with you."

Muttering angrily, Derek thrust himself into the wagon in one motion. A few moments later, Esther came out, and Myles helped her down. "It's a disgrace! That woman's baby just died, and she doesn't even seem to care. Told me to get out, she did. Didn't even want to see the baby! Just wanted to see the captain."

Teresa spoke up quickly. "Mrs. Webber, I'm sure Elisa had a good reason to speak to Captain Arnhardt—and whatever it is, it's certainly none of our business. As for her seeming lack of concern, well, she's probably in shock. Let's not judge her, please. She has enough grief to bear at the moment."

Derek reappeared, this time with Elisa bundled in his arms. Her eyelids fluttered weakly as he handed her down to Myles, who quickly carried her to the wagon where Thomas was waiting. "We'll bury the baby in the morning," Myles said to no one in particular, then dropped to the ground.

"I'll ride with Elisa," Teresa said.

Esther disappeared, eager, doubtless, to spread her story.

"You said you understood why she hates me," Julie whispered when she and Derek were alone.

"It isn't important." He reached for her hand. "Let's go to my wagon. I think you could use a drink, and I've got some brandy."

She shook her head and stepped back. "No, I don't want to. Teresa and Myles will be expecting me back at the hotel soon. I want you to tell me why Elisa Thatcher hates me."

He shrugged, embarrassed. "She feels you're in her way."

Julie blinked and shook her head. "In her way? How?"

"She thinks she'd have a chance if it weren't for you."

"Would she?" Julie challenged, blazing with a jealous fire that appalled her. "Would she, Derek? Or *do* you have scruples that keep you from bedding a married woman? Maybe you do."

"No," he said, laughing. "You know me
83

better than that. But before tonight I hadn't made love to you, or another woman, for quite some time, so she probably felt how lusty I was."

"Well, she isn't pregnant anymore," Julie snapped furiously, "and you won't be making love to me anymore, so when you get hungry for a woman, you know whose wagon to go to, don't you?"

"I guess I do." He sighed. "You know, Julie, you're your own worst enemy. When a person has to lie to herself, there's not much hope for her, and you're lying if you say you don't love me and don't want me."

"Oh, I love you," she flared, "and I do want you, but not on your terms, so it's best we ignore each other from here on. You can inform Elisa," she said finally, tightly, "that she doesn't have to worry any longer about me being in her way."

"I'll do that," he retorted, then turned to walk away, taking big, purposeful strides as he left her alone in the night.

❧ Chapter Seven ❧

A LMOST a month had passed since the
wagon train rolled out of San Angelo.
The weather was cold, as was expected in late
January, and the trail was hard. Fortunately,
little snow had fallen, so there was only
the frigid temperature to endure. Passage
through the Guadalupe mountains was hard
enough without snow and ice.

When they had reached the Pecos river,
they found a small camp of prospectors on the
banks. The men obligingly helped them cross
the river. The night before the crossing, the
prospectors sat drinking with the men, relat-
ing the latest war news. Myles went to Julie
later and recounted the news that Fort Fisher
had been captured by Union forces only a few
weeks earlier, closing down Wilmington,
North Carolina—the last major Confederate
port. The stark reality was crushing. They

embraced for long moments, wordlessly, emotionally, grieving silently for a world they would never know again.

Julie seldom saw Derek anymore. Every day he rode out ahead of the wagons, scouting. He reported to the men at night any obstacles they might encounter the next day.

One morning, as Myles was hitching up the oxen and Julie and Teresa were cooking breakfast at the common camp fire, indignant shrieking broke the stillness.

"Indians!" Esther Webber cried, dropping a skillet of frying fatback. She stared around her in horror, clutching her throat, eyes bulging.

"Esther, it's not Indians," Teresa said, staring down at the spoiled food. "It's Elisa. I can see her standing outside her wagon, yelling."

Elisa was jumping up and down, face livid, fists clutched.

Derek had already ridden out, so the chore of dealing with Elisa fell on Thomas. Like the others, Thomas had grown weary of Elisa Thatcher's rotten disposition, which had become worse since she'd lost her baby.

Everyone followed Thomas as he went to see what was wrong.

"That sorry nigra!" Elisa raged to Thomas. "He's left. Run away. Now what am I going to do? How am I going to handle my wagon and oxen alone? How dare he? I want him found and every inch of black skin whipped from his hide!" She jumped up and down, screaming.

"Now, Mrs. Thatcher." Thomas held up his hands to try and calm her. We don't have time to waste looking for Micah. We've got to keep moving. I'll find somebody to take over your wagon." He looked around, spotted one of Esther's teenage sons, and called him over. "Lonnie Bruce, will you help Mrs. Thatcher?"

Esther quickly stepped forward and pushed Lonnie Bruce behind her. Indignant hands on her hips, her fleshy face bright with anger. She declared, "No, he won't. Micah ran away because of the way that woman mistreated him, always screaming at him and cursing him. I've even seen her hit him with a whip. I'll not have my boy treated that way. She got herself into this mess. Let her get herself out of it."

"She's right," Lonnie Bruce agreed. He had his mother's pinched, critical face. "Everybody knows how she treated old Micah. I don't blame him for running off. I'd have done the same thing. I ain't working for her, no sir."

"Well." Elisa turned cold, condemning eyes on him. "I don't want white trash working for me, anyway."

"Who do you think you're calling white trash?" Esther advanced a step and Thomas moved between them. "Now hold on, both of you!" he ordered. "There's no need for this." He looked around hopefully. "Is there anyone who'll help Mrs. Thatcher out? When we get to El Paso, she can probably hire somebody, but we can't let this hold us up now. We have to keep moving."

No one said a word.

"Come on now," Thomas pleaded. "We agreed at the beginning of this journey that we all have to work together. We're one big family. The captain is out scouting, and I've got a job to do, so somebody has to volunteer to take over Mrs. Thatcher's wagon."

"Let her do it herself," Esther challenged. "She isn't too good to get a few blisters on her hands. All of us women have taken our turns at the reins. She brought this on herself, and I say, let her take the consequences."

A murmur of agreement rippled through the crowd.

"Do I need to remind you that Mrs. Thatcher lost her baby only a few weeks ago?" Thomas glared reproachfully. Damn! How could they be so cold-hearted? Sure, the woman was a spoiled brat. He didn't like her any more than they did, but still . . . "We aren't going to move out until someone steps forward," he warned. "I'm not going to let her take her own reins."

"Well, I'm going to take them!" Elisa cried suddenly, tears of humiliation and anger streaming down her face. "To hell with all of you. What can I expect from white trash?"

Thomas stepped over to grasp Elisa's arm and glowered down at her. "If you don't keep your mouth shut, no one will help you."

"I don't want any help from them." She jerked her arm away. "And you keep your hands off me. You have no right to touch me. I'll take my own wagon."

"No, you won't." Myles spoke up suddenly, giving Julie a beseeching look. "We can't let this hold us up. We've got to keep on moving. I don't want Teresa to have the baby on the trail. Julie, can you handle our wagon and let me take Mrs. Thatcher's?"

Julie nodded, knowing what a rough time she was in for. But, no, they mustn't lose any time.

Suddenly, Lonnie Bruce stepped forward. "Mr. Marshall, if you'll take Mrs. Thatcher's reins, I'll take yours. I just don't want to work for that woman, but I don't mind working for your wife and your sister, not at all."

Esther said nothing.

Grateful, Myles accepted his offer, and Julie said she would be glad to help out. Myles set about harnessing Elisa's oxen, and Lonnie Bruce went with Julie to finish hitching theirs.

Inside the wagon, moving at last, Teresa turned to Julie and sighed. "I wonder what makes Elisa behave as she does? She goes out of her way to turn people against her. It's so sad."

"Well, as you're always saying," Julie replied, "we shouldn't judge people because we never know what is happening inside to make them behave as they do."

Teresa shook her head, her thoughts far away.

They rode in silence for a while, and then Julie decided to go up front and sit with Lonnie Bruce in case he should need help. She soon regretted the move, because the boy had bloody Indian stories on his mind and wouldn't stop talking. He was a great deal like his mother.

"Don't believe everything you hear, Lonnie Bruce," Julie chided after a while. "Sometimes tales like this are exaggerated."

"What I know ain't no exaggeration," he retorted indignantly, " 'cause my granddaddy came out here as a mail rider when the Overland Mail Route got started, and when he came home, he told me what happened to set Cochise and the rest of the Chiricahua on the warpath."

Julie did not like the conversation, but she found it fascinating, anyway. "Tell me what your grandfather said."

"Well"—he took a deep breath, enjoying his big moment—"Granddaddy came out here in fifty-eight, and there won't no real bad trouble with the Chiricahua till sixty-one. Cochise had been friendly, but then he was arrested by mistake for something he didn't have nothing to do with. Some kidnapping, I think it was. Anyway, he escaped, but some of his men got killed, and ever since then, the Chiricahua have been on the warpath. And Cochise ain't the only Indian mad," he pronounced knowledgeably. "Have you heard about the Sand Creek Massacre?"

Julie shook her head.

"According to Granddaddy, the southern bands of Cheyenne were really suffering in the late fifties and early sixties, because they were having trouble finding game and a lot of them were starving. Then there was a Santee Sioux uprising in Minnesota, and a lot of white people got killed, and the whites living on the Plains heard about it and they got scared. A rumor got started that the Southern Cheyenne were moving north to join up with the Sioux and start attacking frontier settlements. Colonel Chivington, from Colorado, started attacking Cheyenne camps whether they were friendly or not. He said, 'Kill Cheyenne whenever and wherever found.' "

"How awful," Julie murmured. "He just gave an order like that?"

Lonnie Bruce nodded. "Last November, about five hundred friendly Cheyenne were camped at Sand Creek, in Colorado, with their leader, Black Kettle. He was one of the three peace chiefs who had signed a treaty. Anyway, he heard about Chivington's orders, but he'd been told by other U.S. army officers that at Sand Creek they'd be safe from attack. Well"—he paused—"that turned out not to be true. Seven hundred Colorado Volunteers attacked, led by Colonel Chivington. He gave orders not to take prisoners. He went charging into that camp waving an American flag, and Black Kettle waved a white flag. Indians were slaughtered—little children hacked to pieces, squaws killed. And the next day soldiers cut up corpses and took scalps and parts of bodies and hung 'em on their saddles and hat bands and rode on into Denver to show 'em all off."

Julie felt her stomach roll with revulsion. "But how could they? These were peaceful Indians."

He snorted. "I know, but you won't be feeling sorry for 'em if they come after us. It's bad enough when they got tomahawks and bows and arrows, but you give one of 'em a gun, and look out!"

Julie shuddered. "I've heard enough for one day, Lonnie Bruce."

Julie could not get the story out of her mind, and later that day, after the wagons had circled into their nightly corral, she drew Myles away from Teresa and repeated what she had heard. He did not seem surprised. "I know, Julie. I heard about it back in San Angelo."

"And you didn't tell us?" she asked, incredulous.

"We knew when we left Savannah that we were going to be heading through Indian territory. Why make ourselves fearful? There's not a wagon train heading west from any point that doesn't face the risk of Indian attack. We just have to be careful. Do you think Arnhardt is riding out every day just to look for fallen trees in our path? Hell, no. He's looking for Indians."

"And has he seen any?"

Myles shrugged, averting his eyes.

"Myles!" Julie cried, grasping his shoulders. "I have a right to know."

Patiently, he said, "As far as we know, we don't have anything to worry about until Arizona. If you want to know more, ask Arnhardt. Though I doubt he'll tell you any more than he tells us men, which isn't much. He isn't going to get people riled or upset unless it's absolutely necessary."

She did go to Derek, and after he had told her more horror stories, he said firmly, "I'm trusting you to keep what I've told you to yourself. The men are aware of the dangers, but there's no point in scaring the women."

"Ah, yes, protect the women from worry," she said sarcastically. "Don't let them worry about anything until a screaming Indian comes at them waving a tomahawk. Then they may worry."

Suddenly, something flashed in his eyes and he reached over to wrap strong arms around her, pulling her close. "Damn it, Julie, you don't have to be afraid. Don't you know I'll give my life, if I have to, to keep you from harm?"

Julie listened for the command of her brain to pull away from him, but there was only the sound of her heart. A warm feeling was spreading through her limbs, a good feeling, a delicious feeling. She found herself smiling up at him. "Yes, Derek. I do know that, just as I know I can't deny what I feel for you."

His mouth claimed hers in a soul-searing kiss, and she clung to him in desperation, wanting the moment never to end.

"You know," he said finally, angrily, "you're in my blood like a hunger that can't be fed. When I'm out on that trail every day, it haunts me—the joy, the pain—every damn thing we had. You feel it, too, I know you do."

"Yes. I won't lie, but—"

"Goddamn it, Julie, we can't go on like this. It's time we talked again. I've come to an understanding within myself, and there's something you have to know . . . something that may help you understand me better. I'm not the cold-hearted bastard you think I am."

Julie was suddenly, gratefully aware that Derek had held a part of himself away from her all along. An intense shudder went through her as she realized the moment of truth was at hand. "Then tell me, Derek," she urged. "Tell me what I need to know, Derek."

"We're going to be together," he said gruffly, tightening his hold on her. "Like it or not. You're going to be mine, and—"

An indignant gasp caused them to spring apart just as Elisa Thatcher stepped from the shadows. "This is disgusting! I come here to talk to you, Captain Arnhardt, about the mess I'm in with my nigra running out on me, and I find what I've suspected all along— you're letting this . . . this *whore* keep you from doing your job!"

Julie struggled against her own fury, grateful when Derek took over. He said, "Elisa, what I do is none of your business, and you would be wise to watch that nasty mouth. Now what the hell do you want?"

Shaken, she stammered, "My . . . my nigra, M-Micah, ran away."

"I heard," Derek replied.

"You'd best find me a driver, then, Captain," she ordered.

"I'll do what I can. Later. If you will excuse yourself now, you're interrupting."

"Oh, I can see that"—she laughed shrilly— "but I'm afraid you're going to have to bridle your animal lust for the moment and treat one of my animals, which seems to have taken ill."

Derek took a deep breath and smiled at Julie apologetically. "I'm sorry, but I'd better check on it. The poor oxen aren't as fortunate as Micah. They can't run away from her."

"Very funny!" Elisa snapped. "You can be sure my husband is going to hear how you've conducted yourself, Captain. You might find yourself out of a job."

He touched his fingertips to Julie's chin and mouthed, "I'll find you later," then turned away resolutely.

Julie watched them disappear, sorrowful because the tender moment was spoiled. What, oh, what had Derek been about to tell her? Wanting to be alone with her thoughts, she began walking among the cactus and scrubs . . . unaware that she was being stealthily followed.

❧ Chapter Eight ❧

JULIE inhaled the crisp, sweet air, gathering her wool cape tighter about her, stepping cautiously among the tiny rocks and rivulets of sand. She had always loved nighttime, exhilarating in the secret mystery of its beauties, never fearing its shadows. Peaceful, so peaceful. Here was the black, velvet shroud to hide her worries. The dancing stars seemed to say, when there is mirth, how can there also be gloom? Standing very still, her gaze became transfixed upon one star, brighter than the rest. Was that the way life was? She wondered, one soul brighter than the others? Some souls who merely provided a backdrop for the chosen one? It was times like this when her infinitesimally tiny existence seemed a sacrilege even to contemplate. Her soul was probably no more nor less significant to God than the faintest glimmer of the tiniest star in His heavens.

There, melting into the night, becoming part of it, she was able to give herself to the thought that provoked her: What had Derek been about to say when Elisa interrupted? In what way had he come to terms with himself? She shivered, not with cold but with anticipation. Perhaps, she thought suddenly, her own position had not been stated clearly enough. Maybe he thought she was bent on marriage. Not true! There had to be time for proper courtship, time to decide whether they wanted to spend a lifetime together. Meanwhile, she would not be relegated to the status of mistress. What kind of marriage would they have later, after she'd been his mistress? It would taint their love forever.

She heard footsteps and whirled about, expectant, happy, then realized it wasn't Derek. A scream began, changing to an angry gasp as she made out the scarred face of Arlo Vance. "Why are you following me?" she demanded furiously. "You frightened me, creeping up on me like that."

"Afraid of Indians?" His voice was arrogant. "No need to be when you're with me, Julie. The Indians are my friends."

"I'm surprised you have any friends," she said impetuously.

"Now, that's no way for you to talk to me, .

honey, not when I want us to be friends. Good friends."

"I don't wish to speak with you, Mr. Vance, and if you don't leave me this instant, I'm going to scream and bring the whole wagon train running."

"Now, honey," he cooed, blasting her with whiskey breath, "I only followed you out here so's we could be alone to talk. I've been trying to get you off to yourself ever since San Angelo. I know you've seen me watching you, but all I want to do is apologize for the other night. That's all. See, I'd had too much to drink before the dance and, well, I guess I was just desperate to be with a woman. You're so pretty. I wanted to be with you so bad, so I just kept saying the wrong things. In my state of mind, I figured I'd lost you before I even had you, so I was just going to go ahead and make my bid right then."

"And you lost, Mr. Vance," she told him icily. "We can never be friends. If you will excuse me, someone is waiting for me."

She started by him, but he caught her arm, giving it a painful twist. "Now listen, Julie, honey, the last thing I want to do is hurt you, but I will if you don't calm down and give me a chance to talk."

"You're hurting me," she cried. "Let me go, please. I don't want trouble, and if I scream, and my brother comes out here . . ."

"You don't want to see him killed, do you?"

He laughed, a nasty, evil sound in the once-sweet night. "So just listen. I want you to forgive me for the other night so we can start over. I'm sweet on you, Julie, 'cause you remind me of my sainted wife. All you got to do is be nice to me. Let me know I've got a chance with you, and I'll let you go."

His next move took her completely by surprise. She suddenly found her lips smothered by his, her neck bent backward. Then, just as quickly, he released her and shoved a hand across her mouth to stifle her scream of protest. "It's my face, isn't it?" he accused. "You like pretty faces, like Captain Arnhardt's face. Oh, I've seen the way you pine for him. I saw you leave with him the night you were supposed to be with me, and I saw how you looked when he was done with you. I know what you two were doing, 'cause I had a yen for the same thing. He got what I was supposed to have—what I *will* have before long. I promise you, I will.

"I want to tell you something." He pressed his hand harder as she struggled to release the rising screams. "I can't help these scars on my face. They're there for a reason. They proved to them goddamn savages that I'm a man. I played their game, and I won. The Apaches said if I could stand red-hot lances cutting into my flesh and not scream, they'd let me live. I wanted to scream. Oh, Lordy, when they stuck those lances in a fire and then put them on my face, and I could feel my own skin burning, the smoke stinging in my own nostrils, everything in me ached to scream. But I knew if I made one sound, they'd stick them lances in my eyeballs, like I'd just seen them do to the men with me. So I didn't scream. They kept on burning me till my whole face was almost in flames. Then they let their medicine man work on me. And when they were done, they told me I wore the brand of a great warrior, and no Apache would ever challenge me or try to hurt me again."

He forced her to the ground, throwing himself on top of her, his hand still pressing painfully over her mouth. "I heard you back there talking to the captain, asking about Indians, and I know you're scared. You want me to fix you so they'll think you're a great warrior, too? Why, when that wagon train goes into Apache country, they'll all be slaughtered except you. All you got to do is be brave, like I was brave."

Her eyes widened in horror, and she felt herself slipping away, for his hand was also pressing against her nostrils, and she couldn't breathe. Soft, gasping whimpers replaced the groans, and he drew his hand away. "Relax, honey, I'm not going to scar that peachy-pretty face of yours. And I won't let those redskins hurt you, either. You're safe with me. I do plan to keep you with me."

When she could force the words out, she said hoarsely, "Arlo Vance, you are . . . insane."

He threw his head back and laughed, the sound echoing in the stillness. Then, in the blink of an eye, his mood became somber. "I'm going to let you go now, Julie, but you will belong to me one day. I will win your heart, remember that. And remember also that if you are repulsed by my scars, they are what will save you from the fate the others will have. Go now. Tell your pretty captain. Tell your gimp-legged brother. If they wish to deal with me, so be it. I'll send their scalps back to you on the end of a spear!"

She scrambled to her feet, then stumbled and fell to her knees. After a moment she was able to stand. She lifted her long skirt and began running through the night to the compound.

She reached the wagon she shared with Myles and Teresa and leaned against the side, away from the glowing camp fires. Reason was slowly replacing panic. Arlo was drunk. Maybe there was no need to be frightened—just wary. No more solitary night walks, no more opportunities for him to accost her. With this soothing thought in mind, she was able to take a deep breath. No need to upset Myles. Why tell him Arlo's lies? What for? They all had enough on their minds without worrying about a drunken story like Arlo's. That decided, she was able to take several deep breaths, smooth her hair, straighten her dress, then step around the wagon and into the light.

"There you are!" Teresa called out brightly. She sat at the front of the wagon, mending one of Myles's shirts, fingers stiff with cold. "I was wondering where you'd disappeared to."

"Teresa, why aren't you beside the fire?" Julie admonished her. "It's much too cold for you out here."

Teresa made a face. "I'd rather be here than over there listening to Elisa. It seems she had some words with Captain Arnhardt earlier and she's been gossiping to the women about catching you and him in a torrid embrace."

Julie felt her cheeks burn, and glanced away. "It wasn't the way she . . . probably saw it, and I wasn't with him just now."

"Oh, you don't owe me an explanation," Teresa hastened to say. "I think it's wonderful that you two are trying to work things out between you, but you certainly don't need Elisa Thatcher spying on you and blabbing to everyone. And I know you weren't with him just now because he was looking for you."

"He was?" Julie immediately brightened, then blushed as Teresa giggled.

"He said he was going to look for you, and if he didn't find you, he'd be back. Just sit down and relax. If you join the other women, you'll just be subjecting yourself to Elisa's sharp tongue."

"Oh, she doesn't bother me," Julie told her. "By now everyone should know the kind of person she is, and nobody should take her seriously."

"They don't now. Oh, in the beginning people were intimidated by her. But now we're thinking in terms of surviving, not of being socially ostracized in Arizona. I think Elisa realizes this, and it makes her desperate. And," she added fervently, "let's don't forget her baby died. That's bound to have affected her, especially since we've heard that's the only reason her husband sent for her. She's a troubled woman."

Julie was only half-listening as she wondered whether to confide what had happened. She decided against it. Teresa didn't need other concerns, not in her condition. It would not be fair to burden her.

Teresa realized Julie was not listening and suddenly inquired, "If I'm not being too nosy, just how are things going with the captain?"

"We're talking." Julie shrugged. "I get the feeling something has stood in the way of our being totally honest with each other. If so, and we can work it out, fine. If not, then I think it's time to end things once and for all."

"But you don't want it to end, do you?" Teresa prodded.

"No," Julie admitted softly. "I don't, but if it must, then I'll accept it. Until we reach Arizona, though, it's going to be difficult to be around him, see him every day."

"Maybe it will be a joy instead," Teresa said brightly, nodding in the direction behind Julie. "Here he comes now."

He walked purposefully to them and, with an absent nod to Teresa, reached for Julie's hand. It was dwarfed by his. Silently, he led her into the shadows far away.

Staring down at her as they moved, he was captivated all over again by her delicate, rare beauty. If he closed his eyes he still saw her vividly in his mind—the misty green eyes shaded by long, dusty lashes, beguiling and mysterious . . . the sensuous lips . . . the perfectly sculpted body, whose mysteries he knew as well as he knew his own.

No woman, he had vowed, would ever capture his heart. His body, yes, but not his heart. He would not allow himself to be enslaved by love.

Julie did not ask their destination. As always, she was content to be in his company.

They reached an outcropping of rocks, and he held her close for a moment, then led her to a private cloister.

He leaned against a boulder, arms folded across his chest. "Now, we talk, misty eyes."

There was scant light, only a quarter moon, but Julie could see his narrowed eyes staring at her intently. She moved back, away from him, sensing that he needed to express himself without the arousal so easily sparked between them. He took a deep breath and began to talk.

"You had a fever on the ship." He reminded her of an incident several years past. "You were delirious and told me all about your past. But I'm the one who should have been so candid with you. Then you would understand why I feel as I do about marriage."

She knew it was best to ask no questions but to allow him to unleash whatever he had been holding inside all this time.

"Long ago," he went on, his gaze transfixed, "when I was a boy, I made up my mind that I would never tie myself to a woman. Understand that I had a happy childhood. I loved both my parents. But what caused me to make that vow was the realization that they never loved each other. Or, if they had, it was long over by the time I got there. They weren't happy together. Miserable was more like it. They never knew my sister and I could overhear through those thin walls—a fisherman's modest house—that we heard my mother's complaining, the violent arguments that drove my father to the sea more often than he really had to go.

"As I grew older, things got worse. My father stayed away more and more. I think I was the only one truly aware of his deep misery, because there were times when we would go out together in his boat, and too much rum would loosen his tongue. He'd confide things I had no business hearing, things he later forgot he'd told me.

"He told me once," he went on, "that the sea was the only place he found comfort, that he would 'welcome the day it gave him eternal peace.' I remembered those exact words when he was lost at sea. Storm warnings were up when he took his boat out that morning, and I later wondered whether he was seeking the solace of a grave at sea. I think my mother finally realized what she had driven him to do. So it was actually her own remorse that killed her soon afterward."

He gave her a long, searching look. "I made up my mind never to get married and endure the same misery. That's why I asked you to be my mistress and not my wife."

It was her turn to speak, she knew, but what words could she find to say that she understood but wouldn't alter her stand? "I'm sorry," she said finally, understanding at long last that their love could never be. "Maybe one day, you'll stop thinking every marriage is like your parents'. Maybe you'll meet the right woman and love her so much you won't be afraid anymore."

She was surprised when he gave her the winsome smile that always warmed her.

"I have found her. I'm looking at her now.

That's what I'm trying to tell you. I want you to be my wife."

It took a minute to sink in. And then she was stretching her arms out to grasp him, heart pounding, as tears of joy streamed down her cheeks. "Derek . . . Derek . . . oh, God, love me, please."

He embraced her hungrily, kissing her soft lips and neck. She clung to him, never wanting to let go. How wonderful his strong arms felt, how safe and good.

He held her a moment longer, then gently lowered her to the ground.

"For the first time," he whispered huskily, "I'm going to make love to you with no ghosts between us. We've a right to it, Julie, because we've committed our souls. Now we commit our bodies."

He spread her cape out on the ground for them, and she watched with heated eyes as he undressed, his body a study in masculine perfection, emanating a strength so fierce as to overpower. He knelt beside her and gently removed her clothing, both of them oblivious to the cold night. His fingertips traced her face, her neck, her firm, supple breasts. He kneaded them possessively. "I love you, Julie," he declared huskily, "and I'm never going to let you go. You're mine now—for always and always."

She pulled his head down to her breasts, and his hands stroked her back and then her rounded buttocks. He teased her nipples with his lips in small, nibbling bites, and they stiffened beneath the sweet assault. His head moved on downward, planting the soft curves of her body with warm, moist kisses.

He reached her thighs, and a spasm of intense joy arched her body as he devoured her with his lips. He tantalized her to her first eruption of ecstasy and then, before the joyful throes within her belly had subsided, he moved to enter her. A cry burst from her at his first penetration, and he continued to thrust mightily until another wave of blessed release left her sobbing.

He lifted her buttocks to meet his movements, and as he became lost in his needs, he was almost savage in his loving ravishment of her, but she urged him on, moaning and clutching, feeling consumed, as she wanted to be consumed for always and ever.

When at last he rolled to his side, arms still around her, he remained inside her, hot, pulsating. Her head was cradled on his shoulder. For long moments, neither spoke, wanting the spell to go on forever. Finally, Derek raised his head slightly and murmured, "Amidst all that moaning, woman, I never heard you say yes."

"Yes!" she cried, gloriously happy. "Yes to being your wife. Yes to giving you all I have to give. Yes to doing everything I can to make sure we'll have the happiest marriage ever."

He laughed, and she had never heard him sound so much at peace. It was as though the end of a long, terrible journey had been reached. Now only rainbows and sunshine lay in their path.

A bit later, he suggested they wait until they reached their destination before marrying. The ceremony could take place in the fort. "I'll resign my position as wagon master and become a pioneer."

She was suddenly apprehensive. "Do you think you will be happy as a farmer, Derek? You've always loved being free to roam. How can you be sure you'll want to work the land?"

"I loved roaming, Julie, but now I realize I was actually searching, not roaming. I've been searching for what I've found, and that's you and the life we're going to have together."

She felt movements within her, and once more they were lost in their passion. Moments later, when they had reached their pinnacle together, he withdrew and raised himself on an elbow to look down at her. He said thoughtfully, "I think it would be wise if we kept our plans to ourselves for the time being. We've rough times ahead. I don't need to tell you that. And I don't need the added worry of people saying I've got my mind on you instead of my job."

Julie quickly assured him she understood.

110

"It's not important that anyone else know. As long as we know, that's all I care about."

Derek felt her shivering and helped her to dress. He dressed, and then they propped themselves against a rock, arms locked around each other. Lost in each other, they didn't at first hear Thomas's cries. But then Derek stiffened, pulling away from her and leaping to his feet. "It sounds like Thomas."

"Here!" Derek called with a robust cry, running toward the voice. "I'm here!"

Thomas raced toward them, a black outline in the darkness. As he reached them, they were alarmed by his agitation. "It's Vance! He caught the Webber boy, Lonnie Bruce, nosing around his wagon and beat him up real bad. He's drunk and he's holed up in his wagon with a gun. Webber and the other men are fixing to go in after him."

Derek spat. "Damn it, I knew there was going to be trouble." The three ran back to the compound, and Derek stalked purposefully toward the scene. The men rushed to meet him, Lonnie Bruce's father the most vocal, as they told him what had happened. In the distance, Esther knelt over her son. Lonnie Bruce was lying on the ground, the other women clustered around him, Esther murmuring.

Julie ran over and, glad to see Lonnie Bruce conscious, asked if he was badly hurt.

"I don't know," he wheezed, blood trickling

from his mouth and nose as he lay on his back, clutching his sides. "He beat me bad, Miss Marshall. Real bad. The men heard me yelling and come running, and he jumped up in his wagon and poked his gun out and said he'd kill anybody that came any nearer."

Elisa Thatcher stepped forward, eyes flashing. "They've been looking for the captain. Now it's obvious why he wasn't here when he was needed, here to do his job."

"Oh, Elisa, shut up!" Julie cried. "This is no time for one of your tantrums."

Elisa gasped and backed away. People did not speak to her in such a manner.

Just then a cry went up from the men, and everyone turned to see Arlo Vance appear at the rear of his wagon, his head and the barrel of a shotgun poking through the opening in the white canvas. "Back off," he roared. "I gave that young pup what he deserved for snooping around my wagon. So you all just leave me be before I blow somebody to bits."

No one saw Derek's hand whip to his holster and bring up his gun to fire the shotgun from Arlo's hands. Derek swung up into the wagon, his fist crashing into Arlo's stunned face, sending him to the ground. Leaping down to tower over Arlo, legs wide apart, Derek cried, "You've got five minutes to get your ass out of here, Vance. If you're still here in five minutes, I'll kill you with my bare hands."

Spitting out blood, Arlo looked up, eyes narrowed, lips quivering. Now was not the time, he told his drunken brain. Derek Arnhardt would get his, but not right then. The odds were too great. He'd be damned if he'd start a fight he couldn't win. Damn it, he should have gone ahead and shot every damn one of them. Saved the Indians' ammunition.

Warily, eyes still boring into Derek's and conveying his message of hate, Arlo wiped a hand across his bloodied mouth, then got to his feet and began harnessing up.

The others fell back a little, and Derek turned and walked over to Lonnie Bruce, who was still on the ground, enjoying all the attention.

"How bad are you hurt?" Derek asked.

"I don't know," Lonnie Bruce whined, arms folded tightly across his chest. "It hurts real bad."

Jasper Wilkins approached them. Jasper, a doctor's son, knew a little medicine. He hadn't been able to help Elisa, but he knew about broken bones. "I checked him over," he told Derek. "He may have a cracked rib or two, but other than bruises and being sore, he'll be all right. A big man like that beating up a young boy! It's a disgrace."

Derek took a deep breath and let it out slowly. Lonnie Bruce wouldn't be able to take over Myles's wagon tomorrow, but Myles had to take over Elisa's, which meant someone else was going to have to help out. Who could be spared? Blast that woman, anyway. If she hadn't caused Micah to run away . . .

"What started it?" he demanded of Lonnie Bruce in a tone that meant he wanted only the truth, and fast. "Why were you messing around his wagon?"

Lonnie Bruce lowered his eyes.

Derek waited. He never repeated himself, especially when he was in this kind of mood.

Intimidated, Lonnie Bruce began to speak, the words spilling forth nervously. "It was just a prank, and he got mad and started swinging. Said I had no g.d. business messing around his wagon and started hitting me."

Derek waited. It was not the explanation he wanted, and Lonnie Bruce knew it.

"It was the other guys," he rushed on, tears springing to his eyes because he knew he was going to get it when his folks heard. "We were over in the rocks drinking from a bottle Hubie Taloe swiped from his father's supply. When we ran out they dared me to get some from Mr. Vance's wagon, 'cause we figured he'd have some, since he's always drunk. So I went over there. He wasn't around, so I climbed up into his wagon. He only had two crates in that big old thing. One was food and the other was whiskey. I just got two bottles, and that's when he came up and caught me and started screaming. I tried to tell him I was just after whiskey. He could see I was

114

holding two bottles, but he kept yelling, asking what I'd found, and then he started hitting me."

Something was nagging at Derek, and he struggled to pinpoint just what it was. Esther Webber was sobbing because her son had been stealing whiskey. Lonnie Bruce's father was threatening the boy with the worst beating of his life once he recuperated from his injuries. The others stood around talking, expressing opinions about the night's excitement.

Derek touched a thoughtful finger to his mustache, eyes narrowed, jaw muscles tensing. He turned to watch covertly as Arlo Vance whipped his horses into a gallop and, wheels kicking up dirt, hurried from the camp.

Derek motioned to Thomas and Myles to follow him, and when they were out of hearing range of the others, he said tersely, "Don't say anything to anyone. Get your horses and mount up. We're going after Vance. We'll wait till he's a good distance from the camp, and then we're going to stop him and search that wagon. I have a bad feeling about this."

Thomas and Myles exchanged looks, and Myles whispered, "What are we looking for?"

"Guns," Derek told them quietly.

Thomas echoed, "Guns? What makes you

think he's smuggling guns? Hell, he wasn't carrying hardly anything in that big wagon."

"Exactly." Derek smiled. "But he has a large Conestoga, doesn't he? Now why is he pulling a big, empty wagon? And why do you suppose Vance went into such a rage when he caught the boy in the wagon?"

"But where are the guns?" Myles wanted to know.

"False bottom," Derek explained with a grim smile. "If I'm right, he's carrying guns. He joined up with us so he wouldn't arouse suspicion traveling alone. Alone in such a big wagon . . . with only two crates in it. . . ."

🎇 Chapter Nine 🎇

THEIR impulse was to gallop ahead, but they held back, moving their horses cautiously as they strained to hear the sound of wagon wheels in the sand.

Derek had told them not to move on Vance until they were far enough from the camp that gunfire wouldn't be heard. He didn't want anyone getting curious and riding out to investigate. This was his job. He intended to do it without endangering others.

Ever alert, Derek glanced around in the black night, watching sprinkles of stars and gliding silver clouds. Wryly, he thought that each star was like an eye. There were so many at night. The sun was the giant star of day, fading at night to be cast out by thousands. He loved the desert and its tranquillity. And, having acknowledged his love for

Julie, something he had struggled against for so long rose within him. Derek knew peace.

He smiled to himself, thoroughly happy. Julie. Spirit. Beauty. Grace. Courage. She possessed, by God, everything he wanted. And he'd be damned if anything would stop him from having her for always.

"Arnhardt."

His communion with himself was interrupted by Thomas's soft whisper.

"If he is smuggling guns, what do we do?" Thomas whispered urgently. "Arrest him?"

Derek allowed his reins to relax. No need to hurry. This trail led straight to El Paso, and while he doubted that was where Vance was headed, he knew the road well enough to know it would be a while before he found a place where he and his wagon could cut off. "Detain him, is more like it," Derek replied grimly. "We'll confiscate the guns for our own use. I'd planned to buy more in El Paso, anyway. We'll turn him over to the authorities there."

Myles unleashed a low, guttural snarl. "If he's smuggling guns to Indians, we should kill the son of a bitch and leave him for the buzzards."

"We'll leave his punishment up to the soldiers at Fort Bliss," Derek said firmly. "All I'm interested in is confiscating the weapons he's carrying. I'll just assume he plans to sell them to Indians, yes."

They rode on for a time. After a while, Myles felt the need to say what was on his mind. "I think you and I need to get a few things straight. I noticed—like everyone else—that you came riding in tonight with my sister."

Derek gazed straight ahead. "Yes?"

Myles, unintimidated, rushed on, "I don't want her hurt, and you seem to have a talent for doing that, so I'm going to ask you to stay away from her."

"That's going to be hard to do, Myles," Derek said quietly. "I'm afraid I just can't honor your request."

Thomas looked at Derek in surprise. Was he actually smiling? Why? Derek Arnhardt didn't goad men into fighting. He stated his position frankly, and if someone differed, then he was ready to defend his beliefs. But Derek never taunted a man into attacking.

Myles was on the brink of losing his temper. "It may be difficult for you to ignore her, since this journey throws everyone together so intimately, but you don't have to take her off by yourself every chance you get. That's what I'm talking about—the little trysts you seem to be having."

Derek responded lightly, "I'm afraid those trysts are going to be more frequent, Myles."

It was only with great effort that Myles was able to keep his tone low. "You aren't going to honor my request? You're pushing me, Arnhardt, and while you may be bigger than I am, I'll not back off."

Derek, unable to conceal his amusement any longer, chuckled. "Now, Myles, is that any way for you to talk to your future brother-in-law? After all, we may be living close to each other once we get where we're going, and it would be nice if we could be one big, happy family." He was grinning happily.

Myles was speechless but only for a second. "Brother-in-law? Are you saying what I think you are saying?"

"Hey!" Thomas whispered urgently but was ignored.

Derek laughed. "I am. Tonight I asked Julie to be my wife, and she said yes."

"Arnhardt—" Thomas's voice was strained.

"I'd like for you to be my best man, but if you're opposed to our marriage, then I suppose it would be awkward for you."

"Opposed?" Myles was ecstatic and reached across to shake Derek's hand eagerly. "I think it's damn wonderful! I've known for some time Julie loved you, but—"

"Damn it, will you listen to me?"

They both looked at Thomas. "I don't hear the wagon anymore."

Silence prevailed. Each man strained to hear.

"He probably just got out of hearing range," Thomas offered worriedly.

"No," came Derek's instant reply. "He couldn't have gotten that far. Let's move on, but cautiously. Don't quicken the pace. If we don't pick up the sound soon, then we'll move faster."

Derek bit his lip. Had Vance been able to hear them? Hell, they hadn't been that close, but the horses' hooves beat into the tiny rocks of the desert floor, and there was no other sound.

With each passing moment it became obvious that Arlo Vance's wagon was not moving. Or had he moved out of their hearing?

Suddenly, an outline loomed ahead. The wagon. Derek reined his horse to an abrupt halt, and Thomas and Myles did the same, all being as still as possible.

Derek slid slowly from his saddle to the ground, and Myles and Thomas followed silently. There were a few boulders around, for they were at the base of a mountain. But for the most part, it was them, the wagon, and the open desert. "I'm moving closer," Derek whispered. "Cover me if he starts shooting."

Hunching so his body was nearly doubled over, Derek stepped away softly. When he was close enough to the wagon he saw that his unspoken hunch was right—one of the horses was missing. Still, that could be a trick. Having spotted a nearby boulder for cover, he darted behind it and broke the still of the night with his cry. "You're covered,

Vance. Throw down your gun and come out with your hands up."

Silence was a thick, suffocating shroud. Derek waited, then hollered again. When there was no response, he fired a shot into the canvas covering over the wagon, figuring that would bring Vance out fast enough.

Nothing happened except for the horses' nervous shuffling. Derek ran quickly to the wagon and threw open the canvas. No one was inside. "He's gone," he called out to Myles and Thomas, who hurried toward him. "He figured out he was being followed and abandoned the wagon. Now, let's take a look. If my guess is wrong, though, why did he abandon the wagon?" Hoisting himself up into the wagon, he began yanking at the thin wooden flooring, and within seconds the cache of guns was uncovered. Gleaming, oiled metal.

"Whew, would you look at that!" Thomas shook his head, eyes wide. "Lord, I'm shaking just to think of it."

"It makes me want to rip him to pieces," Myles hissed. "To think he was riding with us, passing himself off as one of us, and all the time he was bringing Indians the very guns that would have slaughtered us. Damn it, let's go after him. When the others hear about this, there'll be a lynching."

Derek was paying no attention to Myles's outburst. "There must two or three hundred rifles here," he surmised. "Maybe more. He was going to make himself a nice profit. Indians pay in gold or silver, I've heard."

"Let's go after him!" Myles was shaking. "We can't let him get away."

Thomas spoke up quickly. "I'm with Myles. We can't let him get away. He'll only go after more guns. This loss won't put him out of business."

"It might," Derek said matter-of-factly, climbing down out of the wagon and brushing his hands against his thighs. Just touching those guns made him feel tainted. "The Indians will be plenty mad to find out they aren't getting what was promised. He'll have to lay low for a while. It isn't worth our time to go after him. I don't imagine this is his first trip. He probably knows his way around these parts, and there's no telling where he's hiding now. Right now I want to get this wagon back to camp, and then I want us to move and get to Fort Bliss as soon as possible. The Army needs to know about this—and we need to get out of this territory."

Myles stared at him and cried, "You mean you're going to just let him get away?"

It had been a long night. "He's only one man," Derek snapped. "I've got the whole damn wagon train to look after, and right now, what matters is getting those people to El Paso. We've got the guns. Let the Indians deal with Vance. He's no doubt going to be

123

running from us *and* from them. It'll keep him out of trouble for a while. Now let's get going."

Myles and Thomas looked at each other and then looked away. Arnhardt was probably right.

Above, out of sight on an overhanging ledge, Arlo Vance lay on his belly, watching the scene below. As he listened, his fingers had trembled on the triggers of the guns he held in each hand. How he had wanted to shoot, to watch them bleed and writhe in agony on the ground as they resisted eternity. But no. That would be taking a chance. He might not have been able to hit all three of them. He wasn't about to make a stand alone.

Well, they had the guns, but they didn't have him, and he could always get more guns. Arlo Vance watched them until they were out of sight. A coyote on a faraway ledge cried out, a long wail, intensifying and echoing across the desert.

Chapter Ten

O N the landing at the top of the stairs, Julie stood watching the gaily decorated lobby. The people of El Paso were welcoming the wagon train with a warmth that far surpassed previous celebrations.

Directly below, Derek stood with the others, resplendent in a pale blue suit, a red velvet string tie at the collar of his stiff, white shirt. She smiled, thinking of his ruggedness on the trail, contrasted with seeing him dressed like a distinguished doctor or lawyer.

As she watched, Julie noted the admiring glances of the other women. Two young girls stood to one side, exchanging whispered giggles. One stepped to Derek's side, tossing cascades of blond curls as she engaged him in conversation.

He's mine, Julie thought joyfully, for always and always. How she wanted to run down the stairs and throw herself in his powerful arms.

Suddenly aware that someone was beside her, Julie turned toward Teresa. How tired she looks, Julie thought, so drawn, so haggard. She hoped a few days in a hotel would ease Teresa a little.

Teresa touched Julie's arm affectionately. "Are you sizing up the competition?" she teased, nodding toward Derek and his admirers. "They find him as attractive as you do."

Julie laughed softly. There would always be women vying for Derek's attention. "I suppose I'll just have to stay on my toes. It's almost sinful for a man to be so attractive, isn't it?"

"And for a woman to be as beautiful as you are, Julie," Teresa told her sincerely. "He's yours—as I sensed he was from the first time I saw you two together." She nodded with satisfaction. "I just don't know why you're waiting to get married," she went on. "You could have the ceremony here, at that charming mission."

Julie agreed, but she did understand why Derek felt they should wait until they had reached their destination. The way ahead was perilous, and how could he concentrate on his duties if he had a new bride riding in his wagon? There wasn't room for them to sleep comfortably in the supply wagon each night, and if they lived in that wagon,

Thomas would have to find other accommodations. It was not sensible to buy another wagon. Who would take its reins each day? No, Derek was right. They would wait.

She explained to Teresa, who reluctantly nodded in agreement. Then Julie decided it was time to join Derek downstairs. Kissing Teresa's cheek, Julie lifted the skirt of her white velvet gown and descended the staircase. Derek had delivered the gown to her hotel room that morning. She had protested the lavish gift, but he had placed a fingertip against her lips and firmly reminded her that he did what he wanted, when he wanted.

When Derek caught sight of her, he took her hand and drew her to his side, much to the disappointment of the young women hovering around him. "Colonel Thimes," he said to the austere-looking officer he been talking with, "allow me to present to you my fiancée, Miss Julie Marshall, of Savannah, Georgia."

The girls who had gathered around frowned and whispered, then turned away in disappointment. The colonel took the hand Julie presented and kissed her fingertips, bowing. "Had I known Georgia produced such beautiful women, Miss Marshall, I think I might have been tempted to switch my allegiance to the Confederacy."

Colonel Thimes was wide-shouldered and stood ramrod-straight in his dark blue uniform, chest covered by gold buttons and battle ribbons. He wore the lean, hard expression of a man who would not change his convictions for any reason, and she knew he hadn't meant what he'd just said. This man would never be anything but a Yankee.

"The colonel flatters me." She made her tone light, but she looked him straight in the eye. "But tell me, is there news of the war that might be pleasing to Southern ears?"

Colonel Thimes frowned. This was no silly female who challenged him with those bright, emerald eyes.

"War news is never pleasing to either side, Miss Marshall," he responded crisply, his awe of her striking beauty mitigating, a little, the resentment her question evoked. He flashed a smile beneath his neatly trimmed mustache. "If there is satisfaction in all this, it belongs to the Union. We have just learned that our General Sherman has captured Columbia, South Carolina. Fort Sumter, which has the unfortunate distinction of being the scene of the start of this sad war, has been abandoned. Our troops are marching on North Carolina, and with President Lincoln being inaugurated for a second term, we are confident that this tragic war will soon draw to an end. The Confederacy struggles on, but we are bringing them to their knees," he finished firmly.

Derek sensed trouble and placed a warning

arm around her tiny waist, but she wouldn't be dissuaded.

"Colonel, the war may end, but the spirit of the Confederacy will live on long after you and I are dust."

There was a long, uncomfortable silence. Then she continued. "Intelligent people will know the war for what it was, a war of Northern aggression. And as for General Sherman, he's a heartless rogue who orders his men to wreak a path of destruction that would cause a crow to starve in its wake. He allows his soldiers to pillage and murder. Sherman—a soldier? I think *fiend* is more like it."

People listening gasped, and Colonel Thimes's astonishment was clearly mirrored on his frozen face.

Derek, who ordinarily would have stood aside and let Julie's fury vent itself, took mercy on Colonel Thimes and led her into the room set aside for dancing.

"You asked for it, Julie," he told her, "when you asked for news that 'might be pleasing to Southern ears.' "

She gave her long hair an arrogant toss. "I hate to be placated, Derek. It infuriates me."

"You were rude, Julie," he said.

"I suppose I was. I will apologize before the evening is over."

She did. The terrible news had crushed her, but nothing crushed Julie for long. And manners were manners. She found Colonel

Thimes standing next to a refreshment table, and she apologized for her rudeness. After a moment of silent regard, Colonel Thimes forced a smile and said, "I find it refreshing that a young woman can be both beautiful and educated, Miss Marshall."

"Please," Julie said, sighing, "do not patronize me, Colonel. You may feel that you're complimenting me, but I don't feel complimented. There's nothing wrong with a woman possessing knowledge of what goes on in the world. Women have minds, Colonel. Men like you cause me deep distress.

"I'm sorry," she continued wearily, "but you don't seem to bring out the best in me."

To her surprise he laughed, and she felt his indignant facade crumble.

"I do find you refreshing, by God. You've got spunk and spirit. We need more women like you out here. And I'm not being patronizing. I mean it sincerely."

She matched his warm smile. "Why, Colonel, I accept your compliment as such and I thank you. Perhaps we shall not be enemies after all."

"I hope not. What is to be gained if North and South remain enemies after the last gun is fired? No, my dear, we must all work together for peace. We must build our nation again."

"I agree." She nodded.

"Friends?" He smiled.

"The beginning of friendship," she offered.

She and Derek danced for an hour, then another hour, drinking champagne between dances and flirting with each other outrageously.

The only other man she danced with was, to her chagrin, the self-important Lieutenant Hargrove, recently transferred to El Paso.

"I'm afraid there's a good deal of danger on the trail your wagon train is traveling," he informed her. "It's called the Butterfield Trail, in case you didn't know, in honor of the first president of the Overland Mail Company."

"If it's dangerous," she asked bluntly, "why doesn't Colonel Thimes give us an escort?"

"Quite simply," he responded airily, "we have no men to spare. With more and more pioneers heading west to escape the war, the Indians are getting restless. We anticipate trouble, more bloodshed, and our first duty is to the territory here, around Fort Bliss. When the war ends and more soldiers are sent out here, then we can provide troops for escort. You should have waited for a later wagon train," he added, smiling.

Julie got away from him as quickly as she could, and found Derek at the refreshment table.

"I have a right to know what lies ahead,"

131

she told him. "Are we going to be attacked by Indians, Derek?"

"We don't know what lies ahead," he said. "We know there's a possibility of danger from Indians, and we're going to be prepared." He shook his head. "Worrying about it doesn't do a damn bit of good, so will you just enjoy the evening and stop putting every man you meet through an inquisition?"

Julie agreed. Only time could tell her any more, anyway. They danced again, and she reveled in the admiring stares of other women. She allowed Derek to lead her around the dance floor for introductions to townspeople and officers from Fort Bliss. She enjoyed meeting new people.

The evening wore on, and all too soon Myles came up to announce that he was taking Teresa upstairs to retire. Derek suggested Julie get some sleep, too. "Colonel Thimes invited me to his quarters for a brandy with two other officers. There may be a chance I can talk him into giving us an escort at least as far as Fort Bowie. Then we'd be only a little over a hundred miles from Tucson."

"Hurry to me, please," she begged as he held her tightly against him.

"You'll have me as soon as I've talked to the colonel." He smiled. Then he released her and turned her toward the doors leading back into the lobby. "Go now. I'll be there as soon as I can, but it may be a while. Sleep lightly so I don't have to wake up Myles by beating on your door." She made a face at the thought of Myles's reaction to a late-night visit, and then she made her way back through the lobby and upstairs to her room. A happy glow filling her, she undressed and reached for a nightgown. Then, feeling deliciously wicked, she crawled beneath the covers naked. Sinking back against the pillows, she thought about Derek and the visit to come. In moments she was sound asleep. She did not hear the door open, did not hear the stealthy footsteps across the floor.

❧ Chapter Eleven ❧

J ULIE stared in dazed bewilderment at the face looming over her. Cold, dark eyes were glaring down at her. There was nothing in those eyes but hate.

She was not in her bed, not in her hotel room. And then she understood, with heart-wrenching terror, that this was no dream. The loathesome thing above her was real. It had long, coarse black hair straggling around a reddish-brown face. It was a young girl. Her breath smelled foul, and there was a terrible odor around her.

"What do you want with me?" Julie whispered hoarsely, moving just enough to feel herself bound hand and foot.

From the darkness a man said, "She didn't bring you here. I'm the one who wants you."

She knew that voice! Arlo Vance! "You!" She spat, furious, struggling to see around the girl's face. "How dare you? How dare you?" She was too angry to be frightened.

"You belong with me," he said simply. He came into view, flinging a hand out to shove the girl's face away. "Get out of my way," he snarled, and the girl tripped and fell to the floor.

Leaning over Julie, he declared, "You must forgive Sujen. She's jealous. She's been my woman for the past week or so. No doubt her Indian lovers never satisfied her as I have." He smiled. "That's the trouble with Indian men, they take their own pleasure and don't give a damn whether their squaw enjoys it or not. I'm not like that, as you will learn. Soon we'll have the right to consummate our love."

Julie stared at him, whipping her head from side to side as she struggled against the bonds.

"Now, now, you're going to make the rope cut into that lovely flesh." He covered her wrists and stopped her. "Are you wondering where you are? Calm down, and I'll tell you a few things so you won't be frightened anymore. You don't have to be afraid of me, you know. I won't harm you, not unless you make me, Louise. . . ." He froze, then forced a smile. "Listen to me, calling you by my sainted wife's name. No matter. In time, when I teach you her ways, you will become her, and then we'll just change your name from Julie Marshall to Louise Vance.

"Now, then." He settled himself on the side of the pallet she was lying on, careful not to lean against the stakes that bound her ropes. "We're in a little hut that I discovered on a mountain near El Paso. It isn't much, but we won't be here long. You'll see that, other than this pallet, there is no furniture. The floor is dirt. The hut's hardly large enough to turn around in. But there's a roof and four walls to protect us from the harsh mountain winds. There's a pit, for a fire. It's adequate for our needs at the moment, as I'm sure it was adequate for the prospectors who prob'ly built it."

He nodded to Sujen, who crouched in the dirt a few feet away, lips curled back over yellowed teeth. "Don't let her scare you. She knows I won't hesitate to slit her throat if she harms a hair on your head. She's Navajo, one of the Indian women Colonel Kit Carson gave to the Utes in exchange for their helping him and his soldiers make war on her people. She learned to speak English from a missionary who lived in their village for a while. She says the Utes raped her and she got pregnant. They didn't want any half-Navajo brats born in their village, and they don't touch pregnant women anyway, so they kicked her out. I came along and found her and saved her from starving. So I kept her.

"But"—he paused for a dramatic sigh— "now I have you. You're going to be my wife.

You don't have to worry about sharing me with her, but we can keep her for a slave if you want to. What do you think?" He smiled.

She knew better, but she said it anyway. "You're insane, Arlo. And you won't get away with this."

He shook his head in mock sympathy. "Oh, my poor, dear Julie. You've been corrupted by your friends. Why, when I found you naked in your bed, I covered you up. Even my dear Louise, who warmly welcomed my passion, would never have been so shockingly audacious. But we'll change all that, and I'll help you become the decent, well-bred lady you were meant to be, worthy to replace my sainted Louise."

As calmly as she could, Julie said, "Let me go and we'll pretend this never happened."

Arlo pretended to consider that, then once more shook his head. "No. No, I don't think so. See, I went to a lot of trouble for you. I should have left here long ago, but I waited because of you."

He looked at her steadily. "I waited because I knew I could never let you go. You're like Louise. You're mine."

Turning to his squaw, he barked, "I'm going out to get some supplies we'll need for our journey. While I'm gone, give her a bath. And she needs something to wear. I wonder what we—"

Sujen spoke, her voice sharp. "She not wear my skin!"

Arlo wrinkled his nose. "Hell, no, don't put your nasty buckskins on her. You smell like the animal you scraped them from, Sujen. I might as well mate with a buffalo. Wrap her in the blanket I used to carry her in."

Suddenly his arm shot out. His hand wrapped around the Indian's girl's neck so tightly her eyes bulged. He squeezed hard, and hissed, "Heed me, bitch! You treat her well, see?"

He released her, flinging her into the dirt. Turning back to Julie, he was instantly tender. "Don't worry, my love. I'm going to make you happy. You'll see. A few more runs with the guns, you by my side, and we'll find a peaceful place on some lovely mountain. There I will make you my queen. We'll have babies, lots of babies . . . and you will truly be my precious Louise. I will cherish you for always and always."

He leaned forward, lips parted, and a low, guttural sound escaped from someplace deep inside Sujen. Arlo hesitated. Later there would be time for his passion.

He straightened. "Do as I told you, Sujen," he yelled. "I'll be back by dark. Have her clean and warm, and have supper cooking."

Sujen mumbled, "No way to hunt."

"I'm not giving you a knife, you fool," he said sarcastically. "Kill something with your

139

bare hands. There'd better be food cooking when I get back."

A loud shriek split the stillness as Sujen went into an uncontrollable rage. She began screaming in Navajo and threw herself at Julie, who was helpless beneath the pummeling fists. But only a few blows landed before Arlo wrapped his fingers in Sujen's long hair and flung her across the hut.

"I warned you, bitch!" he cried hoarsely, jerking his belt from his trousers. "You need another lesson, and this one you're gonna remember."

Sujen curled into a ball, arms wrapping protectively around her swollen belly.

"Arlo, no!" Julie screamed as the belt whistled through the air and cut into Sujen's flesh. "You'll hurt the baby. Oh, God, don't!"

The leather cracked again and again as Sujen writhed on the floor, not trying to cover her face, covering only her stomach. Blood began to ooze through the buckskin, and Julie sobbed. "Arlo, *damn you to hell!*"

He froze. The belt fell from his hand. He turned slowly to stare down at Julie. "Damn me to hell? Damn me to hell? Is that what you said, Louise? Lord! No!" He fell on his knees beside her pallet. "Oh, Louise, forgive me. To think I provoked you to curse me! I'm so sorry. Say you forgive me, please, please. . . ."

Julie looked beyond him to where Sujen lay moaning and bleeding, tear-filled eyes watch-

ing in terror. She wriggled her fingers frantically above the ropes that held her wrists,
desperately signaling to the girl to get out of
sight. They were dealing with a man who was
really insane. Great care would have to be
taken. Oh, why didn't the girl run?

Sujen understood. Slowly, painfully, she
began inching her way through the dirt toward the door. Julie took a deep breath and
prayed she could distract Arlo. "Yes, Arlo, I
forgive you," she whispered. "It's all right.
Everything is going to be all right." What
should she say next?

"I knew it!" he cried, tears of joy welling up
in his eyes.

Julie watched him carefully, telling herself
to smile.

"You do care about me, Louise, I mean, Julie. Oh, God, I *do* mean Louise, because you
are my precious Louise, resurrected by the
merciful God who knows I can't live without
you. We'll have a good life . . . a happy life.
You'll see. Oh, Louise, darlin', I'm going to be
so good to you. Our firstborn will be a
daughter—Betsy, resurrected, too—and we'll
be as happy as we were. Happier. Oh, Louise,
I love you so. . . ."

"Everything will be all right, Arlo," she repeated, commanding herself to sound calm
and warm. *Oh, please,* she silently prayed, *let
him believe me.*

She took a deep breath and then said, "Go

now. Get me some clothes. It isn't proper for me to be this way. And I'm cold, too."

His eyes narrowed, and Julie panicked. Did he see through her?

He moved closer to her, and it was only by mustering all the self-control she possessed that Julie was able to accept his wet, trembling lips. "Oh, Lordy," he gasped, drawing back, grinning, tossing his head wildly from side to side with glee. "It's going to be so good, Louise, so good. Those other women, it was just animal hunger. With you, it was always a consecration of our pure love. And it's going to be like that again. I know it."

Arlo got to his feet and, without another word, took his coat from a nail near the door and walked purposefully out into the cold dawn.

Julie lay in the dank shelter, the smell of wet earth assaulting her. She continued to struggle against her bonds, but she knew it was futile. It was, she decided, the way worms must feel, surrounded by earth, nothing to do but wriggle and squirm.

The squeaking of the door made her lie very still, eyes squinting in the faint light. The door opened with agonizing slowness. The face of Sujen appeared, and Julie wavered between fear and hope. When the girl had stood there, motionless, for some time, Julie blurted, "I tried to make Arlo stop beating you. I helped you all I could. Won't you help me, Sujen?"

Sujen painfully lowered herself, crouching beside the pallet. Her misery was evident. She winced with each move, continuing to wrap her arms protectively around her stomach.

Julie searched her face for a sign of what the girl might be thinking, but all Sujen did was stare, her face giving away nothing. "Sujen," Julie began once more, raising her head from the pallet. "I begged Arlo not to beat you. I don't want to see you hurt. I'm your friend. You don't want me to be hurt do you? Untie me, and I'll get out of here, and then you can have Arlo. I don't want to stay with him. You see, I have someone else. So Arlo can be yours."

"No!"

Julie blinked. With a rasping gasp, Sujen leaned closer, eyes wide. "Arlo take me into hut, give me food. Now Arlo beat me. Sujen go."

"Where, Sujen? How can you survive?" Julie whispered.

Sujen's chin lifted defiantly, and her black eyes flashed. "Sujen not let baby die."

Good, Julie told herself. The girl wasn't beaten. She had pride, even after all she'd been through. "Then help me escape, too, Sujen," Julie implored. "Help me get back to my people, please." Julie was determined that this proud, strong girl would help her—somehow.

"They're good people. I think they'll take you in, give you a place to live, and food."

The Indian girl's lips trembled slightly as she said, "If Sujen help you, Arlo kill me. Must go."

She started to get up, but Julie's outraged cry stopped her. "You're going to just leave me here, after I begged him not to beat you? If I hadn't been tied, I *would* have stopped him. I was willing to do that for you, even though you'd already tried to hurt me. Yet you're going to leave without helping me?" Her words hung in the air.

Sujen's face remained impassive, but after a moment she said, "No."

Julie was stunned, then, as Sujen produced a knife from inside her knee-high moccasins.

"Must hurry," Sujen muttered, and she began cutting away at Julie's ropes.

"Have you had that knife all the time?" Julie ventured, and for the first time, Sujen smiled. She nodded.

When Julie was free, she tightened the blanket around her and hurried to the door. Staring outside, she saw that the hut was on the side of a rocky slope, and the incline was almost straight down. One stumble and they would roll all the way to the bottom.

"Follow," Sujen commanded, starting to walk up the slope.

Julie pointed downward. "We have to get to town, Sujen, *that* way."

Sujen smiled. "The way Arlo went. You wish to go that way?"

Julie knew what she meant but wondered, "How are we going to find the others if we have to go in the opposite direction?"

"We waste time talking," Sujen said urgently, climbing upward. It was a rough climb, and it was cold in the bleak wilderness. Despite the woolen blanket, Julie was shivering. The wind assaulted without letup. Moving was hard, because she had to keep one hand on the blanket.

After several minutes of climbing upward, Sujen disappeared behind a huge rock, then reappeared. "Now we go down."

Below, in the mist, they could see El Paso and, beyond, the thin ribbon of the Rio Grande river. Watching it, Julie stumbled, twisted her ankle, and fell to her knees. Sujen turned to stare. "No, I'm all right," Julie told her, standing and testing the ankle. It was not hurt very badly, and nothing, not even a broken leg, would keep her there! She forced herself on.

Sujen grabbed a fallen branch and, using her knife to hack at the twigs, created a smooth walking stick. Julie accepted it gratefully, and the Indian girl led them on.

As they drew closer to the bottom, the brush became thicker and denser. Progress was more difficult as they maneuvered their way through the brambles and foliage, but at least there was less chance of Arlo spotting them.

Several hours after they'd escaped the hut, they slid down one last, steep bank and crouched behind thick clumps of bushes. They were right on the edge of the town! Warily, they looked around. Julie was exhausted and shaking. But seeing other people—men unloading wagons, women bundled against the harsh chill—was such a comfort. On the other hand, Arlo could be anywhere and, if he saw them, would doubtless shoot. Did they dare move into the open and chance it? They stayed where they were for a little while, considering.

Feeling Sujen's fingertips on her shoulder, Julie turned to look into the dark eyes. "Why white girl help Sujen, when Sujen wanted to kill you?"

Did Sujen think she had been used again, Julie wondered, as Arlo and so many others had used her?

"Sujen, I want to be your friend," she said. "You've proved you're my friend by helping me escape. We won't think about how you felt before. What you felt was normal, but that's all over now. We're friends."

"Friends," Sujen repeated.

Julie looked over the brush again, and this time the sight made her scream. "Derek! Oh, God, Derek!" She thrashed through the last of the brambles, stumbling down an incline, dropping the walking stick and limping toward him as fast as she could.

Derek had been standing outside the sheriff's office. At the blessed sound of her voice, he turned and ran to meet her, grabbing her against his chest and squeezing tightly. She was overcome by the joy of his strength, the sensation of complete protection flowing through her.

"Derek, Derek, hold me, hold me," she sobbed, tears streaming, her whole body shuddering. "Never, never let me go again."

Derek did not begin asking frantic questions. She needed to be held, and then to be cared for. There would be time, later, to find out what had happened. Just then, he had to get Julie away from the quickly gathering crowd—townspeople, soldiers summoned from Fort Bliss to form a search party, the sheriff. Lifting her in his arms, he started toward the hotel.

Calming a little in his embrace, Julie suddenly cried, "Sujen! Derek, she's frightened, so she won't come out."

Derek stopped, staring down at her.

"She helped me escape," Julie explained. "It was Arlo Vance who carried me off, and if it hadn't been for Sujen, I'd still be tied up in that filthy hut, waiting for him to come back."

Derek set her on her feet. "Where is she?" he demanded, and she pointed to where Sujen was peering out from behind the bushes. Swiftly, he walked toward the girl.

"Don't frighten her," she called to him.

Sujen sank out of sight, and Derek demanded that she come out. Slowly, looking beyond him to Julie, she stood up. Then, cautiously, Julie limped to Derek's side and said, "I promised her she could go to Arizona with us, that we'd take care of her. I couldn't have escaped without her."

He whirled on her. His eyes were tormented. "Did Arlo touch you, Julie? Did he hurt you?"

She shook her head. "He's crazy, Derek. He thinks I'm his dead wife, Louise, or something like her. He didn't touch me in the way you mean. We can't let Sujen go back to him. He'll kill her."

"I'm going to kill Arlo, so nobody need worry about that bastard anymore," Derek said in that deadly voice she knew so well.

From a distance down the street, in the shadows of a saloon porch, Arlo Vance watched, uncontrollable fury whipping through him. He would have his revenge, he promised himself silently. And another name was added to his list—Sujen's. Yes, he thought, smiling to himself. They would all pay, and pay with everything they had. All of them.

❦ Chapter Twelve ❦

THE wagon train left El Paso and moved through southwestern New Mexico toward the Arizona territory. It was late March, 1865, and no one could say which he'd welcome more, the end of the war back home, or the end of the winter that still raged around them.

Winds came, relentlessly whipping dirt and sand up into the sky where it was turned into rain, then thrust back at them in muddy torrents. Some were sure the world was ending when mud fell from the sky.

A troop had been dispatched to ride as far as Fort Bowie with the ten wagons that remained of the train. But when they reached the tiny settlement of Hachita, a messenger from Fort Bliss caught up with them, bearing orders that the escort soldiers were to return to El Paso at once. Commanches had attacked some farms, and a major uprising was feared. Every man was needed. So, with apologies to Captain Arnhardt and the others, military command called its troops back. They couldn't be spared to guard fewer than forty people.

It was a densely overcast morning when Captain Arnhardt assembled his people in Hachita's small general store. He stood before the fireplace, a hole dug out against one wall and a crude mud-and-clay chimney jutting up through the thin, planked roof. Shelves lined two walls, stocked mostly with dirt, cobwebs, and bugs that had frozen to death looking for food. A splintered counter ran the length of the other wall. It was cluttered with dirty glasses, sticky with last night's beer. The store served as a gathering place for the menfolk, since there was no gambling hall or saloon.

As the men filed in, Derek saw that some had brought their wives, though he always meant these meetings for men only. No matter. They would all hear what he was going to say soon enough. As his eyes swept over them, he felt pity, even for the troublemakers, like Elisa Thatcher. Her expression was harsher than usual, and he didn't have to wonder why. No driver had been found in El Paso, and there was nothing to do but insist she get rid of all the things she was hauling, along with her wagon and team, and move in with another family. After much arguing, she'd agreed to dispose of the wagon and horses, but she vehemently refused to part with what she called her precious heirlooms. She obtained the promise of a merchant to store all the boxes and crates and barrels, but Derek doubted she would ever see any of them again. They had probably all been on the auction block before their wagon train left town. Poor Elisa. No matter. He had more important things to worry about. And he knew the real reason for her bitchy behavior. "Heaven has no rage like love to hatred turned, nor hell a fury like a woman scorned." He'd known the truth of that all his adult life. Elisa felt he had scorned her in favor of Julie. But he'd never loved Elisa. Why, he wondered for probably the hundredth time in his life, did a woman expect a man to fall in love with her forever and always just because they'd shared a few hours of passion?

Derek's gaze fell on Colby and Luella Bascomb, and he wondered who was tending the four kids they had left. They had started out with six, and two had died of a raging fever back in the Monahans Sandhills. At the two pitiful graves, which would soon be erased by the shifting sands, Colby and Louella had tearfully said it was God's will. They would keep their faith and go on.

Derek was not a religious man. Sure, there

was a supreme being, Someone or Something, who helped call the shots from Somewhere, but he figured the way things went in life was pretty much up to himself. The Someone or Something would take over when it was his turn to be lowered into a grave, and he would worry about it then. The only faith he worried about was the faith he had in himself. And never had he felt it strained more than it was now.

He overheard Daughtry Callahan tell someone that his wife was still feeling poorly after the birth of their third child four weeks before. Derek softly cursed. Why did women have to get pregnant at the worst possible times? He looked at Myles and Teresa, huddled together off to one side. She looked damned awful, like a rag someone had wrung too hard. Every time he saw her, she looked bigger and sicker. Hell, he and Julie were just damn lucky that she wasn't in the same shape. But maybe it wasn't luck. Maybe it was that Someone or Something smiling down, because life had treated them both so harshly for the last four years.

He caught Julie's eye, and his heart warmed at the sight of her. Yes, life had kicked them in the gut, but they were going to make it one day.

Derek shook his head. He was letting personal desires run away with him, willing to yield his concentration to anything besides having to tell these brave, stout-hearted people what it looked like they were up against.

Frank Toddy yelled, "What's this all about, Captain? We thought we was gonna move out today."

Taking a deep breath, Derek began, and because of his blunt way, he seemed downright cold, though that wasn't really the truth of it. Arnhardt informed them there would be no military escort across the border. He sharply advised any family afraid to continue without the patrol return with the soldiers to El Paso and wait for the next wagon train, which might be larger, or might have an escort. He was brutally honest in describing the threat of Indian attack, and he also pointed out that there were risks with even more people, more wagons. If they were attacked, the Indians could number in the hundreds. All he could tell them was that he would do his damn best to get them through. After all, since leaving Brunswick, they had known the possibility of Indian trouble existed.

They had, he assured them, plenty of guns and ammunition. If attacked, they would try to scare off the Indians by putting every man, woman, and child at the trigger of a gun. They were heading straight through Chiricahua country, about a week's ride from Fort Bowie. With luck, they would reach the fort and obtain an escort into Tucson. From there, he was hopeful the rest of the way would be relatively safe. But there was much open country. Spring would arrive soon, and with good weather, they could make better time. The decision to continue or turn back rested with each individual family. However, those who continued would not find a sympathetic ear for any regrets, no matter what happened to them. He was giving them a chance to change their minds. He ended by recounting everything he knew about current Indian troubles. It involved a great deal of shocking information, touching on many Indian tribes.

Then he took a long pause and said, "I'm going forward. Those who wish to go with me are welcome. To those who wish to turn back, I bid you good luck."

The meeting broke up so that everyone could talk privately.

A short while later, in Myles's wagon, Derek looked at Myles, Teresa, and Julie. His eyes were probing, his demeanor that of a man in the throes of deep concern for those he cared about most. Gravely, he said, "I told the truth. There is danger. Real danger. We may get through all right . . . or we may be attacked. If we are attacked there is a chance we can scare the Indians off—if they don't have guns and there happen not to be too many of them. There is also the very real chance that we may be massacred."

Myles quickly turned to face Teresa. "I think we should go back and wait. You say you figure the baby is due in about two months. We can go back to El Paso and I'll find some kind of work to get us through till after the baby is born. That way, you can even have a real doctor. Then, when you get your strength back, we'll join the next wagon train." He scanned her face, hoping she agreed.

Teresa looked at him as though she had never seen him before. Aghast, she cried, "Go back? To what? We have no home. You can't be sure you would find work! No, Myles, no!" She shook her head firmly, resolutely. "We can build a cabin. We can still get in a late crop this year and have food for next winter. But most of all, I want my baby born in Arizona, in our new home, and I want to get there as soon as possible. God is going to see us through this, Myles. I know He is." She reached to clutch his hand, tears trailing down waxen cheeks. "Please don't ask me to turn back."

Myles looked to Julie.

"I agree," Julie said to him. "She's right. We've come too far to turn back. Have a little faith, Myles."

Derek had reached his limit. Oh, he would go on if need be, guiding those who had signed on in Brunswick to the destination they had been promised. He wasn't about to back out, no matter what the danger was. He was no coward. But neither was he a fool.

155

Would he let the woman he loved and the family she cherished continue on when the dangers were so great? Hell, he'd dance a jig if everybody on the caravan would turn around and head east till things cooled down.

"You're fools," he declared hotly. "I've got a mind to turn everyone back!"

Julie started to protest, but Teresa was quicker. "You can't do that!" she cried, leaning forward. "You signed papers saying you wouldn't quit, that you'd see us through all the way. You can't do that, and you won't. I know you better than that."

"With prudence," he reminded, holding up his hand. "Reasonable judgment. If I think it's too dangerous to continue, I have the right to turn back."

Julie moved toward him. "Derek, don't do that just because you're worried about the three of us. It isn't fair to the others. The Indians have been making trouble for years. Who's to say it won't take many more years before there's peace? Don't you see? We have to continue."

He looked at her, then at Teresa, and then at Myles. "We move out in one hour, those who're coming. Be ready."

Shoving aside the canvas, he saw several men waiting for him. He frowned. There was nothing to do but spar with them over the situation. He'd be damned if he'd make up their minds for them.

Giving Myles and Teresa a chance to be alone to come to terms over the situation, Julie climbed down out of the wagon. She looked warily toward the sky and saw huge gray clouds over the jutting mountains. There was a sharp, damp smell in the air. They were in for either snow or sleet.

Only one man was talking with Derek. Tyler Ford. He shook Derek's hand, nodded, then turned and walked away.

Derek saw her and came over. "Everyone wants to continue," he said matter-of-factly, staring down at her lovely face.

She smiled. With a wink, he hurried away.

Julie went to the Webber wagon, where she found Esther packing up her cooking utensils and dousing their breakfast fire. "Esther, may I speak with you a minute?" she asked politely.

Esther looked at her curiously, puffing herself up a bit. She always felt important when someone asked her advice. "Of course, dear. How can I help you?"

"It's Teresa. I'm worried about her, and I don't even know if I should be. I've never had a baby. But she just doesn't look right. Have you noticed anything?"

"I'll say," Esther pronounced solemnly. She tossed out the dregs of coffee, then dipped the pot into a bucket of water and rinsed it out. "Teresa's much bigger than she should be at this stage. I know she's a tiny thing, so she'd show more than most, but it's not normal for her to fatten up as fast as she has."

"She seems so tired, too," Julie said worriedly, "and her color isn't good."

"Hmph," Esther snorted. "You'd be tired, too, if you were hauling that much weight around all day. You know what I think? I think she's going to have twins."

"Twins?" Julie echoed, stunned.

"Yep." Esther laughed again. It felt good to shock this young woman with her vast knowledge of life. "Myles was a twin, as you should know best. And it runs in families, don't it? Yep." She nodded vigorously, enjoying her moment. "Teresa is carrying two babies."

Julie was trying to absorb the shocking possibility when, eyes glittering, Esther went on, "Want to know something else? Twins come early. Never heard of nobody yet that went to term with twins. I wonder if Teresa has figured it out yet. She should, what with two babies kicking and wiggling around inside her."

"I hope she hasn't," Julie cried then, "and please, I must ask you not to say anything to her about it. It would only make her worry. None of us needs any added worries now."

Esther stiffened with resentment at the very idea. This young girl thought she would do something so tactless? "Of course I won't say anything," she said indignantly. "It's no concern of mine, anyhow. I got my own family to look after."

And the business of everyone else on the wagon train, Julie thought in annoyance. She had hated asking Esther, but she'd known of nobody else who would understand Teresa's problem. And, Julie worried, Esther might be right about the twins. But there was nothing to be done. Teresa wouldn't turn back to El Paso even if she knew she was expecting two babies. Her mind was made up, and a little while ago Julie had seen a stubborn side to Teresa that she hadn't known existed.

Praying that Esther would keep their conversation private, Julie returned to Myles's wagon to help get ready for the day's journey.

Esther finished cleaning the breakfast things, then hurried to Luella Bascomb's to tell her that Teresa Marshall was expecting twins.

Moss-covered rocks surrounded them, a cradle provided by nature. The air was spicy with evergreens jutting from hills above. Chaparrals clumped at the entrance rendered the deserted coyote den private. The night was cold, but in their quiet, secret world, no discomfort intruded.

Derek drew Julie's smooth, naked body against him, one hand firmly on the back of her neck as his lips claimed hers, tongue exploring the delicious, sweet pink mouth. Hot fingertips trailed across her to tantalize, then sweetly pinch, eager nipples that quickened and begged for more.

Slowly, ever so slowly, Derek's finger danced downward to caress her gently heaving belly. As he parted her thighs, she moved her mouth from his, pressing her lips against his thick throat to stifle her moans of anticipation.

He pressed his palm over her pubic mound, massaging in a rhythmic, grinding motion, feeling her moisture on his hand. Expertly, he opened her, seeking and finding that center of ecstasy.

"No," she moaned, reaching to clutch his wrist as he chuckled. She did not want it now, not this way. The pinnacle must be reached with him inside her, all of him, or as much as she could take, and she had never been able to receive all of him. No woman could, for he was too gloriously endowed.

She felt the great shuddering within, and she sank her teeth into his taut flesh, overcome.

Ripples were coursing through her as she maneuvered downward, eagerly taking him with her mouth, teasing, wanting to return the joyful agony he had just forced on her. She could hear his soft murmurs as she pleasured him in the way he had taught her during those wondrous months when they were marooned on the island. When the fires grew too hot, he pulled her up. In a long, slow movement, he entered her and she gasped, nails digging into his flesh. He gave her as much as she could receive, and, together, they crested, spirits touching the clouds and sailing beyond to find the moon, to kiss the stars.

Bodies drenched, they clung together. Derek laughed and touched his throat. "You bit me," he accused. "I'm going to have to watch you, woman. You're getting violent."

"You make me violent." She hugged him tightly, then asked, "Does it hurt?"

"I'll have some explaining to do. And right now you're going to pay." Laughing like children, they rolled on the ground and Derek began to tickle her, but they froze as gunshots split the stillness.

Derek reached for his trousers and, terrified, Julie groped for her dress. They heard shouting.

"Arnhardt, damn it, where are you?"

It was Thomas, his voice high-pitched and unnaturally shrill.

"Here!" Derek yelled, buckling his belt and jerking on his shirt as he stepped through the wall of chaparrals and out into the open. "What in hell is going on?" he demanded. "Why are you shooting?"

Thomas rode up, reining his horse to a skidding stop. "I've been calling, but you didn't hear me, so I fired my gun. You'd better come quick, and Julie, too—if she's with you," he added hastily for the sake of politeness.

He continued, rushing. "It's Teresa. Looks like she might be having her baby. Whatever, she's in a bad way."

Julie rushed out of the den, embarrassment cast aside by fear for Teresa. "Let's go," she cried.

❦ Chapter Thirteen ❦

MYLES was waiting outside the wagon. At the sound of hoofbeats, he turned and ran toward them. Derek reined to a stop so suddenly that Julie was thrown against his back.

Reaching for Myles, she cried, "What's happened?"

Their wagon loomed against the night sky, a lantern flickering inside it, lending an eerie cast. There was the sound of gasping sobs, then a piercing scream. Myles's hands on Julie's arms tensed, tightened, squeezed, and then he set her on the ground and said in a shaking voice, "I was asleep. Her moaning woke me up, and then she admitted she'd been hurting all day, off and on, but she didn't say anything because she didn't want to worry anybody. She figured it was nothing since it's not time yet, and she didn't want Derek to make her go back to El Paso."

He looked at his sister sharply. "It is too soon, isn't it, Julie? It's just a false alarm, isn't it?"

She ached to agree with him, to reassure him, but she avoided an answer by saying, "Did anyone go for Esther?" He nodded, and she said, "Wait outside." He hoisted her up into the wagon, and she dropped down next to Teresa, reaching for the wet cloth Esther held out to her. Each time a pain came, making Teresa's back arch, Julie would try to calm her, wiping her brow with the cloth and murmuring gently. But Teresa was lost in a pain-drenched world beyond Julie's help.

"Too soon," she panted. "Oh, God, it's too soon."

Esther, kneeling at the end of the mattress, corrected matter-of-factly, "Not for twins, dear. Twins always come early."

Julie scowled. "Don't tell her that," she whispered. "We don't know it's true."

Esther's eyes widened indignantly. She was in charge there, and she didn't expect to be challenged. "You'll see I'm right in just a few minutes," she said crisply. "It won't be long."

Moments passed with agonizing slowness, Teresa's screams mellowing to soft moans, then rising again when another pain tore through her tortured body.

Outside, Myles paced, wringing his hands and muttering to himself. Derek stared at the pot of boiling water Esther had ordered, watching the clear bubbles popping in the night and wondering why boiling water was always requested when a baby was being born. He decided it was supposed to give the father something to do.

How much longer till daybreak? Maybe an hour. Lord, this had been going on longer than he'd realized, and that poor girl in there was suffering the agony of the damned. He dreaded the time when it would be Julie screaming, but maybe it would be different with a doctor. Esther probably didn't even know what the hell she was doing. Why couldn't this wagon train have included a doctor? That would have been a piece of good luck. He started to say something to Thomas, sitting nearby, but caught sight of the Indian girl coming toward them.

"Sujen." Derek stood. Sujen pointed toward the Marshall wagon. "Bad trouble. I can help." She was carrying a small bucket, and she stared up at him with that unwavering gaze he'd come to know so well.

Derek cocked his head to one side and looked down at her. She was a tiny thing, probably not over five feet tall. "What can you do to help, Sujen?"

She tilted her head all the way back.

"Sujen help with many births. Help now. She hurt too long."

Touching his arm lightly, she drew Derek away from Thomas. She was embarrassed to talk to a man about woman matters, and the fewer who heard, the better. As best she could, she explained. Derek listened, nodding. What she said made sense.

Aware that Myles was hardly rational, Derek explained carefully. "It makes sense to me, Myles. I figure we should try anything that might help Teresa."

"Yes, yes." Myles nodded, murmuring feverishly. "By all means, get her in there."

Julie and Esther looked around at the sudden intrusion as Sujen climbed into the wagon with her bucket, Derek right behind her. Esther ther cried indignantly, "What are you doing in here, Captain? And get that . . . squaw out of here!"

"This woman," he snapped, "says she's delivered many babies. Her grandmother was a midwife. She taught Sujen all she knew."

"That isn't what we need, I'm sure," Esther said. "It's different with white babies than it is with animals. Now get her out of here. We have work to do."

Derek gave Sujen a slight push toward Teresa. "She's going to try," he said in his best Captain Arnhardt voice. "Now please get out of her way."

"Very well." Esther stood and smoothed

her long skirt furiously. She hissed, "You just go ahead and let a savage take over. I won't be a party to this."

Julie spoke up as Esther began to leave. "Wait! Don't go, Esther, please! We need you."

"Hmph!" Esther grunted, brushing by Derek. With a sharp nod toward Derek, she snapped, "What do you need me for? You've got God Himself—at least that's who he thinks he is!"

Sujen settled herself between Teresa's legs and went to work, there being no point in trying to defend herself.

Derek watched for a moment, then decided it really was no place for a man. He left, reminding Julie that he would be outside if needed.

Sujen greased her hands with the lard in the bucket, then smeared some around Teresa, slowly guiding her hands upward. A few moments later she smiled triumphantly. "It is done! Baby comes feet first. Feet were stuck." She looked warily at Teresa and criticized, "She should sit like this. . . ." She maneuvered herself to a squatting position. "Baby drop out."

"That's not the way white women do it, Sujen," Julie said wearily. She wouldn't pull Teresa into that awkward position. "The baby will come the way it is, and—"

"Now!" Sujen cried suddenly, waving at

167

Teresa. "Push! Push hard. Baby come. Sujen see it!"

Julie watched in mystified wonder as tiny feet appeared. With a gentle tug from Sujen's expert hands, the infant slid out and into the world. Julie's face lit up with a joyful grin . . . but she froze in a second as Sujen pronounced quietly, "Girl-child. Girl-child is dead."

"No," Julie whispered raggedly, scrambling close to the limp body. The baby's skin was a strange, pasty, blue color. She stifled a scream of horror. The cord was wrapped tightly around its neck. It was dead. With a tearful glance at Teresa, who was not aware of what had happened, Julie whispered to Sujen, "Is there any chance?" Her fingers were working, loosening the cord, but Sujen took the baby from her and said softly, "No. Baby dead."

Julie cradled the bloodied body to her bosom and began to cry for the little life that would never be, for the joys never to be experienced and, yes, even the sorrows never to be known. She cried and cried, misery blotting out everything else until she heard Sujen gasp. Julie turned her head, still crying, to see a tiny mound of fuzz appear. Quickly, deftly, Sujen helped the second baby to come out, and immediately its blue face changed to fiery red. Small fists began flailing indignantly, and lusty wails filled the air. "Boy-child," Sujen cried.

Reverently, Julie laid the dead baby girl down on a pile of clothes and gratefully accepted her loudly squalling nephew. "Thank you, God," she sobbed, rocking him. "Thank you, God."

One last pain racked Teresa, and after her scream subsided, she slowly began returning to their world. Tears streamed down her face, and she whispered, "My baby." She whispered the words, too frail to talk.

Julie dried him quickly with a warm blanket, then placed him in Teresa's arms. Just at that moment, Myles's excited cries interrupted the holy atmosphere. "Hey! Did I hear my baby crying? Can I come in?"

"In a minute, Myles," Julie answered, then moved to Sujen's side. Helping to finish clean up Teresa, she pressed her lips to Sujen's ear so she would not be overheard. "Wrap the other baby and move it somewhere out of sight. Don't let Teresa know anything about it yet. She's terribly weak."

Sujen nodded in agreement.

Julie pushed the canvas aside, and Derek lifted her to the ground. Quickly she told Myles about his son. After he had received that news, she told him his daughter was dead. "She was carrying twins, and that's probably why they came early. Miraculously, the boy is a good size and seems healthy, as far as I can tell."

Myles's joy had turned to heartbreak.

"Why?" he choked. "Why did the first baby die?"

"The cord was wrapped around its neck." Julie hadn't wanted to be explicit, but she had no right not to tell him. "She was in labor too long, or— Who knows why, Myles? When I see what I just saw back there, it makes me wonder how *any* babies are ever born and manage to survive. Just be thankful you have your son. And, Myles, I don't think Teresa should be told there were twins, not now. She's very weak." She touched his arm in the age-old gesture from a comforter to the bereaved, then asked Derek, "How far is it to Fort Bowie, or any place where we might find a doctor?"

"A week to Bowie by wagon. Three or four days horseback." He shook his head, dejected. "I'm sorry, but if we send for a doctor and bring him back, she's still six days from his help."

Myles moved toward the wagon. "I've got to see her."

"Wait." Julie went back inside and saw that Teresa was sleeping, her breathing shallow, exhausted. Sujen was cooing over the baby, having bundled him warmly. Julie took him, then handed him down to Myles.

Tears streaming, unashamed, Myles reached for his son, turning away from the others, wanting the precious moment to be his alone.

Julie motioned to Sujen to hand her the pitiful little body she had also wrapped. She gave the bundle to Thomas. "Bury her, would you, Thomas? Please?" she whispered wretchedly, swallowing hard. Derek drew her to him, and she whispered, "Please. Get Esther. I want her to sit with Teresa and watch her. Make her come."

"She'll come," he said positively. "But are you all right?"

"I just want to be alone for a while, Derek."

He kissed her forehead, understanding, then released her, watching as she stepped from the halo of light into her solitary grief.

Streaks of dawn stretched above the distant, shadowed mountain peaks. Faint purple mist webbed the new day. Soon the haze would dissipate as the sun leaped into the sky, exploding. There would be no rain, no snow that day.

Julie wished she could be God, just long enough to bestow the breath of life on that poor infant being buried. Oh, she would give so many gifts to that child: the colors of dawn, the first song of a fledgling bird, a warm breeze, twilight.

"Dear Jesus," she whispered to the ghostly silence about her as her arms crossed her bosom, "I have loved this life, and the longer I live, the more I learn to dwell on the wonders and beauty of the world, not imprison myself

171

within its pain and sorrow. How I have loved the feel of grass under my feet and the soft sound of running streams beside me. I am in love, in love with this world. I have waited for its seasons, climbed its mountains, roamed its fragrant forests, sailed its waters—and always I have known joy and beauty beyond the tears and anguish. Why, God, oh why did the baby have to die without ever living at all?"

Perhaps, Julie reflected, nothing ever really dies. From every death, did not some form of life arise? Leaves fell from trees and were reborn in spring. Stars went down to rise again on other shores.

An infant's cry reached her ears. God had given a life and taken a life. No. He had given a life and canceled a life. There was a difference. And now, now she must pray that he would not take another life . . . Teresa's life.

She fell to her knees and prayed, allowing the tears to come in full measure. When she got to her feet she knew no feeling of comfort.

🎕 Chapter Fourteen 🎕

"SHE'S going to die, isn't she?"
They were sitting on a jutting rock, overlooking the campsite in the late afternoon. Below, the circled wagons looked like a pen of great white seabirds, about to spring skyward.

Myles was clasping Julie's hand, every shred of hope in his touch. His eyes were tightly closed.

The word worked its way from her constricted throat. "Yes." It sounded like a gasp held back until there was no choice but to let it out. "Yes, Myles. I'm afraid she is." She wouldn't lie to Myles.

He pressed her hand to his cheek. "I can't go on if she dies. I swear, I can't. Everything in the past, no matter how bad it all was, is nothing compared to this." He continued to talk, and Julie let him go on.

173

"She asked to hold the baby, and when I gave him to her, she looked like an angel . . . like a holy angel holding that baby. It was like the two of them were going to rise up any second and disappear straight into the sky. But it was eerie, like she was already dead and she wasn't holding the boy, she was holding *her* instead." He folded their still-clasped hands beneath his chin. "Then she smiled the sweetest smile I've ever seen. And she cradled the baby and fell asleep and hasn't woken since. . . ." His voice cracked.

Julie drew her hand away to fling her arms around her brother. They held each other tightly as they cried.

When their sobs were spent, Myles straightened, pushing her gently aside. Then, staring off into the sunset, he declared, "I knew about them—Father and Aunt Adelia." Julie stared at him, shocked. "I figured you knew, too, that you weren't telling me for the same reason I wasn't telling you. If you didn't know, I didn't want you hurt."

"How did you find out?" she asked.

"I was coming down the back stairs one day and saw them kissing in the shadows. They didn't see me, probably never knew I knew. That's why Uncle Nigel killed him. He found out."

Julie hastened to point out, "That was never proven, Myles."

"I know, I know." He sardonically waved

away her protest. "Father was shot off his horse when he was coming back from town. Ambushed. But the fact remains that he and Uncle Nigel had an argument earlier in some tavern on the waterfront. Nobody seemed to know what it was about. But after Uncle Nigel disappeared that night—never to be seen again—it was pretty obvious to everybody what had happened. He killed Father and ran away. It all fits together even if you and I *didn't* know he had a damn good motive. Nobody ever said anything to Mother because they felt sorry for her, but you know something?" He looked at her sharply. "I think she knew."

Julie did not respond. She hated the subject, but if it took Myles's mind off his present heartache, then so be it.

"Yeah, she knew," he continued, more to himself than to her. "She had to. I think Thomas knew, too." He paused a moment before declaring, "He loves you, you know."

Julie nodded slowly. Yes, she knew her cousin loved her, and maybe, had there not been the awful realization of his mother having an affair with her father, she and Thomas might have loved. The truth had stood between them, and it was just as well, for she knew her heart was destined for Derek.

"It's been hell, you know it?" His laugh was short, bitter. "Our lives have been terrible, and you know that's the truth."

175

She remained silent and he said, "I wish I could die with her." His voice broke, and his head dropped to his chest, body heaving.

At last, his sister spoke. "It's not over yet, Myles. You've still got your beautiful son. If Teresa dies, she will live on in him, and you've got to cling to that and remember it through the hard times.

"As for our lives being wretched," she said, "you've got to think of the happy times, the loving times, the good hours."

He looked up thoughtfully and slowly, a sad, little smile coming to his lips. "Teresa said if it was a boy, she wanted to name him for me, but I don't want that. So we agreed to name him for her father and our father. He'll be Darrell Jerome Marshall. How do you like that?" His lips were curved in an attempt at joy, but his eyes were tormented and grieving.

She liked the name and said so.

"We were going to name it after you if it was a girl, Julie, but now I . . . I mean . . ."

"I understand," she said quickly. "But you hate to leave your baby in an unmarked grave out in the middle of nowhere, without even a name. I'd be honored to have you carve my name on that wooden cross Thomas is making. Honored and pleased."

Not trusting himself to speak, Myles nodded mutely.

Moments passed. There seemed to be nothing left to say.

Julie saw him first, hated realizing what Derek's frantic waving at them from below had to mean. But Myles saw and leaped to his feet. They maneuvered their way down the rocks as quickly as they possibly could, and when they reached the ground they broke into a run.

Outside the wagon, Julie stepped into the protective circle of Derek's arms. Myles started inside, then turned to her with beseeching eyes. "Bear it with me," he implored. "Bear one more pain with me."

Derek squeezed her lightly and released her, knowing she would.

Inside, they found Teresa lying very still, her breath coming in shallow gasps. Esther stood a few feet to the right, watching her. The baby was tucked snugly against Teresa. Sujen, hovering nearby, hastened to explain that she had awakened long enough to ask for the baby.

Julie reached down and took him from his mother's weak arms and handed him to Sujen. "Leave us alone with her, please," she commanded softly, praying that Esther would take the hint. She did.

When the two women had departed, Myles sank to his knees beside his wife and gently lifted her, rocking her softly against his heart. Taking a deep breath, he whispered,

"It's going to be all right, honey. You're going to be fine, and so is our baby. We're going to have a good life. I promise." His voice broke on the word *promise*, then he rushed on, "I love you, Teresa. God knows how I love you."

Her lips parted, moving soundlessly.

"Don't try to talk," Myles said, rocking her. "Save your strength, honey."

"Seeds." The word was barely audible. A crippled bird was struggling to sing one last note. "Seeds, Myles. Give them to me."

Julie looked around frantically before finding the small package of flower seeds that Teresa treasured so dearly. She placed it in the frail hands and squeezed her fingers around the package.

"Here they are, darling . . . the flower seeds."

A smile touched Teresa's lips, and she mustered the last of her strength to hold the packet in her grasp. Her eyelids fluttered open, but her gaze was unfocused. "Plant them for me, Myles. . . ." She gasped for breath, a slight rattling within her chest. "Plant these seeds . . . and when the wild flowers grow, think of me . . . and I will never die. . . . Know I am always with you, loving you . . . and our son."

Her head sank to one side. Lovingly, with all the feeling he had for her, Myles lifted her head to press his brow against hers. Teresa's fingers went limp as he did so, and the package fell.

Julie quicky scooped up the package and turned away, no longer able to watch.

Derek came inside, sensing that it was time. He took Teresa from Myles's arms, though Myles was not aware of it. Myles was somewhere else, in that mystic place the mind so wisely knows it can retreat to when we are past enduring any more.

A long while later, when she could speak, Julie showed Derek the flower seeds. "She'll live in the flowers, Derek," she told him vehemently. "We'll plant the seeds when we get to Arizona, and when the flowers bloom, we'll think of her. When the winds scatter the petals over the hills, the flowers will be born there, also. We'll see those flowers and we'll think of Teresa and how we loved her . . . how she loved us."

Louella Bascomb tenderly held little Darrell Jerome Marshall in her arms and blinked back tears as she told Julie, "Of course I'll nurse him. Teresa was such a sweet girl, and I thought so much of her. This is the least I can do." Her voice was shaking.

"Do you think you'll have enough milk for two babies?" Julie asked worriedly.

"I think so." Louella nodded. She was determined that she would.

Julie thanked her. Touching her fingertips

to her lips and pressing them against the sleeping infant's forehead, she left, saying she would come by in the morning to see them. She walked over toward Myles's wagon, stopping suddenly. There, against the wagon, stood her brother, head lowered. She knew the sheeted mound of Teresa's body lay inside the wagon. Myles was hovering over it, protecting Teresa.

Julie turned and left him alone, glad it was so late. The others would not intrude on him, either. As she walked, the faint sound of shovels striking earth reached her, and she trembled uncontrollably. Teresa's grave. Teresa, so warm and loving and full of life, and now it was all over.

She walked toward the supply wagon where Derek slept, and as she approached it a voice rasped, "Julie Marshall! My Lord, but you're a willful, wanton thing! You had Derek out somewhere, groveling like a couple of dogs when I lost my baby. I hear you were doing the same thing when your sister-in-law was losing hers. Maybe she wouldn't have died if you'd been there to look after her. Maybe—"

"Maybe it would be best if you didn't say any more," Julie said so softly Elisa almost couldn't hear. And before Elisa could reply, Derek was there. Elisa flashed him a smile. "We'll find time to talk about everything later, I'm sure." Lifting her chin, she swished away. Julie shook her head and said, "Something snapped, Derek, and I damn near hit her."

He nodded. "Come along now, and get some sleep. We've finished the grave. I saw Myles for a minute, and I figure it's best to just let him be. Let's go bed down near his wagon, in case he needs us during the night.

"Tomorrow," he finished wearily, "is going to be a long day. And a sad one."

🦋 Chapter Fifteen 🦋

AT long last the wagon train crossed into the Arizona territory. The land was awesome; open vistas perhaps fifty miles away seemed close by. Bald mountains, reaching to over twelve thousand feet, screened the desert basin. It looked barren, but to those who had traveled so far for so long, it was hope. They were almost home.

The grasses of the plains swayed like precision dancers in the crisp spring wind. Chaparral and huge saguaro cacti grew near stands of Joshua trees.

It was twilight, and they were camped in a low basin, ten wagons circled around the common fire. Over the crackling flames, the men took turns twisting the *javelina* Derek had killed earlier. The pungent scent of succulent wild pig teased everyone's appetite. Turkey, quail, and dove had been spotted several times, and now that spring was at hand and game was venturing forth, food would be abundant.

Derek sat on a rise, watching Julie near the fire, rocking Myles's baby, cooing to him. He frowned. Myles had not gone near the baby since Teresa's death. It worried Julie and Derek very much because the man was not coming out of his grief at all. He stayed to himself, lost in his own world. Julie even had to coax him to eat. At night, when the chores were done, Myles took his bedroll and climbed beneath his wagon, no matter how bad the weather was. If things did not change, Derek and Julie were going to have a ready-made family, because the care of little Darrell was falling on her.

Derek chewed on a sweet blade of grass, lost in thought, but not so preoccupied that he didn't sense someone approaching him from behind. He knew it was Thomas, had seen him.

Thomas, however, could not be sure of that. He was not about to take a chance and slip up on Derek, so he called out. Derek waved him forward without turning about.

"This weather's really something, huh?" Thomas said cheerily as he settled beside Derek. "If we don't get any spring rain, we should have smooth traveling from here on in."

"This is the desert," Derek said flatly.

"There won't be any spring rain. And I wish I could share your confidence."

Thomas was instantly sober. "I meant only the weather, Arnhardt. I know there's still Indian danger."

"Never more so than now." Derek's teeth were clamped tightly on the grass, and he spat it out and pointed into the distance. "That pass, it worries me, and we're in the middle of Chiricahua country."

"How far to Fort Bowie?"

"Two days' ride to the north once we get through that pass. I'm thinking maybe we'll forget the pass and keep heading west, toward Tucson. Bowie won't give us an escort, not with hell breaking loose all over, and there's no sense wasting our time going there. We've got enough supplies to see us through to Tucson." He stood. "We'd better ride out to the pass and scout it tomorrow. We'll camp here one more night, then head out. I'll feel safer that way."

Thomas understood. Once they rolled out, that was it. The wagons would be in the middle of open spaces, with no protection from attack. And once they entered the pass, they were sitting ducks for an ambush. Yes, it would be best to stay put another day and have a look around.

Derek looked at him thoughtfully and said, "You didn't come up here to talk to me about the scenery, though. It's Myles, isn't it?"

Thomas sighed, impressed all over again by Derek's sensitivity. "Yeah," he admitted, "he's got me and everybody else worried. He's like a ghost. It's like we buried his soul back there with Teresa, and all we've got riding with us is an empty shell." He hesitated a moment. "I figured you'd want to bypass Fort Bowie, and I was thinking maybe we shouldn't. There might be a doctor there who could help him, and—"

"No doctor can help Myles Marshall," Derek interrupted. "I'm not unsympathetic, Thomas, but the fact remains he's got to work out his grief in his own way. I've got to worry about the safety of everyone else. I can't let one man affect my thinking—*any* one man," he added pointedly.

Thomas nodded. "There's something else," he said slowly. "When I got Myles to talk a little, he hinted that maybe everybody would be better off without him. I've got a feeling he may just strike out on his own anytime."

"We can't have that." Derek stared back at the pass in the darkening twilight. "We're going to need every man. Besides, it's much too dangerous for a man to be traveling out here alone, especially one in his mental state. I'll try to keep an eye on him, and you do the same."

They stood in silence for a few moments, and then Derek spoke in such a sharp tone that Thomas instinctively stiffened.

"I think there's something you and I need to talk about, and I think you know what it is. I meant it when I said I couldn't let any man put us in danger."

Thomas stared at the ground, his boot digging into the earth.

"You're playing with fire, Thomas," Derek snapped. "Elisa Thatcher is a married woman. She's also a cunning bitch, and you may get yourself into a lot of trouble."

Thomas raised his chin, refusing to be intimidated. "She's also beautiful, Arnhardt, and warm. And I'm a man. And it's been a hell of a long time—for both of us. We're just giving each other something we both need to get us through the rough times. We aren't hurting anybody."

"You don't have to justify yourself to me. Your personal life is none of my business, but the welfare of the people on this wagon train is. Just don't get in over your head, and don't shirk your duties."

Thomas laughed. "I'm not falling in love with her, if that's what you mean. We both know where we stand. It's like I said—we're just helping each other through some lonely nights." He scratched his chin thoughtfully, then asked worriedly, "How many others know?"

Derek shrugged. "No one's said anything to me."

"Not even Julie?"

Derek smiled. "No, not even Julie, and if she'd heard anything, believe me, she would've said something."

"Well, look"—Thomas gestured helplessly —"I mean, I know she's married, but when we get out there, it'll be over without anyone knowing. I'd just like to know how you found out, because if we're getting careless . . ."

"Don't worry." Derek placed a reassuring hand on Thomas's shoulder. "Let's just say I guessed."

Thomas nodded, and they began descending the hill. It made sense. Derek could see right into people. Always had. He hadn't been the most daring blockade-runner in the Confederacy by being ordinary.

Everyone ate his fill of the *javelina*, its taste exotic but a welcome change after endless meals of beef jerky, potatoes, and cornmeal mush.

When everyone had finished, Derek announced that they would camp one day and one night longer, so that he and Thomas could explore the pass. "Don't start asking me if I suspect there are Apache around," he said. "I'll be looking for Indians every minute from now on, but I will say that this is the pass the soldiers from Fort Bliss warned me about.

"We're in the heart of Apache country," he reminded bluntly, "and I want all of you to be aware of that. Keep your children close to you all the time. Don't let them wander out on the plains, not for any reason. You men keep your guns loaded and ready at all times. Once we start through the pass, it should take us the better part of a day to get through it. Then we're five days' ride from Tucson. But in three days we'll only be a day's ride from Fort Huachucha, so we can go there if need be. I'll breathe easier once we reach Tucson. The rest of the way beyond Tucson should be relatively safe. It's right here that I'm worried about. Everyone stay on your toes."

A murmur went through the crowd as soon as he was finished and women began gathering their children, herding them toward their wagons to tell them what was expected of them. The men went to check their weapons and ammunition.

Derek looked for Julie and found her where he knew she'd be, in the Bascomb wagon with the baby. Without having to be told, Sujen took the infant from Julie and Julie joined Derek outside the wagon. Hand in hand, they moved from the wagon to the privacy of a clump of bushes.

She laid her head against his chest, ripples of warmth moving through her as his arms enfolded her. Nothing could harm her as long as she was in his embrace. She sighed. "You must try to talk to Myles. Please. I didn't think it was possible for him to withdraw any more than he already has, but he gets worse

189

every day." She related a few stories, then said, "Sometimes I hear him crying. And he won't even look at the baby. I think he blames him for Teresa's dying, but he won't talk to me about any of it."

"He's got to work it out for himself," Derek told her firmly. "A man has to handle grief in his own way, and nothing anybody says to him will make any difference."

"But you aren't going to Fort Bowie," she said. "I wanted a doctor to see him."

"A doctor can't do anything, Julie," he said wearily. "Now don't give me a hard time, please. I've made a decision I feel is right for the welfare of everyone. I'll go and try to talk to Myles, though, if it will make you feel better. Then I'm taking first watch. You get some sleep."

Before they parted, he held her tightly against him and said, "Dream about me. Dream of how good it's going to be when we have another chance to be together."

He turned and forced himself to walk away, yearning to stay with her and knowing he couldn't.

He found Myles lying on his back beneath his wagon, arms folded behind his head, staring upward but not seeing anything. He had not even bothered to spread out his bedroll but lay instead on the hard ground. Derek squatted down and peered at him silently. If Myles saw him he didn't acknowledge him.

Finally, Derek spoke. "Have you got your gun and ammunition ready, Myles?"

Myles waited so long to reply that Derek was about to repeat the question.

"No need." His words were barely audible. "I'm moving out."

"No, you're not," Derek countered. "Every man is needed to protect this wagon train. What about Julie? Your son? You want to desert them?"

With great effort, Myles moved his head enough to look at Derek. His eyes were lost, lonely, the reflection of his wretched grief. "I deserted myself the night Teresa died. Or something like that. That's why I want to move on, to try to find something. Then I'll come back. You look after them while I'm gone. You're a better man than I am, Arnhardt."

"When you're down on your knees, it's easy to believe every man you see stands tall. You were a man once," Derek challenged. "Why don't you come out of it and start acting like a man again?"

Myles's eyes flashed, and Derek was pleased to see that much life in him. "Don't push me, Arnhardt. You've never lost a wife, a baby—"

"No, but I've known grief. I like to think it made me stronger. Now get this straight, damn it." He leaned forward. "You aren't going anywhere. You're going to stay and do what's expected of you. If you want to hide under this goddamn wagon at night and feel sorry for yourself, fine. But during the day I'll expect you to act like a man."

Myles didn't say another word. He seemed to retreat all the way into his own world, where he'd been for weeks. But Derek knew he'd heard and understood.

A little later, Julie saw Derek climbing to the rise where he would take first watch. She wanted to talk to Myles, but Louella called to her then, and she had to help with the baby. Sometime later, she made her way to Myles's wagon and called out to him, but there was no answer. Tired, she went inside and lay down on her pallet. Sleep came quickly, and with it, an extraordinary dream.

She was standing before an altar, wearing a dress of shimmering white satin, sheathed in delicate lace. There were tiny diamonds scattered below the waist, like twinkling stars, and cascading ruffles that trailed to the floor and beyond her in a delicately twined train. The bodice teased her breasts, but white netting modestly covered her smooth flesh all the way to her neck. The neck was circled by milk-white pearls.

The radiance of her love for the man walking toward her could not be obscured by the soft white veil that draped from the emerald-studded tiara atop her head to below her hips.

Appearing from a rose-colored mist, resplendent in a coat of sky-blue velvet, he had never been so handsome. Thick wisps of coffee-colored hair curled boyishly round the rugged face, and deep brown-black eyes spoke of all his desires.

He stepped to her side, possessive hands clasping hers, and they turned to face a minister who solemnly intoned the vows of marriage.

Her wedding to Derek. A long dream surfacing finally, to kiss away forever the lonely doubts. Love, always and ever, eternally together, the way it was meant to be.

Then there came a soft cry from somewhere behind her. Julie tried to turn around, to see where the sound came from, so mournful, so wistful, but some unseen power held her. Pain stabbed at the back of her neck as she struggled against the invisible bonds. Then something thrust her head upward, from the rosy mist to golden clouds dancing above. The face of Teresa hovered there, an ethereal glow lighting her lovely smile. Something fell on Julie's face, something infinitely soft, and as she lifted an upturned palm, there fell a delicate pink flower petal, then a yellow petal, then a blue one, then a white one. Suddenly the petals were raining down so thickly they began piling up at her feet, rising to her knees, then to her waist. She saw that Derek, too, was being buried in blossoms.

"My flowers!" Teresa cried. "Give me my

flowers!'' The blossoms became teardrops, and Teresa's smile became a horror-filled grimace. ''My baby! Give me my baby!'' she cried.

Derek was backing away, leaving her alone with the sweet face that had changed so horribly. The tears became flower petals once again, and they were raining down too fast, packing tighter, covering her nostrils, smothering her. Julie couldn't move though she willed every muscle in her body to run, run and be with Derek.

With a muffled cry Julie awoke, clawing at the blankets. It had begun as a dream and ended as a nightmare.

She stared about into the darkness. Something was not right. Something was terribly wrong.

She stood on shaky legs, groping in the blackness for her robe, then made her way among the cartons and boxes to the end of the wagon. The sky was tinged with the pink promise of a new day, but something told her she might not welcome this particular day.

She fell to her hands and knees, whispering Myles's name. There was no answer. She reached out and felt for him, but her hands did not touch his warm, sleeping body. Frightened, she jumped from the wagon and looked underneath it. Even as she knelt to look, she knew he wouldn't be there.

She ran to the supply wagon. There was no

one there. Then she remembered. When Derek completed a watch, he sometimes slept on the rise instead of going to the wagon. She started running, calling out to him, not caring that her cries might awaken the others.

Derek, trained to awaken at the slightest sound, heard her and met her halfway down the slope. Quickly, she explained. "You've got to go after him!"

Derek ran his fingers through his mussed hair until the thing he was trying to grasp hit him all at once. "Where the hell is Thomas?" he demanded of the world around him, then took off down the slope in long, purposeful strides, Julie hurrying after.

Derek ran to the wagon belonging to Eugene Croom, where Elisa Thatcher had lived since she'd sold her own wagon. With one swift leap, he was up and inside, ignoring the startled cries of Eugene, his wife, and two small daughters. As he'd suspected, Elisa's pallet was empty.

His voice split the stillness of dawn as he bellowed Thomas's name, and almost instantly, a low growl of rage emanated from deep within him as Thomas emerged from beneath the Croom wagon, wearing only his long underwear. Julie watched as Elisa, her hair long and tangled, scrambled to conceal herself.

Derek sent his fist slamming into Thomas's stunned face. He fell, and Derek grabbed his

throat and jerked him up, holding him so
hard he could barely breathe. "You son of a
bitch! You were on *watch!*" Derek raged.
"And you sneaked off to be with her! I ought
to kill you!"

His free hand moved to hit Thomas again,
and Julie threw herself between them.
"Derek, no! There's no time for this. You've
got to find Myles before he gets too far away."

Derek released Thomas, and he swayed for
a moment, coughing and clutching his throat.
"Myles is gone?" he croaked, looking at Julie,
not daring to look at Derek.

"If you'd been on watch, you'd have heard
him leave," Derek snarled. "You could have
stopped him."

"Derek, please!" Julie repeated, desperate.
"Don't waste time standing here arguing."

Elisa had crawled out from underneath the
wagon as soon as she had her clothes on.
Coolly, she said, "Really, Captain, I don't
think you're in a position to condemn someone for doing the same thing you've been
doing. I recall a few occasions when people
were looking for *you* and found you . . . missing." She cast a look toward Julie.

"I was not on watch then," Derek growled,
"and we can do without your interference,
Elisa."

"I'll go after him," Thomas offered quickly.
"I'll find him, Arnhardt, I swear I will."

"You damn well better," Derek told him,

turning away. "I'll scout that blasted pass alone today, but don't you come back to camp without him."

"I'll go with you." Julie started away to dress, but Derek caught her and spun her around.

"You aren't going anywhere!"

"He's my brother," she cried, and didn't wilt before his glower. "You can't stop me."

He was suddenly cold. "Yes, I can, Julie. It's part of my job. You may not leave this camp. I've enough troubles without you causing more." He went for his horse.

Julie turned to go, but Elisa's fingers clamped down hard on her shoulder.

"Don't you dare look at me with that self-righteous face, Julie Marshall. I was only doing what you've been doing, and you should know how wonderful it is," she added with an arrogant toss of her head.

Julie retorted hotly, "I wouldn't think it was wonderful if I were married to another man, Elisa. I would think it was shameful—and so should you."

She walked away, wishing she had not said even that much. She kept on going, pretending not to hear as Elisa screamed, "You'll wish you'd never said that, Julie! I'll see you pay for that! You'll wish you'd never said it!"

🦋 Chapter Sixteen 🦋

THEY rolled over the prairie, steadily jarred by deep-baked ruts. The air was thick and still, permeated by the tension that held every man, woman, and child old enough to comprehend the precarious pass just ahead.

Derek had scouted among the rocks and inclines and found no sign of Indians, but he knew this did not mean they were safe. The Indians knew the terrain much better than he did and if they didn't want to be seen, they wouldn't be.

Thomas Carrigan had not returned. When the wagons pulled out, he had been gone over twenty-four hours.

Julie guided her team, felt the firm leather in her hand through her thick gloves. Derek hadn't liked it, but there was no available man, so she'd had to take the reins.

She and Derek had had one brief, fierce argument before pulling out.

"I don't see how we can leave without Thomas and Myles!" she'd said.

He had no patience left. "I told you and everybody else, we can't wait. We've just enough supplies to see us to Tucson. Thomas knows the way. They can catch up with us. There's no choice, Julie." He didn't voice his fears that Myles had gotten too big a start and was farther away than they'd figured.

The pass loomed ahead, and soon proved to be awesome and frightening all by itself, without the anxiety that the Apache might be hiding there. Shadows played against the high walls of jutting rocks. Scrubs grew among the crags and stones. The wind whistled, bouncing from side to side like the songs of mournful ghosts singing their laments.

The first wagon entered the pass and disappeared. The second, with Jasper Jenkins's wife, Esma, at the reins, rolled inside. Julie was third, and she pulled back on her team to slow them down. The path ahead was littered with fallen rocks.

"I do not like the smell of it."

Julie whipped around quickly to stare at Sujen.

"I do not like the smell of it," she repeated quietly. "It smells . . . of death."

Julie shivered. "Please, Sujen. It's going to take most of the day to get through here, and it's spooky enough without you saying how spooky it is."

Onward they plodded, horses and oxen moving cautiously through the narrow, twisting, winding walls. A shroud of silence prevailed. They did not stop for lunch, or even to water the animals. That would have to wait. It had been decreed that once they began the journey through the pass, they would stop for nothing until they'd reached the other side.

The day wore on. Julie winced with pain each time the wheels jounced over a rock, because the reins were pulled tighter, aggravating the blisters on her hands.

Derek rode beside her for a brief spell. She had seen him that tense only once before, when the *Ariane* was running the Yankee blockade out of Wilmington. His face was tight, set, eyes narrowed, all his senses keyed to the slightest hint that anything was amiss. She knew he needed Thomas more than ever but stifled the impulse to say so, even as an attempt at comfort.

It was Sujen who finally broke the silence to say again, "It smells of death. I smell death many times and never forget—"

Her voice was drowned out by a loud, tortured scream. Stunned, Julie jerked the reins suddenly, stopping the horses. The scream echoed, bouncing from one rocky wall to another, filling the pass until it sounded like an entire choir shrieking in rounds.

As Julie sat there, frozen, the screaming woman came running into view from around the bend just ahead. It was Violet Callahan, waving her arms, her face a mask of horror. Her husband, Daughtry, was right behind her, his face white.

Violet Callahan's wail reached them. "It's Mr. Carrigan . . . dead!"

Julie scrambled from the wagon and ran toward the bend.

"Don't go in there, Miss Julie," someone cried.

Julie didn't hear. She stumbled, righted herself, and was just rounding the bend when Derek caught her. He gripped her arms tightly, refusing to let her move. Straining, she twisted her body and looked beyond him. What she saw stunned her with horror.

Thomas was hanging upside down, a rope tight around his ankles, attached to a rock or a tree out of sight. His arms hung loosely over his head, and his body swayed slowly from side to side in the moaning wind. His mouth hung open. His eyes were wide-open but unseeing. The agony of his final moments before death was reflected in those sightless eyes.

Arrows, thick with dried blood, riddled his bare back.

The flesh upon what had once been his

warm, living chest had been peeled and hung in ragged strips of pulp. His heart was visible through the strips of gore.

Derek held her around her waist until she had finished vomiting, then led her back to her wagon.

"Take the reins, Sujen," Derek commanded. "As soon as I get everyone back to their wagons, we're getting out of here."

"No." Julie straightened, snatching the reins from Sujen. "I can do it." Later, there would be time for grieving, but right now there was a job to be done. She would not yield to either weakness or terror.

As Derek prepared to address the others, who were gathering around Julie's wagon, exchanging frightened murmurs, Elisa dashed to the other side of the Callahan wagon, out of Derek's reach, and darted toward the bend. When she looked up and saw Thomas's body, she simply fainted.

Derek got her and tossed her into the back of the Callahan wagon. Then, with swift movements, he scrambled thirty feet up the rocky wall and caught the rope that was holding Thomas's ankles. With a quick flash of his knife, the rope was cut. Gently, he lowered the body to the arms of the three men who had run over to help. Then he roared, "Get the hell out of here as fast as possible, and when you hit the open spaces, just keep going till I catch up to lead you into a circle."

Julie watched as he mounted his horse and waved the first wagon on, urging the Callahans to follow. He looked at Julie anxiously. "Are you okay?"

"Of course." Her voice was high, unnatural, but she was fighting terror. Casting a fearful glance behind her, she wished she could see the Bascomb wagon, wished she had little Darrell with her.

Beside her, Sujen whispered tightly, "Chiricahua. I see the body. I know it is work of Chiricahua—and Cochise."

Julie turned away from Sujen, watching as the wagon ahead moved. Julie popped her reins and the wheels jounced up and down on the rocks. She and Sujen looked upward at the endless walls of rock, wondering if they would ever leave the pass.

The first wagon plunged out of the pass, then the second, and then Julie's. Dust from so many madly turning wheels masked the sinking sun in a cloak of deep burnt orange. One wagon veered from the line, heading north to a mountain ridge that appeared close but was at least ten miles away. Derek rode out after the wagon and turned them back, cursing them for their hysteria.

"You've got to keep your heads," he bellowed. "Join the others, make a tight circle. It's our only hope."

A sharp zinging sound knifed through the air. Bobby Ray Jeeter's arms were flung skyward. He screamed, an arrow sinking squarely between his shoulder blades. He fell to the ground, his neck snapping as he landed. Derek charged over, realized that he was dead, and rode on, screaming for the others to make a circle. Bobby Ray's wife, Susanna, reined up her team and was scrambling from the wagon, shrieking Bobby Ray's name over and over. Derek scooped her up in one arm and grabbed the harness of her lead horses, pulling them into a gallop.

He led the wagons into a circle, and when they were tightly together, the men quickly began to unharness the horses and pull them inside the circle. The women pulled out boxes of ammunition, yelling for the younger children to get out of the wagons and take cover behind barrels and cartons, which the older children were lowering from the wagons.

Julie left Sujen to the task of the horses while she ran into the wagon for weapons. There were five Henry .44 rifles, confiscated from Arlo's cache, and two pistols, Starr Double-Action Army .44s.

Derek's face appeared at the rear of the wagon. "You remember how to use the guns?" he asked, cursing himself for not asking before.

"I don't think I'll have any problem with the rifles, but these pistols—"

"Save them for close range. Get the rifles loaded and then come down here." He grabbed the ammunition box and pulled it toward her, then disappeared.

Julie joined the other women, who were positioned behind a square barrier made of boxes and barrels, in the middle of the circle. Derek had told them their job would be to keep the rifles loaded. As each man emptied his, he would toss it down to them and take a loaded one.

Julie hurried to take Myles's baby from Louella, who was juggling him as well as her own infant. Derek roared, "Hand the small babies over to the older children. You women keep busy loading those rifles. That's all that matters!"

Colby Bascomb rushed up to give his wife some guns, and she asked him if he thought the Indians would attack the whole train. Colby nodded. "The captain said he spotted two Indians watching us from above the pass. They could have massacred us right there. I don't know why they didn't."

"Sujen know why."

Everyone within hearing turned to stare at Sujen.

She declared softly, "Cochise delights in torturing his victims. I have heard this said many times. He watches us as we make ready. He is confident he will overpower us, so he takes his time."

Esther screamed indignantly, "We might have known you'd take their side! Why don't

206

you go join your murdering friends? It's probably you they're after, anyway."

Sujen blinked, then understood what she was saying. "Sujen not Chiricahua. They maybe take me for slave and not kill, but they do not come to get me. How could they know I am here?"

"You . . . you probably sent up smoke signals," Esther blustered, knowing she sounded ridiculous.

"Esther, please," Julie murmured. "We've other things to do."

The bickering ended as Derek joined the group, looking calm and unruffled. Only Julie, who knew him so well, could discern the hint of fear in those dark eyes. He glanced briefly, silently, at the dazed Elisa, his brow knit in vexation, then beckoned to Julie. She walked away with him, so the others couldn't hear them.

The distant mountain range was shadowed in the purple of early evening. It looked like a painting, but it wasn't a painting, this desert wilderness. It was an arena of death.

"It's bad," Derek told her, his gaze sweeping their pitiful little compound where the men were taking up their positions, lying down on their bellies behind barrels and anything else they could find. "It's almost sundown. They won't attack at night. They have some idea about their gods not being able to find their spirits if they're killed in the dark. Dawn will be another story."

Julie leaned against him. "So we're just waiting to die?" she asked bitterly.

He gave her a fierce shake. "Don't talk like that. Don't give up on me. We're going to fight. Do you hear?"

She nodded. Of course. She would be brave—for him, for Darrell, for herself, but her courage felt like a very small thing.

"Right now I need your help. I want you to see if you can do anything with Susanna Jeeter. Bobby Ray was killed and she saw it happen. Give her a drink of whiskey and see if you can calm her down. There's no time for tears, not now."

No time for tears. The words echoed in her mind. No, there would be no time for crying in the hours to come . . . but there would be time later. "What about Myles?" she forced herself to ask, fearing the answer. "Is there any chance he's alive?"

"A very good chance. He must have left early in the night and had several hours' start on Thomas. There's no telling where he is, but I've a feeling he's safe." Then he looked down at her, eyes hungrily, lovingly devouring her face. "I'm not going to let you die. Or the baby. I'm getting the two of you out of here somehow."

Julie's words were drowned out by the sound of shouting, and they looked around to see Daughtry Callahan running out of the compound, waving a white flag. His face was frozen in a ghastly grin of hope. Derek yelled for him to stop, but he kept on going.

"Let him go, Arnhardt," Colby Bascomb cried. "We're giving up. We'd rather be slaves to the Indians than be killed and scalped!"

"You fools!" Derek started running toward the compound. "The Indians don't want slaves, they—"

There was a piercing scream, and all eyes locked in horror on Daughtry Callahan as he fell backward, two arrows piercing his chest, one in his heart. His wife tried to break away from the men holding her, then collapsed on the ground.

"Here they come!" Derek's voice rang above the chaos as the Indians made their first charge. "Every man to his post! You women take cover and get ready to load the guns!"

So! They weren't going to wait for morning! They would fight in the dusk.

Julie scrambled to join the others, praying that Darrell was safe, feeling a wave of relief as she saw Sujen crouched behind a barrel, both babies held tightly against her bosom.

The men began firing, and soon empty rifles were tossed to the women, freshly loaded ones tossed back. The Indians were circling the wagons, screaming. Their arrows filled the air. One fell, then another. Julie looked up long enough to calculate that there were a hundred Indians—and the wagon train numbered only eleven men, thirteen women, and some teenagers and children. Was there no chance, no chance at all?

Suddenly flames lashed skyward as a fire arrow pierced canvas. Someone started toward it, and Julie recognized Frank Toddy, knew the wagon was his. Derek shouted for him to get down, but he kept going until an arrow struck him through his right eye and he pitched forward with an agonized scream, his body jerking in spasms until death took him.

Everyone kept working, the tasks of firing and loading giving the mind something to concentrate on. Madness would surely have taken over without those tasks. They were doomed, and they knew it.

"They're leaving," someone shouted above the clamor. "They're going back to the pass!"

Martha Toddy scrambled from the barricade and ran to her husband, falling beside him in a sobbing heap. One of the men went over to pull her away, gently explaining there was nothing to be done. They all had to stay under cover till the captain told them it was safe.

Moments later, when the Indians had gone, Derek waved everyone around him, horrified by the desolation in their faces. These were the same buoyant spirits he had led from Georgia, a lifetime ago. As he looked at them now, it was as though some inner light had been extinguished. Taking a deep breath and letting it out slowly, he told them, "We have until morning. They left because it's dark, and they don't like to fight at night. At dawn they'll be back, and then they won't quit until we're all dead."

"Well, goddamn it, man, do something!" Colby Bascomb shrieked. "We ain't just gonna sit here and wait to die."

"We aren't," Derek told him soberly. "You are going to leave now and ride due north to Fort Bowie and bring soldiers back."

"Me?" Colby echoed weakly, glancing around nervously, retreating a few steps. "Why me? They'll get me, like they got Carrigan. I got a wife, a family. . . ."

"Everyone here has a family, Bascomb," Derek pointed out icily. "No one wants to go, but someone has to."

"Yeah?" Colby was blinking furiously, daring anyone to call him a coward. "Well, what about you, Captain? Seems to me you got us in this mess, and you ought to be the one to risk your ass out there."

The other men chimed in, mostly agreeing, a rumble going through the stillness.

Derek looked at each in turn, then said, "All right. I'll ride out and leave you to fend for yourselves, if that's what you want."

Patricia Hagan

Elisa Thatcher stepped forward. "No! You can't leave us. You're our only hope. If you go, we won't have anyone to lead us." She waved her arms beseechingly at the others. "You can't let him go. There's no one else who can lead us out of here if we make it. No one who knows the way."

"She's right," someone admitted.

"Yeah," echoed another. "We got to have Arnhardt. We can spare another man but not him."

"Go, Bascomb," someone shouted. "Don't be a yeller-belly!"

Derek waved them to silence. "If he won't go, who among you will volunteer?" he challenged.

There was silence, then the crowd parted as a tall, thin boy pushed his way through and stood before Derek. Lonnie Bruce Webber, Adam's apple bobbing, announced with all the courage he could muster, "I'll go, Captain. I'm a good rider, and I got a good horse. You draw me a map, show me which way to go, and I'll ride like hell to get there."

"No! Not my boy!" Esther ran forward to grab him, but he wrestled away from her.

"It's my decision, Ma," he cried, pushing her away firmly. "I'm the best rider here. You know I am, and I've got the fastest horse by a damn sight. I can make it."

"Stop cursing," she said automatically, then turned tear-filled eyes on Derek. "Don't

212

you let my boy go. He'll be killed. You can't let him do it."

"He's going." Lonnie Bruce's father approached. "He wants to go. And he's right, he is a good rider—a damn good rider. He's got a better chance than anybody. And I'm proud of him."

Lonnie Bruce swallowed hard. "Just give me an idea of which way to go, sir. I'll leave right away."

Derek placed his arm across the boy's shoulders and led him away. Esther cried harder, and her husband took her to their wagon, trying to soothe her.

Colby Bascomb melted into the darkness, cowed by the looks of the others.

Julie felt a hand on her arm and turned to find Sujen beside her, the baby cradled against her chest. Julie took him, kissed his forehead, then asked suddenly, "Sujen, you know about the Chiricahua. Is there a chance they will spare us?"

Sujen shook her head. "No. They will come at dawn, and we will all die. They never take prisoners, not even babies. The women they will kill last, after the braves have made them pray to die." She saw no reason to lie to her friend.

Julie swayed, clutching the baby so tightly he whimpered.

"There is one chance," the Indian girl pronounced.

Julie waited, not daring to let hope rise.

Sujen seemed to change in an instant from a young girl to a wizened woman, black eyes hardening, head tilting as though mustering all her defenses to withstand the misery ahead. "I will go to them and ask for refuge. They will take me in, make me a slave. Because no squaws travel with them, they will use me. It will not matter that I am swollen with child, for they are hungry. While they do this, you and the others may escape. It is a small chance."

Julie was horrified. "No! I won't allow it, and neither will Derek."

"It is only way I know of," Sujen said stonily. "Only way for you and baby to hide until your pony soldiers come. It must be done."

Derek approached and Julie explained. "We won't use human flesh to buy our way out of this," Derek said. "No more of this talk, Sujen. Understand?"

Sujen merely bowed her head and turned away.

"That . . . that was a brave thing for her to offer," Julie stammered, holding the baby tighter. But Derek had other things on his mind. He steered her back into the center of the compound, yelling for the others to join them. When he had their attention, he told them, "Tonight I'm taking the women and children out of here, to hide them somewhere."

"No!" Susanna Jeeter moved to the center of the group. She stood, shoulders stooped, before Derek. Her voice was strong as she proclaimed, "I'll not run away. My husband is dead, and I intend to fight those murdering savages with every breath within me till they kill me, too. And my children will fight. I'll not run, not as long as I've strength to pull a trigger!"

"I'm not leaving, either, Captain." Louella Bascomb spoke up in a small, weak voice. "I don't reckon I've got a life without my old man, anyway, and I'd just as soon die with him as live without him."

"I feel the same way," one of the other women said wearily. "We were going to make new lives out there. What good are we without our men? I say, if it has to end, it ends here, with all of us together."

The women's voices rose together in unison as the men shouted angry protests. Derek watched, listening, until he couldn't stand it anymore and roared, "You're all crazy. If you women stay here, you are going to die here." He allowed his words to sink in before continuing. "Even if the boy reaches Bowie, there's a chance the soldiers won't get here in time anyhow, because the Chiricahua will attack at the first light of dawn."

Without pausing, he looked down at Julie and commanded, "Tell them. Tell them what fools they are. Tell them you aren't going to sacrifice yourself and the baby."

When she did not respond, he said it again. "Tell them, damn it."

She touched the soft down of the baby's head. Oh, God, didn't Derek know that she had no life without him? How could she live without his love when he had taught her that was all there was to live for? Finally, with everyone watching, she whispered tremulously, "I can't, Derek. I can't leave you."

He closed his eyes against the pain. What could he say?

Feeling his despair, she asked, "Could you leave me to die, Derek?"

He squeezed his hands till the knuckles turned white. "I'd step in front of a goddamn arrow and die for you, but I sure as hell wouldn't jump in front of one if you were already dead so I could die *with* you!"

Julie heard one of the women gasp. She didn't care who it was. She was too stung by Derek's cold proclamation to care that others overheard her heart breaking.

"Stay and die here," he told the women furiously. He turned and walked away then, leaving them to their final hours.

❧ Chapter Seventeen ❧

JULIE had been only temporarily stunned by Derek's harsh candor, for she knew how easily his emotions could erupt, then subside. She stood there with the baby and slowly she realized he was all that was left of her family. She felt a sudden wave of guilt. There was no doubt in her heart that her love for Derek was so overwhelming that life without him seemed impossible. Yet, did she have the right not to protect this child? Who had given her the right to play God?

God. She lifted her face to the heavens and silently prayed for the strength to do what she knew He would have her do.

She loved Derek with all her heart and soul and every breath she drew, but she could make it without him—without any man—and by God and by heaven, she would do so if she had to.

She looked for Sujen and found her as easily as her shadow. Handing her the baby, she whispered, "See if Louella will nurse him. He'll waken soon, and he'll be hungry."

Then she hurried after Derek, calling to him as he was about to climb into the supply wagon. Bracing himself for another confrontation, he turned to face her.

"I will go," she told him resolutely. "Tell me what I should do."

He started to reach for her, a relieved smile touching his face, but drew back, hating the wall that had sprung between them but knowing it was, for the moment, necessary. "Midnight," he told her. "Get food and water and be ready to leave then. Sujen will go with you. She knows how to trail and can lead you to safety." He knew there were caves among the rocks on the outside of the pass. "You will hide there until it's safe to come out."

Shivering shook her all the way to her toes. It would be "safe" to come out when the wagon train was completely destroyed.

"Go now," he said, turning his back. "I've got things to do, and so have you. There isn't much time."

Neither moved. Suddenly Julie could bear it no longer and threw herself against his back, feeling the rippling of his muscles. "Don't," he commanded gruffly. "Don't make it any worse, Julie. Don't say anything."

"I must!" Her fingers dug into his arms. "I

must tell you how much I love you, Derek, how I wish we hadn't wasted so much time fighting with each other."

He whirled about to grasp her wrists, holding her. "You always loved me. I knew it from that first night we met on the *Ariane.* You melted what you called my heart of iron, just as I melted your heart. You were mine, always mine. Even when you said you hated me, you were lying. You loved me." He shook his head slowly from side to side. "So independent."

He jerked her roughly against him, bending his head over hers. "You were the strongest, most independent woman I'd ever known, but after you realized you did love me, you lost some of your independence. It wasn't the war that made you weak, it was your love for me. Now you've got to give up that love and find your strength again—and that's what scares you, not the thought of me dying."

"No, Derek, no!" She shook her head wildly, horrified. "I do love you, and that's why I don't want to leave you. Being alone doesn't frighten me. I know myself. I can make it on my own. But, you see, I don't have the right to let the baby die if there's any way I can help him to live. But no matter what the future brings I will always love you. I'll always be grateful for what we had together."

His eyes filled with tears as he clasped her

tightly against him. "I never thought I was capable of loving any woman, Julie. I did have a heart of iron, but you taught me what it is to let love in. With my dying breath I'll give thanks for having known such love. It'd be so goddamn easy to take you and run and leave these others, but if I deserted them I'd never know another moment's peace." He smiled wryly. "It's an old tradition that a captain goes down with his ship. I couldn't live with myself if I didn't protect these people. So I'll stay here. Let's just be glad we had this time together, rejoice for the good times and not be bitter because it ended before we had a chance to live all the joy we would have had."

She was overwhelmed. "I can't live without you," she breathed, barely making any sound at all. To find love and then lose it so soon to death! "Derek, please . . ."

Derek grabbed hold of his will. "You can live without me," he said firmly. "There's no more time to argue. Be ready at midnight or, so help me, I'll drag you out of here. You *are* going, Julie."

He released her abruptly and stepped back. Before she could say any more, Elisa Thatcher appeared, her face twisted by anger and fear. "Listen to me, Derek Arnhardt. My husband is waiting for me, and it's your responsibility to see that I get out of this. I am not going to die here, and if I'm the only one of these idiotic women willing to leave, then I demand you take me out of here."

Derek regarded her coolly and said, "Julie has changed her mind. I'm taking her and the baby and Sujen out of here. Get several canteens of water, as much food as you can carry, and dress comfortably and warmly. Be ready to go at midnight."

Elisa's response was cut off as one of the men ran toward them, yelling. "Captain, there's a horse and rider coming in fast."

Derek ran with the messenger back to the center of the compound. Julie started after him, but Elisa caught her arm and held her. "Listen to me. Once we get out of here, I'm leaving you and the Indian. I'm not going to take you to the fort, because I know you'll tell Adam . . . lies about Thomas and me. So just be ready to go your own way."

Julie nodded, there being no point in arguing with Elisa, even when she was in a normal state. She ran toward the center of the compound just as the horse and rider reached the compound from the other side.

The horse leaped into the circle. It was Lonnie Bruce's horse, and the boy's arrow-riddled body slumped off the animal and fell to the ground. His mother's screaming echoed clear across the plains to the pass.

❧ Chapter Eighteen ❧

THE sounds of weeping mingled with the nightwind wind whisper. The angel of death hovered over every man, woman, and child within the wagon circle. Esther Webber sat, trancelike, beside Susanna Jeeter, neither speaking. Half the men had sought oblivion in whiskey, but oblivion eluded them, for the time being. The children slept, apparently unaware that they might wake up only one more time before the final sleep.

Julie looked for Sujen and, not finding her, decided she would be waiting at the supply wagon. Her rations were heavy and clumsy, strapped to her back, as she maneuvered to hold the baby tightly against her bosom. Derek had warned her that the baby must not make a sound, even if that meant gagging him.

Elisa, wrapped in a heavy woolen cape,

turned away as Julie approached the meeting point. Derek appeared out of the darkness and asked, "Where's Sujen? Damn it, we've got to leave now if I'm to be back by first light."

Julie's worry was evident. "She knew what time we were leaving. I haven't seen her."

"I saw her," Elisa said, explaining that she had spotted Sujen crawling beneath one of the wagons two hours earlier. "She's gone. It's just you and me, Julie," she said.

Julie whirled on Derek. "You must go after her. Maybe she's decided to do what she offered to do. We can't let her!"

Derek swore. "There's no way I can go after her. It'd be suicide. She's not going to buy us any extra time, anyway. They'll be done with her by dawn," he finished brutally.

"Oh, she must have gone to the Indians," Elisa said airily. "She wouldn't admit it, but she'd gladly submit to every single one of those savages if it meant saving herself."

Julie almost allowed herself to be goaded into fury, but she mustered restraint. There was no time for anger, no time even to mourn Sujen's brave but foolish decision.

Derek gave them their orders. They were to remain close behind him, moving swiftly and as silently as possible, dropping to their knees to crawl if he signaled them. They would be moving directly toward the Indians, and that was the only thing in their favor, for the Indians would be watching in the directions that led away from them. He was confident they could make it to one of the caves on the outside of the mountain pass, where he would leave them.

They crept through the night, the only sound that of gentle footsteps on the tiny rocks and sand of the desert. Derek walked between them, guiding their way now and then with gentle tugs on their capes. Julie held the baby close, a soft rag ready to press against his lips should he make the slightest sound.

A loud shriek split the air, and Julie froze instantly. Elisa gasped, and Derek whirled angrily. "It's a mountain lion," he whispered. "Don't ever cry out like that. The Apache are alert to every noise. They always know an animal sound from another sound."

The hulking shadow of the mountain pass loomed out of the darkness, and they were about a mile from the wagon train. Suddenly Derek jerked them to an abrupt halt. Before Julie had time to wonder why, they heard noises from somewhere ahead of them and upward—high-pitched wails, bursts of guttural laughter. A chill shook her. The Apache had Sujen. Derek had to tug at her to start her walking again. "There's nothing you can do," he whispered. "Keep moving."

Heavy, smothering clouds obscured the moonlight. The total darkness was a blessing.

Using instinct and memory, Derek groped his way around the rocky ledges and crevices. At last he found an opening that satisfied him. After abandoning them a little while to explore the inside, he returned to guide them inside. After they'd groped along for thirty feet or so, he announced, "I think it's safe to speak in here, but keep it low."

Immediately Elisa whined, "This is dreadful. How long do we have to stay here? That sour smell! It's horrid, like . . . like wet animals."

"Blood smells worse," Derek said brutally, then turned to Julie. "Leave the baby with Elisa and come with me for a moment."

Julie didn't want to leave Darrell with Elisa, but she knew it would be for only a little while.

He took her hand and led her on back toward the front of the cave. Finding a smooth place on the cave floor, he drew her down beside him. Each was aware of how precious and how final was this last time together. "Do you hear that?" He was smiling at her. She shook her head.

"It's the sound of the sea," he went on softly. "Listen. The waves rolling and crashing, the stabbing cries of the sea gulls, the wind. See how the wind ruffles your hair?" He twined her soft tresses around his fingertips. "Taste the salt on your lips. It's the taste of you and me, misty eyes, because

our love was born on the sea. We are the sea
. . . its stormy depths, its gentle rolls and
swells. Perpetual. Endless. Forever."

She sobbed, unable to hold back any longer.
"Not forever. We are ending, Derek. Here.
Now, as you go to your death. Stay with me,
Derek. If you love me—"

His hand moved quickly to cover her lips.
"Don't say anything more," he commanded.
"I'm doing what I have to do. And you're
wrong, Julie. We aren't ending. We'll never
end, because our love can't be destroyed. Our
love will become a spirit, and it will roll with
the tides and blow gently with the winds. No.
We'll never end. We'll live forever, Julie. I
love you."

As he held her, kissed her, Julie began to
hear the sea . . . the cascading swells birthed
into breakers to crash in white foaming triumph on the shore . . . creeping slowly back
to be recreated as waves again, to be reborn,
to know glory once more. They would not die,
could not die, and this ethereal moment
would live forever, like the sea.

Bitterness overtook her, though, as he
stood to go. "I lost my home, my mother, then
Teresa, and a niece I never had time to know.
And my dear brother. "But"—she shook her
head wildly—"I didn't think God would do
this to me, make me lose you."

"We lost the mountaintop, Julie." He

grinned down at her in the blackness. "The mountaintop was ours, and we lost it."

"I don't understand." She was weeping.

He held her hands very tightly. "I'm mad that God yanked the mountain out from under us, but I sure as hell appreciate the trip up. At least He didn't just let us stand at the bottom, staring up, wondering what it would be like to climb to the top of the mountain. We know what it's like at the top. We know. Most people never do find out."

And then he was gone.

She stared into the darkness, but he was gone.

She sat there a very long time, then she got to her feet and made her way back to Elisa and the baby. Elisa's whining voice droned on, but Julie didn't hear. She took the baby and walked away. As she stood in the black cave, holding her nephew, she heard the sea all around her, crashing. She could smell the salt and see the foam, hear the sea gulls and the wind. She thanked God for the trip to the mountaintop . . . and prayed for the strength to rise from the terrible fall she was about to take.

Julie stared out into the faint dawn light. Blackness turned to dull gray, then faint gray. Soon the sun would leap over the mountains, above the junipers, heralding a new day.

The baby stirred, whimpered. He was going to wake up any second and need to be fed, and what was she going to do? Her breasts had no milk. He would cry, the Apache might hear. She looked at Elisa, saw that her lips were moving. But she couldn't hear her. Then her gaze moved to little Darrell. His mouth was open, but she couldn't hear him, either.

Irritably, the baby was snatched from her arms. Julie watched as Elisa took something from a pouch and stuffed it in the baby's mouth. He began to suck eagerly, and it came to Julie that Louella Bascomb had told her how to make a sugar tit. Had she made one and brought it along? Strange. It was hard to remember.

A bird circled high overhead, catching Julie's eye, swooping and swirling, setting a circular orbit. A seagull? No. A seagull would be white, not black. She continued to watch his determined flight.

Beside her, Elisa gasped softly. Did Julie imagine those other sounds, the whoops and shrieks? No. They were riding out of the pass, red-skinned men with wide shoulders and deep chests—bareback, smooth chests. Their bareback mustang ponies were kneed to a full gallop, no doubt urged on by the screaming as well. The men were sinewy, powerfully built, their long black hair flying in the wind, held away from their faces by headbands.

Elisa, holding the baby tightly, shrank

back inside the cave, but Julie couldn't stop watching. Her whole being was riveted to the scene below.

Apache arrows rained through the air as the riders approached the wagon train and the men inside the circle began firing their guns. One brave fell, then another, bodies flailing in the sand.

The air exploded with the demented sounds of thundering hoofbeats, war cries, the cracking of guns. One wagon was set on fire, the flames spreading to the next wagon and then the next. The pitiful little compound became an inferno as white canvas blazed skyward.

The Indians, circling the wagons, broke through to the inside, tomahawks and knives slashing. They leaped from their ponies, crying shrilly as they moved among the wagoneers.

It did not take long. Soon only one white man was left, standing on top of the remains of a barrel, fighting without even any ammunition. He was taller than his attackers, brawny arms and shoulders glistening as he swung an empty rifle at the Indians.

Something bounced off his forehead, slicing his skin, and blood poured into his eyes. He could barely see the men closing in on him. How many? Two dozen? Three? They could take him any time they wanted to. He had only seconds to live. Yet he felt no terror. He was too goddamn mad to be scared. With his powerful right arm he swung the rifle butt again and broke open the face of a brave jumping close by him, knowing he had sent one more to death before he faced his own death. But why didn't they take him? What the hell were they waiting for?

A roar from the pit of his soul rose above the din. "Take me, you sons of bitches! Go ahead and kill me!"

The Apache fell back, looking to their chief, who still sat, regal, upon his horse, witnessing the unusual defiance of a doomed white man who ought to have been begging and was not. The braves had been ordered to take the white man alive, and the chief had not changed his mind. He barked a sharp command to a brave directly behind Derek, who felled him with a quick blow of his tomahawk.

Julie stood transfixed. Her eyes saw two Indians drag Derek's body to a horse and sling him up and over. She watched as the others gathered the dead wagoneers' guns and ammunition. Her eyes saw the Apache ride away, out across the plain, into the desert, toward the mountains beyond. Derek was with them, lying across a horse.

Her eyes saw everything, but her mind took in none of it.

On a ridge to the south, Arlo Vance crouched behind a rock and smiled. The sons of bitches had paid, as he had sworn they would. The Indians had guns now, and he had his revenge. A frown creased his forehead. The only thing he didn't like was their taking Arnhardt with them. But no matter. Arnhardt must've been wounded, and if he wasn't hurt bad enough to die, the Apache would kill him later.

He saw the buzzards swooping down toward the bloody bodies. The settlers wouldn't have liked it out there, anyway, he reflected wryly. It was tough out west.

❧ Chapter Nineteen ❧

FOR two days, the women remained in the cave, sometimes looking down at the swooping vultures with dull, glazed eyes. Julie was in shock, Elisa decided. Even the grating crying of the baby couldn't wake her from her stupor. When it became obvious that Julie was unreachable, there was nothing for Elisa to do but tend Darrell as best she could. She complained endlessly, but Julie didn't hear. She was blessedly removed, in another world, far, far away.

On the morning of the third day, as the sun rose in a fiery blaze, Elisa said, "I'm not staying here any longer, do you hear? I'm getting out of here." Her hair hung listlessly about her dirt-streaked face. She was exhausted. And she could no longer stand Julie's eerie, silent staring at the decomposing bodies below. Even the vultures had gone. "If the Indians were coming back, they'd have been here by now. Fort Bowie is north, and that's where I'm heading, no matter how long it takes me. If you want to stay here, it's up to you." She looked down at the baby, who was, thank God, sleeping for the moment. She supposed she would have to take him. Something was tickling her mind, something she could not quite put her finger on, but it had to do with the baby, she was sure. She would figure it out later.

Julie didn't answer. How could she even hear Elisa when she was on Derek's ship, moored off the coast of Bermuda?

Shaking her head, Elisa set about gathering what supplies remained. The baby whimpered, and she railed, "Damn you, shut up! I've enough misery heaped on me without your whining!"

Hurt, frightened, hungry, the baby began to howl. Elisa slapped him. "If you don't shut up, I'm going to wring your goddamn neck, you little brat!"

Julie turned to look at the baby. "Don't hit him," she commanded coldly, ominously. "Don't hit him again."

"Then you tend him," Elisa cried, picking him up and thrusting him roughly into her arms. "Keep him quiet, and let's get moving. If we must die, at least we'll die moving."

She started down the rocky incline, and Julie stumbled along behind, clutching the

baby. He snuggled his little body close
against her bosom, feeling better.

Elisa remembered the direction in which
Lonnie Bruce had been told to ride, decided
that was north, and began trudging that way.
Julie walked behind, allowing her to lead
their way.

When the shadows of night spread across
the flat, vast plains, the pitiful trio was
hardly out of sight of the wagon train massacre. There were no mountains, no shelter, and
they lay down on the rock and sand floor and
slept in exhaustion, the cold desert winds
whipping across them.

The next morning, Elisa chewed a piece of
hardtack till it was mushy, then forced the
baby to eat it. He promptly spat it up, and she
cried, "We don't have food to waste, you little
bastard!"

"Don't you call him that!" Julie said
quietly. "I'll kill you if you hurt him."

Elisa stared at the woman threatening her
and felt chilled. Was Julie insane? Her first
impulse was to leave both her and the baby
there, but if they did encounter Indians, she
might use them in some way. And she didn't
want to be alone in the desert, so she would
keep them with her.

Julie drank water, but she couldn't eat.
Food had no appeal. She was in the bottom of
a deep, deep pit, with walls of sand that collapsed upon her each time she tried to climb

out. It was easier just to stay in the pit, allowing the tiny grains to slowly cover her, bit by bit. At some point, she supposed, she would disappear.

"Drink some water and let's go." Elisa got up when Julie had finished drinking, and began to plod along, shoulders already hunched against the merciless sun.

That scorching day bled into cold night, and the next day was horribly hot. It was midmorning on the third day when Elisa fell to her knees and sobbed, "I can't go on. I can't. We're going to die here." Her fingers opened and closed in the tiny rocks as though grasping for strength and finding none.

Julie stared down at her in confusion. The warm buzzing that had been filling her for the past several days had become a hot, giant roaring. She could not see, could not speak. It was becoming difficult to understand anything at all. Who was this woman?

She continued to watch the woman beating her fists against the ground, and after a while, she laid the baby down beside her. Maybe he would like to wriggle and kick, too. But, no, he just lay there, opening his eyes against the glaring sun, then squeezing them shut and moaning.

Shading her own eyes against the glare, Julie gazed toward the ridge in the distance. They had wanted to reach it by sundown, but they weren't going to if that woman didn't get up again. She could not understand why they were going to the ridge, anyway.

With parched, painful lips grinning, Julie waved at a man who was waving wildly at her. He was on a big horse, and he was wearing blue, a blue uniform. She watched quietly as other soldiers appeared on the ridge and then began to ride down after him. One of the men carried a flag that snapped smartly in the wind. There were two dozen men riding hard, fast, headed straight toward them.

The soldiers descended the reach and kicked their horses into a full gallop, their shouts of triumph splitting the air across the plains. Elisa struggled slowly to her knees, eyes wide. As realization swept over her, hope lifted her to her feet and raised her exhausted arms above her head. The cavalry! Dear God, the United States Cavalry!

"Thank God!" Elisa cried as the big burly man with the stripes on his shoulder brought his men to a halt, then dismounted. "I thought we were done for," she called to him in a quavering voice.

The soldiers all got down off their horses, and the sergeant motioned to one of them to see if the baby was alive. The soldier lifted the child in his arms and called, "He's breathing, Sarge, but he seems awful weak."

The sergeant stared at Julie, who continued smiling at him vacantly. One fine-looking woman, he thought, despite her

haggard appearance. Too bad she was so . . .
wretched. Something was very wrong. He
had seen it happen before, out there. He
turned to the other one. "I'm Sergeant
Lasker, A Company, Fort Bowie. Are you
from the wagon train that left El Paso a few
weeks ago?"

"Yes, yes," Elisa sobbed. "We're all that's
left." Tears of joy streamed down her cheeks,
which the soldiers mistook as grief for her
lost companions. "The Apache attacked back
there. Four days ago. Five. I've lost track."

"Apache Pass," the sergeant said, sighing.
"Damn, I wish we'd gotten word sooner.
Maybe we could have gotten here in time."

Elisa blinked. "Word? You heard about the
attack?"

"Not about the attack, ma'am," he explained, motioning her toward his horse. "We
just heard there was a wagon train on the
way. We were on alert for it. We'd better start
back now. The baby needs tending to. We can
talk on the way." He looked worriedly at Julie. "What's the matter with her? She don't
seem hurt, but—"

"She's tetched," Elisa said, dismissing Julie. "I'm Mrs. Elisa Thatcher, Sergeant. My
husband—"

"Hot damn!" The sergeant released her
suddenly, jerked off his hat, and threw it to
the ground to stomp on it. "Did you hear

that? We got her! Only three survivors, and
the captain's wife is one of 'em. Boy!"

Elisa stared. "I don't understand," she said
slowly. There had to be a mistake. "My husband is Lieutenant Adam Thatcher, and he's
stationed on the Gila River, almost on the
California border."

"No, ma'am!" The sergeant informed her
importantly. "Your husband is now a captain, stationed at Fort Bowie. He received a
telegram from Fort Bliss saying you had
passed through there a while back, and we
been riding patrols looking for you. He
wanted to make sure he intercepted you before you went on out west with the others."
He looked at the soldier holding the baby,
and smiled. "So that's the captain's baby!
Well, he hoped your time wouldn't come till
you got here, but seems like everything's
okay, huh? There's a doctor back at the fort,
and he'll take good care of you. Gee, you've
sure had a rough time of it, ma'am." Elisa
looked down at the ground modestly.

As they rode back to the fort, Elisa's mind
worked frantically. Julie might never come
out of her stupor. And if she didn't, what
would happen to the baby? An orphan's
home. No need for that, not when she could
pass him off as her own. Who would know dif-
ferently, or care? Everyone else was dead.
Myles surely was. He would be no trouble,
and the only reason Adam had agreed to take

her back as his wife was the baby—which was dead. She had not wanted Adam to know she had lost their baby and hadn't allowed Derek to send Adam word when she gave birth. By letting everyone think Darrell was hers, her marriage was secure for as long as she wanted it to be. Later, if someone better came along, well, who could say what might happen one day? For the moment she was safe.

She reminded herself that had it not been for her holding herself together they would probably all be dead. That baby owed his life to her, by God.

✖ Chapter Twenty ✖

JULIE stared pensively through the narrow window. The sweet-faced woman who had helped her with a hot, delicious bath the night before and brought her a clean pale-blue wool dress had also explained where she was, but it meant nothing to Julie.

She watched as six cavalry companies filed out of the stables toward the parade ground, the officers' harks crisp in the still air: "Column right! Left line! Company, halt!" Horsemen paced briskly, raising dust from the hard ground. Each of the six companies marched into regimental front lines, mounted on horses of matching colors, the guidon of each waving colorfully from a pole fixed into the stirrup socket of the guidon corporal's stirrup. The men sat in disciplined form, double ranks of mostly mustached and sunburned faces, all stern. They faced the company commander and the adjutant, who took his report. Then the adjutant turned his horse and trotted him about fifty feet forward, halting before a man who sat regally atop his mount, apart from the others.

Lieutenant Colonel Wendell Manes answered the adjutant's salute with one of his own. Words were exchanged, and then the band exploded into quick, spirited march. The band marched down the front of the regiment, wheeling and returning. Finally the buglers lifted their trumpets to the sky and sounded retreat.

"It's a lovely ceremony, isn't it, dear?"

Julie whirled around to see that Mrs. Flora Manes had entered her tiny cubicle. A small fluff of a woman, she was all kindness. Apparently, she saw only the good in things. She reminded Julie of someone—but who? "Yes," Julie responded finally. "It's quite lovely." She heard how hollow her voice sounded.

Mrs. Manes rushed forward to give her a hug. "How terrible it must be not to remember anything, my dear, but it will all come back to you one day. Doctor Mangone says you're suffering from shock, and no wonder. We must give thanks to God that you and Mrs. Thatcher and her baby were spared. One day it will all be behind you. We must think of the future now."

The future. Julie turned back toward the window. How could she think of the future when she couldn't remember the past and didn't understand the present?

"Come now," Mrs. Manes was saying. "My wonderful Mexican cook has prepared a delicious meal for you."

Julie did not want to eat, did not want to do anything but sit in her sparsely furnished room and try to sort out her thoughts. That dreadful roaring in her head had subsided, leaving a void in its place. Something told her that, if she were given enough time for thinking, she would figure out who she was and where she was and why things were the way they were.

But she obediently followed Mrs. Manes down a short corridor and into a larger room. The walls were of thick, splintery planks; the floor covered by smooth stones, dirt packed between to hold them in place. A large flag adorned one wall, and beside it was a large portrait of President Abraham Lincoln. Julie stopped. "Why is the portrait draped in black crepe?"

Mrs. Manes turned around and saw what she was looking at. "Oh, my dear child, our president is dead. Assassinated. Such a terrible thing. He was a great man."

Julie continued to stare at the portrait. Bits and pieces were coming back. There had been a war. Between North and South. She was a Southerner. "The war," she felt a sudden, driving need to ask. "Is it over?"

"Oh, yes," Mrs. Manes said. "At least Mr. Lincoln lived long enough to see the war end. General Lee surrendered to General Grant on April ninth, just five days before Mr. Lincoln died."

Julie blinked. "But what day is this? What month? What year?" She felt tears spring to her eyes, and she didn't know why.

"It's 1865, dear." Mrs. Manes took a step backward, suddenly a bit apprehensive. "And it's April twenty-seventh."

"Correct." Lieutenant Colonel Wendell Manes's voice boomed as he walked to the end of the long trestle table. Thick wooden benches ran down each side of the dining table. "And I have just received two wonderful items of news. The Confederate Army in North Carolina surrendered yesterday, and the President's assassin has been shot and killed."

Flora Manes led Julie to her place on the bench and gently scolded her husband. "You know I don't like to discuss anything distressing at the table, Wendell, dear."

"Yes, Flora, yes." He gave a mock sigh. "I know your feelings about dinner table conversation. I'll wait until brandy and cigars with my officers." Smiling at Julie, he asked pleasantly, "And how are you feeling, Miss Marshall? I must say you look much better today."

Julie was glad they talked so much. She wasn't up to talking at all.

The outer door leading to the parade ground opened, and Captain Adam Thatcher and Elisa entered the dining room. The captain gave a sharp salute, which was returned by his commanding officer. Adam Thatcher made a fine show in his dress uniform. His broad chest displayed a tight, brass-buttoned coat with a white wing collar and black cravat. His long legs stretched the straight sweep of dark blue trousers with broad yellow stripes. Adam's face was lean, angular, with an olive complexion. He wasn't as deeply tanned as the other soldiers. A neatly trimmed mustache rimmed straight, firm lips. His eyes were dark and narrowed, as though constantly brooding. He was a military man through and through, rigid posture, a no-nonsense set even to his jaw. And though his skin had not darkened to a leathery hue from constant sun, his hair was bleached to a cotton white. It curled in a mischievous little-boy style about his ears and collar, the only hint of spontaneity in Adam Thatcher's austere manner.

He was handsome and he knew it, but was not preoccupied by it. He merely acknowledged it. As he looked at Julie Marshall, he was appreciative of her gifts—full, voluptuous breasts rising from the bodice of a dress made for a smaller woman, limpid green eyes

peering up at him curiously from beneath
thick, dusty lashes. Her hair, so black it
shone with sparkles of blue, hung loose and
soft around her delicate face. She had rare
beauty, indeed, but the quality that struck
him the hardest was her all-encompassing
look of gentleness. She would be soft, warm,
loving, nothing like the shrewish woman beside him.

. Wendell Manes made the introductions between Julie and Adam Thatcher, and Julie
was all too aware of the way his eyes caressed
her, the clasp of his hand. "I am so pleased
you're safe and well, Miss Marshall." His
voice was as rich and satisfying as fresh-
brewed coffee on a cold winter morning, and
his smile was concerned, even probing. She
felt it all the way to her heart.

"Thank you," she murmured, pulling her
hand away firmly. She hadn't missed the way
Elisa narrowed her eyes coldly. Julie did not
like that woman and was eager to remember
if there was a reason.

They took their seats, and Flora Manes
lifted a tiny silver bell to ring for the Mexican
servants. They brought in platters of chicken
and dumplings cooked in a rich, red sauce,
boiled potatoes with bits of onions, deep-fried
corn balls seasoned with paprika.

"How is the baby, dear?" Flora asked of
Elisa as she helped herself to a large portion
of chicken. "Is he stronger now?"

Elisa shrugged. "Yes, I think so. I'm afraid I'm not very good with children. Adam found a young Mexican girl to look after him, and I haven't heard him crying much. He's all right."

Adam's eyes shaded. "You are his mother," he said crisply. "You must learn to care for him yourself."

Elisa laughed nervously. So far it had been quite easy to pass the baby off as hers, and she was going to have to continue the ruse for quite some time. She needed time to decide what she wanted to do with her life, and the only thing she was certain of was that she didn't want to be on that dismal little post in the middle of nowhere. "Now, Adam," she cajoled, "I told you I didn't have milk to nurse him. There was nothing for me to do but allow one of the mothers on the wagon train who was nursing her own to take over his care. I really haven't had much time with the baby."

"Well, that's going to change," he said gruffly. "I never believed in the ridiculous Southern custom of women handing over their children to someone else to care for."

"Oh, I agree," Flora interjected. "Wendell can tell you—we had the money to afford nursemaids, but I just wouldn't allow it, would I, dear?" She waited for her husband's obligatory nod before continuing. "And I'm so glad I didn't. Now that our sons are grown, I give thanks to God for every precious moment I had with them when they were growing up. You'll feel the same way, Elisa. And it will give you something to do out here, too. I'm afraid there's not much social life on this post."

Elisa looked near to tears. "I thought all military posts had balls and teas." She looked about the table. "Don't you?"

Wendell Manes attempted to explain. "This fort is in the middle of Apache territory, and as more and more settlers come west, our importance here will increase. We really haven't time for—"

"Never a social function, sir?" Elisa asked incredulously, feeling the sharp nudge of her husband's boot beneath the table. "Why, I should think a gala ball would be in order, so I might meet the other officers' wives."

"There aren't many officers here, Elisa," Adam snapped, "and not many of the enlisted men are married."

Flora Manes looked uncomfortable. "Perhaps," she offered gently, casting a pleading look at her husband, "we could have a little something. It would be a nice change, and it might be good for poor Julie."

Suddenly Wendell Manes grinned broadly. "Well, maybe you're right, dear. We'll have a welcoming party for Mrs. Thatcher—and a going away party for us."

Flora stared at her husband openmouthed. The others fell silent.

"I was going to tell you later," Wendell said to his wife, and then looked at Adam, "and I was going to make a formal announcement to my officers when we meet later. But I may as well tell all of you now that I have received orders to report to Washington."

"Oh!" Flora gasped, hand flying to her throat. She laughed, ecstatic. "Wendell, darling! My prayers have been answered. Washington! Oh! We'll leave this dreadful place, at last!" She turned to Elisa, oblivious to the younger woman's envy. "I have wanted Wendell to be sent there for so long. Washington!"

"Congratulations, sir," Adam said quickly, raising his wine goblet to his commanding officer. "I know you'll do well there."

Wendell gave him a wry smile. "Just as you would have, Adam, if you'd accepted the transfer offered you last month."

"You had a chance to go to Washington?" Elisa exploded. She had lifted her own glass to join in the toast, but now she set it down so quickly the contents sloshed over onto the table. "You turned it *down?*"

"I had to wait for you, didn't I?" Adam mumbled.

"Well, I'm here now," she snapped. "Just send word to Washington that you'll gladly take the next transfer. I don't want to stay here in the middle of nowhere any more than Mrs. Manes does. Why, nothing to do, and those savage Indians all around us. . . ."

Wendell interrupted cautiously. "I'm afraid there's no chance for your husband to be transferred now, Mrs. Thatcher, unless he wants to give up the chance for a promotion. You see, I requested that he be placed in charge here. It's a wonderful opportunity for him, very important to his career."

Elisa got to her feet, cheeks flaming. "I don't give a damn about his career, sir. I've been through hell these past months, and I'm sick of this blasted wilderness, sick of death, Indians, hard times—all of it. I want civilization. It's easy for you to talk about how wonderful it is for him to be in charge of this ratty little fort, because you're leaving. I'm the one left behind with nothing to do but turn into a leathery old sun-wrinkled hag like every other woman I've seen out here."

While Wendell stared, stunned by her outburst, Flora touched her fingertips to her cheeks and whispered, "Why, my dear, are you referring to me? I've tried to stay out of the sun, and I had no idea. . . ."

"Allow me to apologize for my wife." Adam Thatcher rose stiffly, furious. "She's not herself, which is to be expected after her ordeal. I'm sure when she's rested, she'll be as happy as I am over a promotion that means so much to my career."

"Oh, no, I won't," Elisa blazed, backing away as he held out his hand to her, meaning to lead her from the room. "I'm not going to stay here, I promise you that."

Adam apologized again quickly and, as his gaze swept over Julie, he saw the deep sympathy on her gentle face. Then he turned and clasped Elisa's shoulders and pushed her toward the door.

Wendell Manes rose. "Adam, I'm sorry," he called. "This was obviously not an appropriate time for me to say anything."

"Don't worry about it, sir." Adam made his voice pleasant as he pushed Elisa through the door, "I'm very pleased for your good fortune and my opportunity to command this fort. I'll meet you for brandy later." He closed the door after them, but Elisa continued her tirade, the angry sounds fading as Adam moved her along the corridor.

"I'm shocked," Flora Manes murmured as soon as they were alone. "I'm not at all sure that woman was meant to be a military wife. The very idea of such an outburst in front of her husband's commanding officer!"

"Most unfortunate." Wendell sat down and resumed eating. "Adam Thatcher is a fine officer, and he could have a fine military career, but not with that millstone around his neck."

Flora nodded.

They finished the meal, and Flora suggested Julie retire. "I have some sewing to do, and Wendell always sits up with his offi-

cers. They'll have a lot to talk about tonight!"
She looked at her husband, her face shining.
"How long before we go? Do I have time to get
letters off to the boys telling them we're coming?"

"Well, I think we'll just surprise them,
dear, because we leave on the next stagecoach east."

"I've so much to do!" Flora cried, jumping
up. "Come along, Julie. I'll walk you back to
your room."

Julie waited until Flora had bustled away,
then found her way outside her room to the
quiet parade ground. It was a nice night, a
half-moon illuminating the purple-black sky.
Drinking in the sweet, clean desert air re-
vived her spirits.

The fort was a shabby collection of sad
buildings, all of cottonwood. It was surrounded by a pointed stockade made of logs
set upright in the ground, topped at each corner by bastions where sentries could see the
countryside day and night. The ground had
been worn smooth, and there was no vegeta-
tion within the fort. What a drab place it was!

"Miss Marshall."

She turned and saw Adam Thatcher approaching from the shadows. Standing a couple of feet to her left, he began by apologizing
for Elisa's behavior. "What she said was in-
excusable. If the lieutenant colonel were not

so understanding, I'm sure my promotion would be in jeopardy."

"Don't worry, Captain. I'm sure Elisa just hasn't gotten over our ordeal. When I remember everything, I'll probably be the same way."

"Oh, I doubt that," he said quickly.

His lips turned upward, and an appealing dimple appeared in his face. She was reminded of how handsome he was.

"I think," he said, so softly that it seemed he was touching her, "you would be quite understanding, Miss Marshall. I can't imagine your ever causing your husband such unhappiness."

She murmured, "I don't think I have a husband. I'm not sure of anything, but I have a feeling I'm alone in the world."

He did touch her then, for only a brief moment. His fingertips touched her face, then withdrew quickly. "As lovely as you are, you never have to be alone. Several of my men have asked whose permission they need to court you."

"I don't want to be courted," she told him quickly, stepping back, disturbed. "I would prefer to be left alone. Maybe I should leave here, go on to Tucson. I've no reason to stay at this fort."

His eyes narrowed slightly. "I'd hate for you to leave, Miss Marshall. But may I call you Julie?" He waited for her to nod before continuing. "I've talked to Dr. Mangone, and he assures me your memory will return. Until it does, you need someone to look out for you, and I would be honored if you would allow me to be that someone."

"That's very kind of you, sir." Oh, why was he affecting her this way? It wasn't just his good looks. There was something else, a quality, a gentle manner she found most appealing. She needed friendship. And he was right, she did need a protector until she could sort things out. Later she was sure she could take care of herself.

"Please," he said laughing and looking at her closely, "I do consider myself a gentleman. I don't intend to seduce you—though I would be less than honest if I said the thought hadn't occurred to me. You are a beautiful woman and you appeal to me very much. But I want to look out for you. Will you allow me to do that?"

Julie couldn't help smiling at his frankness, and she was warmed by his concern. "Of course," she told him, "I'm honored. But are you sure your wife won't mind?"

"Elisa doesn't like anything I do," he said tightly, then dismissed the unpleasant subject with a wave. "Tomorrow, I'll take you on a grand tour of our modest little fort. Do you ride? I'll show you the countryside. There's a large lake not too far from here, and it's safe to go there as long as we take a patrol."

"I wonder whether I'll ever feel safe again," she mused, more to herself than to him. "There's so much I need to remember. The war. I can't remember anything about the war. I assume I'm a Southerner, but I don't know where I came from. And, in a way, I don't want to remember my past at all."

"The wagon train left from Brunswick, Georgia, so perhaps your home is not far from there. It will all come back," he said hesitantly. "Just don't rush things. I'm from the South, too, but when the war broke out, I joined the Union forces."

He proceeded to tell her what problems that decision had caused among his Southern friends and, particularly, with Elisa's family, who were believers in slavery and the Confederacy.

Julie was deeply sympathetic as she listened to him. "I don't feel I would have believed in slavery," she said firmly.

"As gentle and compassionate as you are?" he said. "No, no, Julie Marshall, not you. There's too much warmth in your heart. You couldn't stand to see anyone hurt."

Julie realized she liked Adam Thatcher. He was a fine man, gentle in his way, yet severe when it came to defending something he truly believed in. She wanted his friendship. "Thank you," she said sincerely. "Thank you for wanting to help me, Adam. I know we're going to be good friends."

He gazed down at her, moved by her radiant, ethereal beauty. Moonlight filtering through the drifting silver clouds above bathed them, transforming the ugly stockade into a lovelier scene. He wanted to touch her, to hold her, but he didn't dare.

Julie felt something happening to them, something that shouldn't happen if they were going to be friends. "I'll say good night now," she murmured softly, knowing she had to leave right then. "Thank you for talking with me, Adam. I'll look forward to seeing you tomorrow."

She turned and walked into the building where her room was, and she didn't look back.

Adam's eyes stayed hungrily upon her until she had disappeared. Then, sighing, he went to check on the sentries, the errand that had brought him outside in the first place.

Unseen, Elisa stood in the shadows, fists clenched at her sides. She had heard only part of their conversation, but what she'd heard had been enough.

🦋 Chapter Twenty-one 🦋

JULIE managed to avoid Adam for a whole day and a night, keeping to her little room and asking Mrs. Manes to send a little food in rather than chance a dining-room encounter. But another meeting was inevitable, and when she was obliged to attend a tea for the departing Lieutenant Colonel and Mrs. Manes, she found herself just as glad to see Adam as she had feared she would be. She knew his feelings for her were dangerous, but she was so lonesome, so badly in need of his warmth. She needed a friend. Surely that was no crime, was it?

So it was both pleasurable and frightening to find herself alone with Adam, in a corner of the dining room, sipping champagne and hoping Elisa didn't see them together and make a scene. The other guests were gathered around the Maneses, laughing and talking, everyone caught up in the excitement of their leaving—and everyone wistfully envious of the older people.

No one could hear them, so Julie boldly asked the question that had been bursting inside her for some time. "Adam, why did you marry Elisa when you constantly find fault with her?"

He was taken aback by her candor, but he answered honestly. "Our families wanted it, and to be fair, Elisa is a lovely woman. She can be quite charming and desirable when she wants to be. Unfortunately, she doesn't want to be . . . anymore. And I didn't see the nasty side to her until it was too late. I'd thought she was just, well, temperamental." He paused, then finished explaining. "It was over for us long ago, and I'd made up my mind the marriage had to end. I requested duty out here and left her behind, but when I made a visit home, I'm afraid I let my male weakness betray me. She became pregnant, and we have to stay married. So now you know the situation."

Julie felt sorry for the man. Elisa was cruel and selfish. But, in fact, they did have to stay married because of the baby. Her head began to ache, and she said tightly, "Please, Adam, I have no right to hear these things. Your marriage difficulties are your own and should be kept private."

"But that's what friends are for, isn't it?" he asked irritably.

She looked up in amazement. He was angry with her. Why?

"Perhaps, someday, you'll feel the need to confide in me. I assure you, I won't be as unsympathetic with you as you've been with me."

He turned and left her, joining the other officers who were gathered around their departing commander, making toasts. She stared after him, bewildered by the outburst. But there was little time to dwell on Adam because Elisa suddenly appeared, slightly tipsy on champagne. "I could tell by that stiff-necked walk of Adam's that you did something to make him mad, Julie, dear. What happened? Did you refuse to meet him later to do what you do best—roll around like a bitch in heat?"

Julie was stunned, but she wasn't going to let Elisa goad her into a quarrel. "I don't have to take that from you, Elisa. Just leave me alone."

"Alone?" Elisa echoed. "My goodness, you certainly don't want my husband to leave you alone. Why, he spends almost as much time with you as he does with our son—which leaves no time for me." Her eyes narrowed. "I don't like that."

"Elisa!" Adam called sharply. "The stagecoach has arrived. We're going outside to see Lieutenant Colonel and Mrs. Manes aboard."

"Excuse me." Elisa wrinkled her nose scornfully. "Wifely duties, something you wouldn't know anything about. So you just keep standing there in that pitiful little patched-together dress, while I take up my rightful position as wife of the post commander."

As soon as they'd all gone outside, Julie fled the parlor for the sanctuary of her room. Flinging herself across her bed, she allowed the bitter tears to flow. It wasn't fair, any of it. If only she could understand her feelings for Adam, her bewildering attachment to Adam's baby, her longing for— what? She couldn't get a grip on any of it.

She stared up at the ceiling, images running through her mind. Finally sleep came.

Darkness was covering the window as a knock caused her to sit up, groggy. Without thinking, she called out, "I want to be alone."

"Open up, Julie," Adam called, "or so help me, I'll kick this door down."

She sensed he would do just that, so she got up and unlatched the door, standing back as it swung open. Adam stepped inside, kicked the door closed behind him, and placed strong hands on her shoulders. "I must talk to you, Julie," he said simply. She kept her gaze on the floor, fearing what was coming.

Releasing her, looking down at her, he

breathed, "I've wanted to kiss you since the first time I saw you, Julie Marshall. You're the most beautiful, most gentle woman I've ever met. I never knew I would want anyone the way I want you."

Shaking her head firmly, she said, "No, Adam. I am not going to let myself get involved with you. You're married. And even if you weren't, I have a feeling deep inside me, deep in my heart . . . a feeling that I belong to someone, *someone,* though I've no idea who. Until I find out the truth, I don't intend for any man to touch me."

He reached for her and held her against him. "Julie, I love you. If you were my wife, I'd never let you out of my sight. I'd love you every minute of every day for as long as I live. . . . I won't let you go, Julie."

The tears spilled forth, and Julie tasted their saltiness as she parted her lips to speak, to protest again. But the words were stifled by his kiss. His hands cupped her face, and his mouth devoured hers. She felt his tongue, probing, possessive, and a warm, liquid fire was ignited within her. She was unable to stop herself from pressing against him, and her hands had a will of their own as they pulled him closer, while her mind cried for her to push him away. In another moment they would have been lovers but for the sudden commotion outside. Shouts and cries followed gunfire. Then there was stillness, followed by more shouting.

At once, cursing, Adam gave in to his military training.

"Later," he promised her. Then he dashed from the room. Julie took a deep, grateful breath. She'd been helpless, the betrayal of her body nearly overtaking her. She was shocked. How little control she had! Uncomfortable with herself, she dashed outside rather than face herself alone in her room.

She found herself standing next to Sergeant Lasker, who informed her that the excitement was over an Indian girl the sentry had seen stumbling toward the stockade gate. The girl had fainted just outside, and they had brought her inside. She was barely conscious, pregnant, and apparently about to give birth.

"She's Navajo. I know a little of the language," Adam was saying to the officers and soldiers. "Where's Dr. Mangone? Let's get her inside. Lift her gently, now."

Elisa came running up just as the Indian girl was being lifted. Looking at the Indian girl, she went into hysterics. "Get her out of here! That dirty Indian is one of them! It was her people that attacked the wagon train. I won't have her on this fort. Get her out, Adam!"

Adam snapped to his men to get moving, get the girl to the infirmary, and then he said very tightly, "Elisa, she may be an Indian, but she's a human being and she's going to have a baby. We're going to do what we can to help her. We'll figure out what to do with her later. Right now I'm not going to stand for any of your outbursts. Do you hear me?"

Julie stared. Elisa looked almost insane. Why was she reacting so viciously? The Indian could do them no harm, certainly not in her present condition. Did memories of the massacre plague Elisa so horribly? Julie wondered whether she wasn't, maybe, better off not recalling anything.

Back inside her room, Elisa allowed herself to vent her fury and panic. She would have to get rid of Julie Marshall once and for all. And what if Sujen told anyone about little Adam actually being Darrell Marshall? Would anyone believe her? Elisa's world was falling apart. She had to act fast. She sat by her window, staring out at the night sky, her mind whirling.

⚘ Chapter Twenty-two ⚘

THE infirmary was one small, narrow room, located in a corner of the fort's square complex. It contained only two narrow cots and a table on which instruments and supplies were laid out. There were no windows and no fireplace, and when the chilling winds of winter seeped in through the split-log walls, Dr. Mangone ordered buckets of smoldering ashes and chips of wood brought in for warmth.

Dr. Mangone was short, balding, and sometimes quite hard to get along with. Behind his back, the soldiers—not affectionately—called him "The Boston Crab." A private practice in his native Boston would have been far easier, but the doctor had felt called to duty in the wilderness after serving in the Union Army and realizing the dire need for medical men on the frontier. His decision, and his harsh life, made him irritable with himself and everyone else.

"What's this?" he snapped when Sujen was brought in. He removed his thick glasses so he could glare more harshly. "Now you bring me Indian squaws about to give birth to Indians who will grow up to scalp me?"

Adam was used to the doctor's crankiness and knew him for the nice old codger he really was. "What are you worried about, doc?" he grinned. "There's not much on your bald head to scalp, now, is there?"

"I don't need your smart lip, young man," Dr. Mangone snapped, motioning to the soldiers to put the girl down on a cot. "Where'd she come from and what's she doing here?"

Adam told him what little there was to tell, and then they noticed Julie standing uncertainly inside the doorway. "Well," he demanded gruffly, "what are you doing here? Are you a doctor?"

"Hey, doc, go easy on her," Adam said. "She's the only female help you've got, I'm afraid. The others won't help an Indian."

"I'll do anything I can," Julie assured the doctor, who grunted in reply. Adam and the other men left the room, and the doctor said, "Stand by and do what I tell you to do." He lifted Sujen's eyelids, closed them, then stepped back, recoiling. "Damn it to hell, would you look at her? See those bruises and scars? Looks like someone tortured her. She's been beat, cut, and I'd say she's even been burned. God almighty, it's a wonder she's alive! Who could've done this?"

Julie stared at the pitiful little body. To think what the poor girl had endured . . . "Will she live?" she asked him.

"Maybe." He set to work stripping Sujen of her ragged, dirty buckskin dress, then covered all but her legs with a blanket. With skilled hands, he pressed down on her abdomen, waited for a contraction, then pushed harder. "She's unconscious, so I've got to do all the work," he explained.

Julie watched, tense, ready to do whatever he asked. The doctor pressed Sujen's abdomen again and again.

"All right . . . it's coming," he cried at last. "Get a blanket from that other cot over there and be ready to take the baby in the blanket when I hand it to you."

Julie got the blanket and positioned herself behind him, his body blocking her view of the girl. Very slowly, he turned around to face her. He was holding a tiny, motionless being, staring down at it. The umbilical cord was wrapped tightly around its neck. The baby was dead.

"It's already started decomposing. Probably been dead several days. Hand me that scalpel over there."

Dizzy, Julie moved toward the table, found the instrument, and gave it to him. He deftly separated the dead baby from its mother, then quickly wrapped the body in the blanket and thrust it into Julie's trembling hands. "Give him to the guard. Tell him to see it's buried right away."

Julie turned to obey.

"And tell him to send word to Captain Thatcher to get someplace warm ready for this woman and to find somebody who'll look after her. I'm going to do all I can, but I'm not sitting up with her all night, and she can't be left in this cold infirmary."

An hour later, Dr. Mangone stepped back from his patient, wearily wiped his hands on a towel, and announced, "She's weak, but with proper care she might pull through. Indian women are stronger than white women. They have to be. Now," he said, sighing, "I'm getting back to my fire and my brandy."

"Wait," Julie called after him as he headed for the door. "The guard hasn't come back. What am I supposed to do with her?"

"Stay with her and keep her warm."

"But I can't do that in here."

"Julie, I'm leaving her in your care," he said wearily. "The captain'll find a place for her."

Exasperated, and more than a little angry, Julie tucked the blanket tightly around the Indian girl and then went outside in search of the guard. Another guard was standing not too far away, and she called to him, "Where is the man who was here earlier? He was to send for Captain Thatcher."

The man shook his head apologetically. "I'm sorry, ma'am, but he couldn't get through to the captain, so he went to bury the baby. He sent me to relieve him on duty till he could get back. They went outside the post on the burial detail, so I don't know when he'll be back."

"But I need to see Captain Thatcher!" She waved her arms wildly. Good Lord, what was she supposed to do on her own?

"Ma'am, what can I do?" he asked, hoping to soothe her.

"You would be helping a great deal," she said in a more controlled voice, "if you would carry the girl. Follow me, please."

The first golden fingers of dawn stretched from beyond the eastern mountains as the bugler sounded reveille, bringing the fort to life.

Julie was awake. She hadn't slept at all. She sat in a ladder-back chair near her bed, watching the rise and fall of the Indian girl's chest. Sujen was on Julie's bed, carefully covered in blankets and quilts. Dear Lord, she dreaded being the one to tell her the baby was dead, but there was no one else to do it. No one, it was obvious, wanted anything to do with this girl.

Shortly after reveille was sounded, Adam knocked and called to her softly. Anxious for company, feeling more lonesome than she had since coming to the fort, she hurried to let him in. "Oh, Adam, what happened last night? The baby was born dead, and I couldn't get a message to you—"

"Elisa and her damn social life," he said brusquely, entering the room and closing the door. He walked to the bed and stared down at the girl. "Is she going to live, do you think?"

"Doc Mangone thinks she may, but she hasn't awakened once. Now that everyone is awake, I'd like for some hot broth to be brought in, and hot tea. I'm going to force it down her if I have to, because she's got to start getting some strength back."

He nodded. "Of course, and I'll have her moved right away so you can get some rest."

"Oh, no." She was quick to quell the idea. "No one really cares what happens to her, Adam, and you know it. But I do. I feel so sorry for her. I want to look after her."

His smile was forced. "That's kind of you, Julie, but I can't allow it. She's an Indian, for God's sake, a savage. I'll have her moved to the stockade, and the guards there can look after her. When she's strong enough, I'll question her, see how much information I can get out of her."

Julie was horrified. "You can't do that! Those men won't really look after her like I will. Look at her! Her body scarred by what someone did to her . . . she's lost her baby. She can't be dangerous to me or anyone else!" she challenged indignantly.

He looked at her with tenderness, but he would not be dissuaded. "Not only am I not going to take a chance with your safety, I also don't want you wearing yourself out, Julie."

Exuding his best military air, he declared firmly and unequivocally, "I'm having her moved at once, and I want you to get right into bed. I'll have your breakfast sent in, and you can rest all day. Later"—he flashed a tender smile—"I'll find a way for us to be together."

She was about to reply when a sudden knock interrupted. Adam looked startled. "Ask who it is," he whispered. "I don't want Elisa to find me here."

Julie called out through the door and heard, "Corporal Timothy Posey, ma'am. I heard the squaw had been brought here, and I've got something that belongs to her."

As Julie opened her door a little, the soldier held out a dirty, worn leather pouch. "The squaw had it with her. One of the men found it in the dirt outside the gate. Nothing in it we can make anything of, but she might want it if she wakes up."

Julie thanked him and closed the door, then laid the pouch aside. She turned to Adam, wanting to settle things between them once and for all. Her voice firm and unwavering, she said, "What happened yesterday should not have happened, Adam, and it won't happen again because I won't let it. We must forget this. We must not become involved."

"Forget it?" he echoed angrily. "Julie, I want you to understand. *I love you.* We have to be together." He stepped toward her, but she moved away, holding up her hands to stop his progress.

"Adam, you have a wife."

"I know," he replied quietly, painfully. "I'm reminded of my miserable marriage every moment of every day. I don't love Elisa and she doesn't love me, but now there's my son, so I can't divorce her. But you and I can still be together, still love each other, still find happiness." Eyes beseeching her, he held out his arms.

She made her voice cold. "Don't touch me, Adam." Remember his baby, she told herself.

"Very well." His eyes reflected despair as his arms fell to his sides. "But I do love you. I wish I were free to marry you, but I can't give my son to Elisa. You know very well what kind of mother she'd be without supervision. I can't bear the thought of her raising him without me around." He shook his head as he implored, "Julie, bear with me, please. As much as I love you, I can't give up my son. But we'll work something out. I know Elisa, and she's not going to stay here. She'll leave eventually. Just be patient."

She wanted to grab him and shake him and make him understand. "You aren't listening to me. I'm not *asking* you to divorce Elisa. I'm not *asking* you to give up your son. There can never be anything between us, Adam. You've got your life and I've got to make my life. It's too late for us, and we have to accept that and forget anything ever happened between us."

She was searching his face, praying for a sign that he understood. It would be so easy to love Adam, to fall into his embrace. But what she couldn't tell him was that his marriage was not the only thing holding her back. There was another reason, and it would all come clear one day why she couldn't love Adam Thatcher.

"Go now," she whispered, her back to him. "Please. Leave me, please."

As quick as a striking rattlesnake, he grabbed her and spun her around and crushed her against him, his mouth possessing hers. As he released her he cried, "I'll never let you go, Julie, never. By God and by everything holy, I'm going to have you. Maybe not this moment, or this day, but you will belong to me. Remember that." He left before she could muster a reply.

As the door slammed shut, the girl in the bed stirred, moaning. Julie turned. She was awake, a startled expression in her eyes, as though she could not believe what she was seeing. For an instant, Julie was frightened. Hesitantly, gently, she asked, "How are you feeling?" Good heavens, would she know any English?

The faint words that came in response made her heart stop.

"Julie. It is you!"

Julie blinked. Had she heard correctly? "You know me? How do you know me?" Her body began to tremble.

"You do not remember Sujen?" The girl lifted her head, then fell back upon the pillows. She moaned, "The baby. It is dead?"

"I'm sorry." Julie sat down beside her, smoothing her long, dark hair back from her forehead. "You had a little boy. He was born dead. There was a doctor, but there was nothing he could do. I'm so sorry. Please believe me, we tried."

"I feared that my baby had died inside me," Sujen whispered mournfully. "For days I did not feel him move, but no wonder. The Chiricahua were very bad. Even the Utes were not as cruel when they took me from my people. These men were." Her voice trailed off. She looked suddenly at Julie and cried, "Your man. They did not kill him. He lives, Julie, he lives!"

"My . . . man?" Julie couldn't understand why her body trembled so violently. "I don't understand you. How do you know me? Who are you?"

Sujen suddenly realized that Julie truly did not remember. "Derek Arnhardt." She tried to sit up, all her attention on Julie's face. "You do not remember? Captain Arnhardt. The wagon train. Arlo Vance. He came to the Chiricahua while I was there. He helped them find the guns and kill the wagon train. Julie, you remember?"

Julie felt like sobbing, but she didn't know why. "Please," she begged, reaching out to clutch the Indian girl's shoulder. "Tell me what it *is* that I should remember, for I swear I remember nothing of my life at all."

Sujen glanced around the room. When she saw the worn pouch, she gestured to it, and Julie quickly picked it up and handed it to her. "Perhaps now you will remember." Sujen rummaged in the bag. "This is something I have kept with me, for I was so touched by the girl's dying words that I took part of what she left you. Forgive me if it was wrong, but I hoped to keep her spirit alive."

Tenderly, she held out a small packet, which Julie took. She looked at it curiously. Then she poured the contents into her hand, and as the seeds touched her flesh, a voice whispered, "Plant these seeds . . . and when the wild flowers grow, think of me . . . and I will never die. . . ."

"Oh, God . . . ! *Sujen!*" Julie wrapped her

arms around her friend, tears flowing freely, her body quaking as memory washed through her. It was all rushing back. Images danced through her mind one after another, crowding each other out. Teresa's death after giving birth . . . Myles leaving, grief overwhelming him. . . . Amidst the stabbing pains of awareness, buried in the past that her mind had attempted to shield, there was Derek. "He's alive." She had to hear her own self say those words. "Derek is alive."

Sujen nodded. "He is well. The Apache chief wants him alive. Derek is a great warrior. You see, he was hurt, and his mind is still hurt. He knows not who he is . . . just as you knew not your own heart before you held the seeds."

Julie said all there was left to say. "I love him."

Sujen nodded. "He is held by a powerful magic, the peyote spell. Even if I could get to him, there would be nothing I could do to help. But perhaps you—"

"I will find a way to him, Sujen," Julie said, and there was no arguing with her.

Sujen closed her eyes and fell back against the pillow. She had done her job. She had lost her baby, but she'd given Julie back her life.

❧ Chapter Twenty-three ❧

CAPTAIN Adam Thatcher sat behind the large mahogany desk in his small tidy office. A tray to his right held a stack of paperwork yet to be done. That stack was much smaller than the tray of completed work to his left. Adam was fastidious. He abhorred disorder and wouldn't tolerate indolence. He maintained a firm hand with those ranking below him and acquiesed respectfully to officers above him. He'd been comfortable during his years at West Point, comfortable with the military way of doing things. That spilled over into his personal life.

Everyone around him knew Thatcher was ambitious. He had felt cheated because he'd missed heavy action during the Civil War. Requesting assignment in the West had been looked upon with favor by higher-ups, and he'd received a great deal of praise when he asked for the transfer. He wasn't surprised when Wendell Manes named him post commander. Only the usual time- consuming military paperwork lay between Adam and a giant jump to the rank of major—and permanent command of the fort.

In part, the transfer west had been to escape his miserable marriage. He believed in a family and he wanted one, but he'd discovered, too late, that Elisa was a selfish nag, cold in bed, a thorn in his side. Had he not carelessly gotten her pregnant, he'd have been free months ago. But freedom from Elisa was no longer possible.

That morning, as ever, Adam appeared coolly collected and ready for anything that might challenge him. But he was grateful for the training that cloaked his feelings. For right then, Adam's world was being torn apart, and there wasn't a thing he could do to stop what was happening.

Before him sat the only woman he had ever loved deeply, the one he wanted with all his eager heart. Julie. And now he knew he couldn't have her.

She was insane. She hadn't just lost her memory, she was insane. And she threatened his son, the only good thing in Adam's life. He could not let her do it.

He rose from the desk and began pacing in measured, heavy footsteps. He didn't want to think about Elisa, but she'd been right about Julie Marshall all along, had tried to warn him off. He pushed that thought aside and cleared his throat.

"Julie," he began sternly, "you mustn't think I'll let you get away with this ridiculous story. Of course Adam is Elisa's—Elisa's and mine." He held up a hand to prevent her speaking.

Tense moments had passed since she'd finished her incredible story, and he had tried to appear as calm as possible while his mind scattered, then collected itself.

He made his voice as tender as possible. "Julie, you've been through a terrible ordeal. It was so horrible as to make you lose your memory, so I'm sure that this hallucination you're having was also caused by the ordeal."

Her green eyes sparked with fury, and she leaped to her feet. "Adam, it is not an hallucination! Talk to Sujen yourself. She'll explain. I have my memory back. I know who I am, and I know the baby you call your son is my nephew—my brother's child. I'm sorry for you, Adam, but your own son died at birth. We both know the only reason you allowed her to come out here was the baby. When the massacre happened, when I didn't know my own nephew, Elisa leaped at the chance to pass Darrell off as hers."

Struggling for control, Adam said very softly, "Julie, I realize you believe what you're saying, but I know it's all part of your illness."

"*I am not ill.* And I know you don't like it, but I'm telling the truth."

"Sit down!" he yelled, and she had no choice but to obey. "Will you talk to Sujen, Adam?"

He nodded, smiling a false smile, confident that nothing a squaw could say would make any difference. In the girl's weak, vulnerable state, Julie had probably had no trouble coaxing her to back up her hallucination. He wondered what Julie had promised in exchange. "And if I believe Sujen," he asked smoothly, "what then? Do you wish to raise my—your nephew? Do you want the baby, Julie?"

Julie shook her head. "I haven't decided what to do about him, Adam. First I have to find Derek. The Apache are keeping him prisoner."

Adam walked over to the window, something in her voice making his heart burst all over again. "Derek?" he repeated. "Who is this Derek to you?" He waited, nerves taut, for her answer.

"I love him. I've loved him for a long, long time, but it was only on the wagon train that we both came to realize how much we meant to each other. No one is going to stop me from finding Derek."

He stared out the window at the barren

land between him and the mountains. At that moment, he'd had all he could take.

He went to the door, summoned a guard, and ordered, "Take her to her room, lock her in, and post a guard outside the door. No one is to see her or talk with her except myself or Dr. Mangone. Move the squaw to the stockade and see that she's looked after. The minute she's well enough, I want her off this fort!"

"Adam, no!" Julie sprang to her feet, running to him, but the guard restrained her. Adam left the room. Struggling, she screamed at him as he walked quickly down the hallway, "You can't do this! I'm not crazy. I'm telling the truth! Talk to Sujen! Listen to her, *please.*"

"Ma'am, I don't want to hurt you," the guard warned as she continued to struggle furiously. "Please calm down."

"Oh, damn you, let me go!" Julie twisted, trying to break his grip. Two soldiers, hearing the commotion, rushed to the guard's aid. The three men dragged her away.

Adam kept on going, heading straight for his quarters. When he got there, he found Elisa having tea with Katrina Melling and Mina Tooley. The women looked up, startled by his appearance. Even Elisa knew better than to argue when he said, "I apologize, but if these good ladies will excuse me, it's very important that I speak with you alone. Now."

As soon as the door closed behind her guests, Elisa cried, "Just what was that all about, Adam?"

"Where is my son?" he demanded coldly.

"Why, with Carlita, I suppose." She shrugged. "Why?"

"Have you even seen him this morning?"

"What?"

"You heard me!" He was fighting himself to keep from grabbing her and shaking her. "Have you seen him at all today? Did you give him his breakfast? Did you give him his bath? Have you even held him? Did you hold him yesterday? Did you play with him?"

"Adam—" She backed away as he advanced menacingly.

"Answer me!" He was dangerously close to slapping her, and he hated himself for the temptation. "You never do anything for the baby, yet you told me not to listen to Julie's story. *Is* Julie telling the truth?" His voice cracked. "Is that baby my son? Tell me!"

"That conniving whore will stop at nothing!" she cried, desperation making her sound righteous. "She bedded every man on our wagon train, and now she's after you, so she's trying to cause trouble between us. How dare she say Adam isn't mine? Dear God, when I think how I suffered giving birth! Well, I'll take my son and leave here before I'll let you abuse me this way! The idea!"

She began to cry, flinging herself against

him. Adam couldn't face the possibility that the baby might be taken from him. He held her to him, folding her against his chest, letting her cry. He felt like the biggest hypocrite of all time. He despised Elisa and he loved Julie, but he was not going to lose his son to either of them.

When Elisa's hysteria subsided, Adam led her to the sofa to lie down, then brought her a glass of sherry. She gulped it eagerly, and he saw how overwrought she really was. He sat down beside her. She looked up at him with red-rimmed eyes and proclaimed hoarsely, "I hoped our marriage would be strengthened by the birth of our son. Please don't let that crazy woman come between us."

He did not meet her gaze. "You've got it all wrong, Elisa."

"Do I?" she challenged. "If I have to, I'll take little Adam and leave here. I've known Julie Marshall much longer than you have, and I know she's capable of anything. I'll take the baby and run away if I have to, I swear it. If you want Julie, take her. But you'll never see your son again."

Adam still didn't meet her gaze. "All right, Elisa. I understand."

❧ Chapter Twenty-four ❧

IN the end, it was Elisa who unraveled the
tangled skeins, Elisa who helped Julie escape her prison and sent her away from the
fort on horseback. Oh, she didn't think of it as
helping Julie. She meant only to be rid of her,
for she knew she couldn't put an end to
Adam's infatuation without getting rid of Julie.

Elisa knew that by letting Sujen and Julie
go she was taking a chance on Julie's coming
back for her nephew. But she guessed that
neither Julie nor her Indian friend would survive for very long. No, she decided, there was
no great risk in getting the women away from
the fort—and Adam. But there was a terrible
risk in letting them stay.

So it was that Julie and Sujen found themselves miraculously freed and sent away
across the desert with horses, some water,

and a little food. It was a hard trek, nevertheless, and Julie worried about Sujen. Could she muster the strength she needed, so soon after her ordeal?

Julie herself felt strong, sure of herself, full of hope. An hour passed, then another, then another. They were riding bareback, but no matter. She suddenly seemed to have all the will, all the fire she'd been without since the massacre.

Sujen slowed their pace only after the land became rougher, with hills to climb and holes the horses had to avoid. Riding beside Julie, Sujen asked, "You are tired?"

Julie shook her head, but confessed, "I'm hungry, and I could do with a drink of water. Is there any nearby, or should we use the little we have with us?"

Sujen answered, "Spring has thawed the mountain snows, and the streams are too muddy to drink from. Take just a little from the canteen."

Worried, Julie asked, "Are you sure you're all right, Sujen?" But even as she asked, Julie realized that Sujen would never admit a weakness.

A little later, Julie quietly told her friend the story of the wagon train massacre, as much as she knew. It brought startled gasps from Sujen, who was usually stonily composed.

When Julie finished, Sujen was too disturbed to say anything about the Indians. She turned the subject to Derek. "It is wise that I lead you to the Apache camp. Captain Arnhardt will surely sink further under the spell the medicine man casts upon him with peyote. I do hope your face will make him remember who he is. But . . . this is strong magic. I fear for your life, Julie, yet I can think of nothing to help you."

"Sujen," Julie said sharply, "I have to find Derek, no matter what happens. But if you're afraid of Cochise's people, what will you do? Is there anywhere you can go? Will you hide nearby and wait for . . . for whatever happens to Derek?"

Sujen did not reply. Instead, fingers wrapped tightly in the horse's mane, she steered her horse suddenly to the left, down into a brush-filled ravine. "We go this way and hope we do not awaken rattlesnakes, for with the warm spring sun, they no longer sleep soundly. Then we will climb the mountain and take shelter to hide us when dawn comes."

"But, Sujen—" Julie persisted.

"We talk then," was Sujen's curt response. "Now we must be quiet, to listen for the rattlesnake's warning."

As night fell, Sujen found a small cave. There were no signs of recent animal occupants, so they prepared to spend the night there.

Patricia Hagan

"You certainly know this country," Julie marveled. "I would never have gotten this far so well on my own."

As she spoke, she turned in time to see a very dark look cross Sujen's face.

Julie prodded, "Must you go away? You could speak Apache and . . . and . . ."

Sujen shook her head. "When the sun rises, I can do no more for you. If the Apache see me, they will surely kill me."

Julie groped for, and found, Sujen's hand in the darkness. Squeezing it tightly, she fervently told her, "You've already done too much and suffered too much."

Silence hung like a shroud for a long time, and then Sujen said, "When the first light of dawn comes, I will leave you. Forgive me if you think I abandon you, but I do what I must do."

Julie swallowed hard. "Tell me what I should know about the medicine man, about peyote."

Sujen shrugged helplessly, searching for words. "In the beginning, I do not believe the shaman meant to confuse Captain Arnhardt by giving him so much. But the great Cochise saw what a giant he held captive, and who knows what he was thinking when he ordered more and more peyote."

After a moment's reflection, Sujen continued, "Cochise feels your man is a brother, a friend. He does not want Derek to leave, and

288

he won't let him be killed. What else to do but keep him safe by keeping him drugged?"

"How is the peyote given to him?"

"In food, in drink."

Julie took a deep breath and let it out slowly, not wanting to ask her next question. "Has Derek ridden with the Apaches on any of . . . their raids, Sujen? Please tell me. I have to know."

Sujen smiled. "I know why you ask me. When I was a little girl my father took me with him on a hunt. We saw raccoons, and I watched how they wash their food before they eat. I asked my father if they did this to make food taste better, and he told me yes, it would taste better if clean. That is how it is with love. To know that your warrior killed your brothers would make your love taste not as clean. But be at peace, my friend. I am sure he has not been part of Cochise's raids."

Julie hoped desperately that Sujen was right. She would learn the truth soon enough, she reminded herself.

Another question tormented her. "What . . . happens to a person who takes peyote?"

"We believe," Sujen told her, "that if a man is not morally true, he cannot use peyote. The cactus that brings visions is like a teacher or a healer, a great spirit. My people have used mescal, which is both like and unlike peyote.

"My father was called a giver of visions. He

took them both. He told me of dreams, visions of the future. People would go to him with great problems, and he would dream the answer.

"It is said," she went on, peering out of the cave toward the horizon, "that once two warriors were lost, and their sister looked for them and did not find them. She fell to the ground, exhausted from searching. A dream came to her that her answer would come with the dawn. When she awoke, she found the peyote plant. She ate it, only because she was hungry, and she had a vision that told her where her brothers could be found. There are many stories like this."

"But can't it harm him?" Julie blurted, frightened. "If they keep on giving it to him, over and over—"

"I never heard of anyone dying from peyote. Too much makes a man loco, yes. I think they do this to Captain Arnhardt because they fear him—for if he comes back to his true self, he will fight to the death. Cochise does not want this. It would be a waste. He keeps him a prisoner of the drug until he thinks of a way to make him one of them. He wants no fights, nothing to put danger in Derek's path."

After a while, Sujen asked the question Julie had been asking herself for two days. "What will you do when you find Derek?"

Julie's voice choked. "I don't know, Sujen.

I'll stay hidden for a while and watch them. Maybe something will come to me." She flashed a wry grin. "Maybe I'll find a cactus and eat some peyote and have a vision."

Soon enough, the blackness outside their cave became a bluish-gray. Sujen sprang to her feet. "I must go now. When you leave here, climb on up to the top of the mountain where it is flat and runs either way as far as the eye can see. There are mesquites and creosotes that will hide you, but be cautious. From there, is not too far to return here at night. But be very careful always, for the Apache have many eyes."

She led the horse to the entrance as Julie scrambled to her feet, calling, "Wait! You can't leave, Sujen." Tears filled her eyes as she embraced her friend tightly. "I may never see you again! We've been through so much. You're my sister." Her voice caught.

Sujen pulled away gently and mounted the horse. Silhouetted against the gray sky, the young woman looked like an apparition. "It is said among my people that when two hearts have touched, they become one. Once this happens, though the two walk different paths—never to cross again—they are always as one, for their hearts beat together, even in death." She reached beneath her buckskin dress and brought out a knife. Handing it to Julie, she said, "Take this. There was one of the Apache group who was not all evil. Dark

Buffalo speaks English, which he learned from trading with your people. He gave this to me the night I was dragged from the camp. He gave it to me, not for protection, but to end my life before the wolves killed me. I did not have to use it. Perhaps it will give you protection . . . or end your life if you must."

She held out her hand for one last clasp, and Julie grasped it. "My friend, our hearts have touched. We are one. Even in death."

She turned and rode away, disappearing as a rosy mist began to overtake the gray shroud.

Great clouds crowded the horizon, and the ringing mountains stood like attentive spectators as Julie crouched behind a thick clump of pale, feathery mesquite. She surveyed the plateau she had stealthily climbed. Like a flat-topped fortress, the plateau was dark, solid against the morning sky. Along the edges, gypsum rock shimmered silver in the sun.

She was lost. In either direction, there was a maddening maze of gullies and ravines rimming the desert.

Raising her head ever so slightly, she saw gentle wisps of gray smoke rising in the distance. Creeping along, darting between the bushes, she moved toward the smoke. After a while, she reached a ridge and knelt behind a clump of brush, looking out, her heart skipping wildly. Below, in a wide, flat gulley rimmed by rocks and ridges, was the Apache camp. Tepees held by tall poles dotted the ground, their sides pulled out and stretched by stakes. Squaws, hair falling down their backs, wearing buckskin dresses, hovered near small cooking fires. The air was filled with the thick scent of cooking meat as they prepared the morning meal. Children ran, shouting in the early chill. Men, dressed in breechclouts, moved about, preparing for their day.

Where was the lone white man among all those copper-skinned ones? She clenched her fists. Tension, the smell of cooking food, her own hunger, all combined to make her feel horribly ill.

The sun rose higher, singeing the earth. The heat was torture, but she crouched there, rigid, camouflaged by the brush. She couldn't go down into the camp. She could only hope for a glimpse of Derek, to know where he was—and be certain he was still there at all.

A movement to her right made her turn quickly, and she drew her body into a tight ball, cringing at the sight of an ugly brown-and-yellow lizard. It was ominous, repulsive, and she slowly closed her fingers around a large rock and threw it, missing him but sending him scurrying away.

Just then, she felt a sting on her leg. A

small many-legged creature had bitten her, and she brushed him away with a sharp gasp of pain. Blinking back tears, she told herself not to cry, not to give in. There was nothing to do but to endure.

After an eternity the sun began to sink, and the brilliant turquoise sky became pale lavender. Then the horizon faded to blue twilight.

It was time to return to the cave. She made no attempt to leave the plateau, though, continuing to stare out into the gathering twilight, then down at the camp. Time passed. It was getting too dark to find the cave easily, and then, without being surprised, she realized she wasn't going back to the cave, wasn't going to retreat, not now. Now she knew where to find Derek, and though she knew Sujen would be horrified, she was going to do the only thing she could. She was going after Derek. Now.

Before she stood up, ready to climb down into the camp, she called on the memory of Teresa's face for strength, and on the memory of Myles's voice, and on the picture of Derek's eyes she carried, always, in her heart. She prayed for a long time, and then she rose and left the safety of the plateau, making her way carefully down into the camp. It was getting cold, and she pulled her black cape around herself tightly, wondering fleetingly if it would hide her until she wished to be seen. She climbed down through the rocks and brush and walked toward the camp, the journey taking about half an hour, yet seeming like only a moment.

The Indians were gathered around several fires, cooking and eating. Julie counted six fires, and guessed she saw four or five people, including children, around each one. She stopped at the entrance to the camp, gathered her cape more closely against her trembling body, then stepped into the camp.

The first to see her was a heavily muscled man with shoulder-length black hair and a smooth chest. He wore only a breechclout. His eyes lit up at the sight of her, and after he had looked her over, he stepped toward her, reaching her in a few powerful strides. Julie willed herself to stand her ground, and she didn't flinch, even when he took her arm and led her forward. She steeled herself for the astonished quiet that fell over the camp, and the ensuing eruption of shouts. She returned every stare, reminding herself to stand straight and tall. But after a while she couldn't bear the possessive hand on her arm any more and shook it off. He scowled and reached for her again, but there was a commotion behind him and he turned around, then dropped his hand. Julie turned more slowly, knowing something had happened behind them.

As she turned, she saw awe in the faces of those around her, and when she saw the warrior they were looking at, she understood. This must be Cochise himself, for no one else could seem so entirely in command. Even the brave who had been holding her arm, so sure of himself, was subdued. The camp was utterly still. Even the children stopped talking and stood, poised, ready to hear Cochise speak.

Julie stared at Cochise. He was taller than most of the others. His shoulders were broad, and he had a deep chest. But it was his face that held her gaze. There was a special intelligence in his black eyes, not the arrogance she'd expected. His nose was large and straight, and he had a very high forehead. His black hair, which hung to his shoulders, was shiny and hung straight. Strings of beads adorned his neck. He stood as though planted there, strong thighs spread apart, hands on his hips.

Julie decided to chance communicating with him. What else could she do? "I am the white man's woman, and I have come to take him home. You must set him free."

She felt so foolish, knowing he didn't understand. Sujen had told her he didn't speak English, and she knew not a single word of Chiricahua. She threw her whole heart into the declaration, hoping desperately that he would understand the language of her eyes. She was so intent on getting through to him that she almost didn't hear the voice behind her.

"I will translate for you, if Cochise wishes me to."

She whirled around and saw an Apache looking at her with—what? Pity? It bewildered her. Who was he? As though he could read her mind, he said softly, "I am Dark Buffalo. I will ask Cochise if he wishes to talk with you."

He spoke a few words to his leader and, receiving a nod, began to translate for Cochise and Julie.

In what Julie thought an amazingly gentle voice, Cochise spoke to Dark Buffalo, who told her, "Cochise says you are a goddess, as beautiful as the warm, golden sun and the cool silver moon. He asks that you tell him how you found your way to us, and why you risked your life to come here."

"Tell him that my love for my man, your white captive, is so great that I do not fear death."

Dark Buffalo translated, and, as he spoke, Cochise listened intently. When Dark Buffalo was finished, he turned again to look at Julie, who said hurriedly, "Tell him he must let the white captive go. He belongs with his own people, as *he*"—she nodded at Cochise—"would want to live among *his* own kind." As she finished, she kept her gaze resolutely on Cochise.

They looked at each other, the warrior and the young woman, and their eyes held each other for an eternity. Cochise spoke a few words, and Dark Buffalo waited until Cochise nodded before translating.

"Cochise decrees," he said slowly, "that your man has a right to claim you because of your love for him. But, when you came here, you were claimed by one of us."

The man who had held her arm so possessively grunted, and she knew it was he Dark Buffalo meant.

"Storm Face also has a right to claim you, and this means there must be a settling of claims. This will be done according to our law—the two men will fight until one is dead and the other remains to take you for his own. If Storm Face is the victor, you must remain here and serve him as his woman."

She felt the warrior's eyes on her back and shuddered, but she refused to turn and look at him.

"But," Dark Buffalo went on, "if your man wins, then you both will go free. It has been decided by Cochise."

At that moment, a tall man emerged from a tent on the far side of the camp. He was unsteady on his feet, but there was no mistaking the one she loved above everything on earth. "Derek!" she cried. He looked at her, registered nothing, then disappeared back into the tent.

He didn't know her! If he didn't, then all Sujen had said must be true. Every nerve directed her to Derek; every bit of strength she had impelled her toward his tent. But he *was* drugged or he'd have known her. And if he was drugged, then she had to deal with Cochise before she could go to her love.

She turned again to the leader and said, "It's not fair! He's been drugged, and he's not able to fight. Can this be Apache law? To let a strong man fight a sickened one? Is that Apache honor?"

Dark Buffalo, obviously taken aback, was hesitant about saying such things to Cochise, but Julie cried, "Tell him! Ask him if this is Apache honor!"

Slowly, carefully, Dark Buffalo spoke to Cochise. The great warrior looked at Julie appraisingly, nodded to her with a look that held respect, and bade Dark Buffalo tell her what he replied.

"Your . . . the man will be given no more peyote. By morning he will be himself. Cochise wishes you to know that we have honor in all our laws—even when it doesn't seem so to your people. And he bids me say that your people have not been . . . truthful, or honest . . . with us."

Julie nodded. She could hardly dispute that. She knew, too, that there was no hope of persuading Cochise to change his mind. He was leaving, disappearing into the shadows. The others began to move away as well. Storm Face shot one blazing look at Julie, and then he went into his tepee. There was no one left but Dark Buffalo and Julie. He was looking at her with the look he'd had all along. Was it pity? She couldn't decide. He said quietly, "I could not say this while Storm Face was near. Cochise says you may remain in your man's tent until morning."

She was too stunned to reply, and he left her standing alone in the clearing, walking swiftly to his tent.

Somehow, going to Derek was going to be harder than all the rest. She had mourned for him, longed for him, risked herself to get to him. But now that she was only a few steps away from him, she couldn't move. Knowing he didn't recognize her made it impossible to approach him. What if his eyes were blank when he saw her? What if he wouldn't let her touch him? What if he ignored her? She wouldn't be able to stand it.

But she had to stand it. She had to force herself across the clearing, make herself approach the tent, and confront Derek. She had to. Slowly, every step an agony, she went to the tent and called softly, "Derek? It's Julie."

He came outside, as shaky as he'd been when she first saw him. But there was a flicker of recognition in his eyes, just a flicker. It was enough.

"Derek, I'm coming inside to spend the night. All right?" She made her voice steady and, without waiting for an answer, stepped inside. He followed her.

🏵 Chapter Twenty-five 🏵

THE tent was small, nestled beneath a craggy overhang, apart from the camp, as indeed the man who lived here was a being apart. She stood inside the tent and stared up at him.

"I love you," she whispered. "God knows how much I love you, Derek."

Derek squinted, trying to fathom her by staring hard at her. The drums in his brain were not quite so harsh. Colors were not as vibrant, but he could see more clearly. She was glorious. She was beautiful.

They stood staring at each other, the woman devouring the man's face and the man looking more and more weary, as though he was trying too hard to remember something, something that remained beyond his grasp. When he couldn't recall whatever it was and was tired of trying, he lay down on a pile of buffalo hides and went to sleep. Julie sat next to him, as near as she dared, keeping watch over him as he slept. It was cold, and she pulled her cape closer and covered herself with a buffalo hide, but she didn't lie down. She stayed next to him, her eyes never leaving him, watching him breathe and wondering what his dreams were about.

The night wore on, but Julie couldn't let herself sleep. It was as though she had to force him back to himself, using all her will to battle the drug.

She thought about Myles and prayed he was alive. She wept for Teresa. She wept for the baby with Adam and Elisa.

Derek stirred, and she snuggled close against him. He awoke. Darkness clothed them. Julie felt his warm breath on her, and soon his lips found hers. She yielded to him, and their bodies came together, rocking softly, then building to a wild crescendo.

"I love you, Derek," Julie breathed against his neck as, afterward, he held her close to him. "I love you with all my heart, and I always will."

It seemed so right to be lying close, whispering love words, that it took her a while to hear him.

"Misty eyes," he whispered.

She sat up abruptly. "Derek! You . . . You know me?"

He shook himself. He still couldn't think

very well, but there was so much that she had brought back to him. It flooded his mind, images and feelings rushing through him.

"Julie," he said. "Julie."

She hugged him as hard as she could. "Yes, my love, yes. It's me, and we're together, and we're going to live. We're going to live! Oh, Derek, Derek, I love you so."

Suddenly, he pulled away from her, hastily throwing her cape over her body. He covered himself with one of the hides.

"What is it?" she asked.

"Dark Buffalo," a voice whispered, and she hastily pulled one of the buffalo skins around her, over the cape. He stepped inside and looked first at Julie and then at Derek.

"I cannot help you very much, but I wanted you to know that you have my heart."

"Your heart!" Julie echoed. "Derek can't defend himself, and you expect us to welcome your sympathy?"

Dark Buffalo whispered, "There is something I can do."

Julie reached out to clutch his arm in desperation. "Anything! Do anything. Just help us, please! There's so little time."

There was a pained look on his hawklike face as he held out a small clay pot. "I took this from our shaman when he was away from his tent."

Julie cautiously took the pot. The smell was horrible, and she swayed. Dark Buffalo reached out to steady her, then withdrew his hand as she steadied herself. "How long since you have eaten?"

She shook her head. "I don't know. Between my empty stomach and the horrible smell of whatever is in that jar, I feel sick."

He reached for the leather pouch that hung from his belt. Digging inside it, he brought out a handful of white stalks. "Squaw cabbage. It's better boiled, but you can eat it raw. I also have this, a loaf made from breadroot, mesquite beans, and flour. It will give you strength, and there's enough for him," he said, nodding at Derek. "The night before warriors go out to battle, they take peyote. Afterwards, when the shaman gives them this, they are no longer possessed by peyote."

Julie eyed him and said frankly, "I have no choice but to trust you, Dark Buffalo."

He shook his head firmly. "I do not lie. I grieved for the way the Navajo squaw was treated. It was I who cared for her and fed her. We became friends, and she told me about you. Yes, I know it is you she talked about. I do not lie to you. I risk my life to be here now, but I wish to help you both."

Julie listened quietly, warmed, and said, "I thank you, Dark Buffalo. You've given us a chance to live, just as you gave Sujen a chance to live. She is alive, and by now she is probably safe." She guessed correctly that he had been afraid to ask about Sujen. His eyes glowed as he learned Sujen was alive. Then he looked at Derek once more and left the tent without another word.

Derek drank all that was in the pot, then lay back and looked at Julie. He reached up and lovingly touched her face. "Misty eyes, it is you. . . ."

She smiled, her whole heart in the smile. Then she gave him the loaf and the rest of the squaw cabbage, and as he ate, she told him whatever he hadn't been able to recall himself. Finally, desperately, she asked, "Are you able to fight, Derek? Is there a chance for us?"

Derek answered matter-of-factly, "I think so. You see—I'm mad," he said. "I'd say I'm as goddamn mad as I've ever been in my whole life." This, she thought joyfully, was her Derek—fighting mad and ready for battle! Her heart swelled with love and pride. They had a chance.

In a level voice, he told her what he planned for their future, after the morning battle. "Misty eyes, it's a new life for us. God knows, we've been to hell and back, and now it's time for a little bit of heaven. It's not going to be easy, but for us it never has been. We're going to that fort, and we're going to take Myles's and Teresa's baby whether Thatcher likes it or not. Then we're going west. California. We'll make our life together there. And we won't look back. The past is a cobweb that holds people in its miseries and keeps them from going on to the future.''

He kissed her for long, precious moments; all the love, tenderness, hope, and promise of a better tomorrow was in that kiss.

When he finally released her she whispered, ''Derek, if you should die . . .''

He silenced her with his fingertips. ''That's not going to happen.'' His lips twisted in that familiar, arrogant grin, the grin that had once annoyed her so. ''After all, I mastered the winds and the tides. And I conquered your love—just as I swore I would. How can anything stop me now?''

She matched his grin with an incandescent smile, but there was nothing she could do about the tears that followed.

🎕 Chapter Twenty-six 🎕

THERE was a strange, unnatural stillness in the air. Not the slightest breeze stirred the feathery mesquites or ruffled the burr grass. The Apache men, bare-chested, wearing only breechclouts and moccasins, ringed an area in the middle of the camp, their eyes upon Derek as he and Julie approached the circle. Their faces were stony. The women stood far behind the men, clearly observing but not taking part in the ritual. The children were nowhere to be seen. This was deadly serious, no place for children.

When Julie and Derek reached the circle, two warriors approached and removed her from Derek, positioning her behind the circle of men, one on each side of her. She was caged. It was very little comfort that one of the men was Dark Buffalo. Derek leaped for her but was stopped by a warrior with a lance.

"It's all right," Derek called to her. "You won't be harmed. They're just holding on to you while the fight takes place." He tried to give her a reassuring smile.

Dark Buffalo, without any of the previous night's friendliness, spoke to Julie. Lips set, as though he had only contempt for the impudent white squaw, he said, "It is expected that I speak with you, for it is known we speak the same language. I can help you in no way now, so do not ask. Now, I must be one of my people. You understand?"

She nodded. She couldn't expect him to endanger himself more than he already had.

She was about to ask what they were waiting for when Storm Face emerged from one of the tents, striding toward the circle. The other warriors and the squaws stepped aside for him, but some didn't move quickly enough, and he shoved them aside. His face was heavily painted—white streaks beneath his eyes, black down his nose, and an arrowhead of ochre painted on each cheek. He looked vicious. His eyes locked with Derek's, transmitting his message of hatred . . . and the solemn promise of death. Derek, unflinching, returned his stare. There was no hatred in Derek's face, but his eyes were just as deadly.

Satisfied that he had made a public display

of his courage, Storm Face turned conspicu-
ously and looked at Julie. She was shocked at
the look he gave her. This man wanted her,
believed in his right to her, and meant to
have her. Before she could react, the watching Apache began murmuring among themselves. In a moment, Cochise appeared. He
walked slowly, arms folded across his chest.
Unlike the others, he did not wear a breechclout. He wore long buckskin trousers. His
chest was bare but adorned with even more
necklaces and beads than he'd had the day
before. A rag was tied around his forehead,
holding back his shining, straight black hair.
Moving directly to the middle of the circle, he
stopped and gazed at Derek for a long time.
Then he spoke to him, calmly, melodiously.

Julie did not even have to ask Dark Buffalo
to translate. He spoke loudly, so Derek could
hear him. "Cochise repeats his decree. If
Storm Face is victorious, the woman will remain here to do his bidding as long as Storm
Face wishes. If the other wins, the two of you
will go in peace. He says he has looked upon
the white man as friend, and his heart will be
sad however the battle ends, for Cochise and
the white man will not meet again."

Derek yelled to Dark Buffalo, his eyes on
Cochise. "Tell him I have something to say."

The message was relayed, and Cochise signaled his willingness to listen.

"Tell him," Derek commanded, his voice

crackling through the air, "that I am very angry with the Apache for the slaughter of my people. But though I am angry, I am grateful that he saw fit to spare me, and glad he has looked upon me as a friend. I have no intention of returning to this place, nor will I tell any of my people where to find it. If we meet again one day, I hope we can smoke the pipe of peace. No more blood must be spilled between our peoples."

Dark Buffalo translated rapidly, but there was no visible reaction from his leader. With a final look around, Cochise withdrew a knife tucked in his waistband. Holding it high above his head, he made one quick, downward thrust, sending the knife into the ground.

Storm Face screamed a piercing shriek and leaped for the knife, and in that instant, Derek understood. There was to be only one weapon, and they would fight over it. He lunged, and the two men reached the knife together. Storm Face's hands clutched Derek's throat and his knee came up to smash into Derek's crotch. Derek groaned, fingers squeezing the Indian's wrists with all his might. He felt a bone snap, but Storm Face neither cried out nor loosened his hold.

The two fell over and thrashed in the dirt, rolling over and over, the spectators moving back cautiously as they rolled beyond the boundaries of the circle. Storm Face, shrieking his death cry again, saw the large rock before Derek did. He grabbed the rock and brought it smashing down, just as Derek jerked to one side. The rock scraped his ear, a glancing blow. Storm Face swung again, and Derek was stunned—just long enough for Storm Face to leap forward and grab the knife.

Derek rallied, stumbled forward, and caught his ankles. Storm Face fell onto his back. Rising a little, his powerful arm plunged the blade toward Derek's back.

In one movement Derek caught Storm Face's wrist in mid-flight, twisted it upward, and forced the warrior's hand to drive the knife into his own chest. Derek felt the thud as flesh was split, and he pressed harder, driving the knife all the way in. Blood spurted, covering Storm Face's chest and running down into the sand.

Cries of shock and disbelief rose all around. Mouth gaping in a silent scream, Storm Face stared up at Derek, eyes wide with pain. Then the eyes went blank. The women began wailing their grief, but the men all stared, stunned, making no move or sound. It was as though they expected Storm Face to rise from the ground.

Derek got to his feet and looked around for Julie. Sobbing, she wanted to run to him, but found she couldn't move. Adoration, relief, love, all kept her rooted where she stood. God had given them their one chance, and that was all she could comprehend.

Beside her, Dark Buffalo remained coldly composed. "It is over and you are free to go. Go now. Do not look back. Keep your word that you will not tell your soldiers where to find us. We will move to another camp, but we will still know if you have not kept your word. You have been given the chance to live. Do not live foolishly."

Derek beckoned to Julie, and then she came alive, running into his waiting arms. He held her but only briefly. "We must go— now."

Cochise, having looked at the dead Storm Face for only a moment, had left. They wouldn't see him again.

It was Dark Buffalo who led them to a horse, tethered just outside the camp, and left for them on Cochise's orders.

"Do you know the way to the fort?" he asked.

She shook her head.

"Go east, down the mountain, and follow the great gully to the south." After Dark Buffalo had told them where water could be found, he nodded to them and left, walking briskly toward the center of the camp, his back rigid. He didn't look back.

Derek threw his arms around the horse's neck and swung himself onto its back, then grasped Julie's arms and pulled her up behind him. They held their breath as they left the camp, but no one tried to stop them. Julie clung to Derek, head pressed against his broad back. The azure sky was clear, the winds warm and gentle. She lifted her face to the sun and gave silent thanks for the day . . . for their chance . . . for their freedom.

They found the water Dark Buffalo had promised within an hour, and drank their fill. Before they got back on the horse, Derek searched Julie's eyes. "You look . . . very tired. Are you worried about getting the baby from the fort? Don't be. I promise you, we won't leave that fort without him."

With a brilliant smile straight from her heart she said, "We still have rough times ahead, I know it. But right now I can't feel anything but joy."

They rode hard, straight for the fort and the baby. Later, they would search for Myles.

The sky went from azure to turquoise, and the desert stretched on forever, daring them to find its end. But they would. Hadn't they come through the slaughter of their wagon train, the death of Teresa and disappearance of Myles, Derek's captivity, Julie's torment? When everything seemed lost, hadn't they found each other?

It came to Julie as they rode into the horizon that only one thing had ever really kept them apart—their own stubborn pride. Only her pride and his had ever threatened their love. *Their* love. It wasn't her love and his any longer, but their love, the two made one through fire and death and grief and endless trials. One love: theirs.

Derek turned just a little, looking at her face for a moment. "It won't be easy making Thatcher understand, but we'll get the baby, Julie. And we'll find Myles, I swear it. And then . . ." He paused for so long that she thought he wasn't going to finish. "And then," he said, "we'll go. Maybe California, I don't know. Wherever it is, we're going back to the mountaintop, Julie." He reached for her hand and squeezed it, and she squeezed back with all her might.

"Julie . . . come with me. We'll go to a new life, a place at the top of the mountain. We'll go to where the wild flowers grow."